AN OBVIOUS FACT

By Craig Johnson

The Longmire Series

The Cold Dish

Death Without Company

Kindness Goes Unpunished

Another Man's Moccasins

The Dark Horse

Junkyard Dogs

Hell Is Empty

As the Crow Flies

A Serpent's Tooth

Any Other Name

Dry Bones

Also by Craig Johnson

Spirit of Steamboat

Wait for Signs

The Highwayman

Stand-Alone E-Stories
(Also available in Wait for Signs)

Christmas in Absaroka County (Four Stories)

Divorce Horse

Messenger

CRAIG JOHNSON

AN OBVIOUS FACT

VIKING

VIKING

An imprint of Penguin Random House LLC
375 Hudson Street
New York, New York 10014
penguin.com

ISBN 9780525426943 (hardcover)
ISBN 9780698157521 (e-book)

Printed in the United States of America
1   3   5   7   9   10   8   6   4   2

Set in Dante MT Std
Designed by Cassandra Garruzzo

For my brother, Greg,
who had his head run over once,
which explains a lot.

"There is nothing more deceptive than an obvious fact."

Arthur Conan Doyle,
The Bascombe Valley Mystery

ACKNOWLEDGMENTS

When I was very young, my father, who was always tinkering with something, brought home a model 841 Indian Scout motorcycle in a half dozen peach baskets and set about rebuilding it with my mother, brother, and me in attendance, none of us ever questioning how the thing had become unassembled in the first place.

The Scout had an intriguing past—the U.S. Army had commissioned it during World War II for desert fighting, and, in response, Indian designed and built the 841—8 standing for the new motor and 41 for the year. In fact, the parts that Dad labored over looked as if they might've been shipped from Cairo during the war, but with the ubiquitous red paint giving the impression that this Scout had been decommissioned and sold out of the surplus warehouse in Springfield, Massachusetts.

My mother said it was painted that color to hide the blood.

For weeks my father assembled and reassembled the parts, cleaning Linkert carburetors with toothbrushes, rewinding copper wire on the generator, and trying to find spokes that would fit the even then antique motorcycle. Finally, after hours and hours of intensive labor, the Scout was finished, and the three of us stood on the porch steps out of the way of trajectory as my father attempted to kick it into internally combusted life.

My father, a man of considerable strength and vocabulary, began stomping the starter lever on the Indian and when it proved to be uncooperative cut loose with a streaming commentary not fit for polite society.

Operating a motorcycle of this particular vintage was a tricky proposition with a shift lever that sat alongside the gas tank and a shift pedal that required a heel-toe pattern, and a kick-starter, all of which were familiar to my father.

Kicking the living daylights out of the old motorcycle again, my father swore some more and redoubled his efforts. A couple of the things he might not have been aware of were two of the primary reasons the 841 had been turned down by the army—a quixotic clutch and a faulty gearbox.

He kicked again and then paused in action but not in word.

The other thing he might not have known was that the 841 motor was built for the rugged conditions of the wartime desert, where fuel was not plentiful and so designed to run on a low compression ratio of 5.1:1, something he might've considered if he had been aware before adding a high-octane booster into the gas tank.

Mounting another Herculean effort, he tried again, and the twin-cylinder, side valve engine roared to life as he stood there holding on to the handlebars and revving the throttle, his grease-stained face grinning for all it was worth. It was at that instant that the 841 Scout decided it was off to war and took my father with it. Bursting into full, high-octane throttle, it managed to engage its faulty gearbox and shot away with my dad barely holding on with one hand.

We watched as he made the corner of the house and then turned in a sharp left angle up a hillside populated with pine trees with trunks of varying thicknesses. He bounced off a few before the rear tire caught traction and flipped him over backward, the two of them entangled and tumbling back down the hill.

My mother was horrified.

My brother and I couldn't wait to try it.

Thus began a lifelong preoccupation with things that are fast—horses, cars, trains, women, and, yep, motorcycles.

I'd like to throw a two fingered salute out to my riding partners for all their help in getting *An Obvious Fact* up on two wheels starting with super agent Gail "Gear-Grindin'" Hochman and her henchwoman, Marianne "Smooth Rollin'" Merola. The sidecar over at Viking Penguin couldn't be fuller with Kathryn "Chrome Queen" Court, Lindsey "Wall of Death" Schwoeri, Victoria "Skid Mark" Savanh, Brian "Hold My Beer I Want to Try Something" Tart, Olivia "T-Bone" Taussig, and Ben "Pedal to the Metal" Petrone.

I know a little Arthur Conan Doyle but not as much as my friend Leslie Klinger and was glad to loan Henry a copy of Klinger's *The New Annotated Sherlock Holmes: The Complete Short Stories*. Thanks to Jamey Gilkey of Old Man G Performance and John Stainbrook for keeping me honest on the two-wheel thing. Thanks to my backup men, Michael Crutchley and Curt Wendelboe, for the motorcycle accident technology and the great K-9 stories. Thanks to Linda and Bob Prill and Dr. Frank Carlton for the lowdown on skeet and trap shooting—those ashtrays are elusive and need to be put on the non-endangered list.

Hey, if you haven't ever visited Devils Tower you need to head over that way, and a great place to hang your hat or grab a meal is in Hulett, one of my favorite towns in Wyoming. Thanks to Chef "Jersey Boy" Dean and the Ponderosa Grill & Cafe, which serves one of the finest cheesesteaks west of the Schuykill River, just ask Vic. Thanks to The Golf Club at Devils Tower, which really isn't the den of iniquity that I make it out to be. . . . And in Rapid City, SD, a shout out to Piesano's Pacchia for the great pizza and Ron's Cafe for the marvelous pancakes, which kept me going on this marathon, iron-butt ride.

Music is really important to me when I'm writing, and I want to thank Rickey Medlocke for providing the soundtrack and the friendship—you know you've made it when you get an email from Lynyrd Skynyrd. And by the way, I don't think you guys sound like a garage band.

Finally, there's the only one whose arms I want wrapped around me as I take on the hairpins of life, my wife, Judy "Vincent Black Lightning" Johnson.

AN OBVIOUS FACT

1

I tried to think how many times I'd kneeled down on asphalt
to read the signs, but I knew this was the first time I'd done it
in Hulett. Located in the northeast corner of the Wyoming
Black Hills, the town is best known for being the home of
Devils Tower.

I looked at the macadam blend, the stones shining in the
mix that was still wet from the early morning rain, and sighed.
With the advent of antilock brakes, it was hard enough to
properly estimate the speed of a vehicle involved in a traffic
accident, never mind in the rain.

"Do you see anything?"

I nudged my hat farther back on my head and turned to
look at the large Indian leaning against the door of Lola, his
Baltic blue '59 Thunderbird and my granddaughter's namesake. "How about you come over here and take a look for
yourself."

Henry Standing Bear didn't move and continued to study
the large book in his hands. "I am on vacation."

I was kneeling at the apex of a sweeping curve on state
route 24 where the road veered off toward Matho Tipila, the

Cheyenne name for the first United States National Monument, so declared by Teddy Roosevelt in 1906.

"There is traffic coming."

I didn't hear anything, but that didn't mean he wasn't right, so I walked to the edge of the road and watched as a phalanx of motorcyclists came around the corner and descended toward us like a flock of disgruntled magpies.

They slowed—not for me, I wasn't in uniform—but because of the corpuscle-red Indian motorcycle with the modified KTM extended rear-axle dirt bike that roosted on the flatbed trailer behind the Thunderbird.

The leather-clad cyclists thumbed their horns and gave a collected thumbs-up to the Cheyenne Nation as he leaned there, looking as if he were negotiating a treaty, with his muscled arms folded over his chest, the first volume of Leslie S. Klinger's *The New Annotated Sherlock Holmes: The Complete Short Stories* in one hand.

"You could have waved back."

He shook his head. "That would not fit with the tourist's stereotypical vision of the stoic, yet noble, savage."

I glanced at the book. "Is that mine?"

"Yes, I took it from your shelves. I did not think you would mind if I borrowed it."

I glanced back at Devils Tower crowding the horizon. The geologic area around the megalith is not of the same composition as the tower itself, and the belief is that about fifty to sixty million years ago, during the Paleogene period, an igneous intrusion forced its way up through the local sedimentary stone, some saying it was an ancient volcano, some saying it was a laccolith, an uncovered bulge that never made it to the surface. "You know how it got its name, right?"

"Yours or ours?"

I ignored him and started back toward the T-bird. "When Colonel Richard Irving Dodge led an expedition back in 1875, his interpreter got it wrong and referred to it as Bad God's Tower, which then became Devils Tower, without the apostrophe as per the geographic standard." I opened Lola's passenger door and eased in.

The Bear climbed into the driver's seat and studied me.

I reached back and stroked Dog's head. "You don't care."

"About what?"

"The apostrophe."

He hit the ignition on the big bird. "I care that a delegation of my people attempted to have the name restored to Bear Lodge National Historic Landmark, but your U.S. representative killed it. 'The name change will harm the tourist trade and bring economic hardship to area communities.'"

I knew the man he was talking about, and I had to admit that his nasal imitation was spot on. "But as an expert, what's your feeling on the apostrophe?"

He grunted and placed the book between us. "'There is nothing more deceptive than an obvious fact.'" Pulling the vintage convertible into gear, he patted the book. "Sherlock Holmes."

"Did you borrow all three volumes?"

He pulled onto the vacant road. "Yes."

"Oh, brother."

• • •

It took a while to drive the nine miles into Hulett—eighteen minutes to be exact—because thirty miles an hour was as fast as Henry Standing Bear was willing to drive Lola (the car), especially while towing Lucie (the motorcycle), and Rosalie (the dirt bike).

The Bear liked giving vehicles women's names.

We skipped Hulett's main street to avoid the fifty thousand or so motorcycles parked on both sides of the road. The town's population of just around four hundred multiplies under the August sun as bikers from around the world arrive for the nearby Sturgis Motorcycle Rally, which pulls in close to a million bikers each year.

Held in the town of the same name just across the border in neighboring South Dakota, the rally lasts a week. On the Wednesday of that week, Hulett throws what they call the Ham 'N Jam, offering free music and a thousand pounds of pork, three hundred pounds of beans, and two hundred pounds of chips; they also celebrate something they call No Panties Wednesday, though nothing in the official literature mentions the missing undergarments.

Our destination was the Ponderosa Café and Bar and the Rally in the Alley, which was handy because the gravel back street was the only place where there was a parking spot large enough for the car and the trailer. Henry eased the Thunderbird through the crowd and parked behind a tent set up to sell T-shirts, patches, do-rags, and other souvenirs.

"Today's Monday, right?"

"All day."

I glanced around at the hundreds of people milling about. "And the actual Ham 'N Jam doesn't start until Wednesday?"

"My thought exactly."

"Do you think you should put the top up?"

He shut his door and looked at the very blue sky. "Why? I do not think it is going to rain again this morning."

I shrugged and glanced at Dog, the hundred-and-fifty-pound security system. "Stay. And don't bite anybody."

A woman in a provocative leather outfit, a lot of hair, and a multitude of rose tattoos paused as she passed us. "Is he mean?"

"Absolutely." As I said this, he reached his bucket head over the side door and licked her shoulder with his wide tongue. "Well, almost absolutely." She smiled a lopsided smile, which revealed a missing tooth, and continued on down the road. I looked at Dog. "Just so you know, you could get a disease."

He didn't seem to care and just sat there wagging at me.

Moving to the trailer, I watched as the Bear used a chamois cloth to remove what dust had collected on the Indian motorcycle.

"Why do people ride these contraptions, anyway?"

He checked the tie-down straps and stood. "Freedom."

"Freedom to be an organ donor." I glanced up and down the crowded alley. "T. E. Lawrence died on a motorcycle. You know what I make of that?"

"He should not have left Arabia?" Henry climbed over the railing and stood next to me. "Where are we supposed to meet him?"

"Here." I looked around. "But I don't see him."

The Cheyenne Nation took a step and glanced down the alley, choked with bikers of every stripe, and plucked the *An-*

notated Sherlock from the fender rail where he had left it. "Maybe he was called away."

"The only police officer assigned to a fifty-thousand-biker rally?" I smiled. "Maybe."

He carefully placed the book under his arm. "There is always the Hulett Police Department." He glanced around. "If I were a police department, where would I be?"

"At 123 Hill Street, right off Main as 24 makes the turn going north."

"Far?"

"Almost a block."

He started off, intuitively in the correct direction. "The game is afoot."

I shook my head and followed as we made our way, taking in the sights, sounds, and smells that are Ham 'N Jam. "Doesn't smell too bad, but maybe it's because I'm hungry."

He nodded and smiled at two lithesome beauties in halter tops as they grinned at him.

"What happened to your Native stoicism?"

"Well, anything can be taken to excess."

The crowd in front of Capt'n Ron's Rodeo Bar on the corner was spilling onto the street in joyous celebration of the open container law, which allowed alcoholic beverages to be consumed in the open air during rally week. The party was in full swing, the sounds of the Allman Brothers' "Statesboro Blues" drifting through the swinging saloon doors.

I looked back at the Bear. "Two of the Allman Brothers died on motorcycles—what do you make of that?"

"That if you are an Allman Brother you should not ride a motorcycle."

I sidestepped a short, round individual who was wearing a Viking helmet and drinking from a red plastic cup, but Henry got cut off.

"How you doin', Chief?"

The Cheyenne Nation half smiled the paper-cut grin he reserved for just these situations. "I am not a chief. I am Henry Standing Bear, Heads Man of the Dog Soldier Society, Bear Clan." He leaned in over the man, the bulk of him filling the sidewalk. "And who are you?"

The Viking didn't move, probably because he couldn't. "Umm . . . Eddy."

The Bear extended his hand. "Good to meet you, Eddy. The next time we see each other, I hope you remember to address me in a proper fashion." They shook, and Henry left Eddy the Viking there, utterly dumbstruck—not that I think it took much.

"Oh, this is going to be an interesting two days."

We rounded the corner, the crowd thinned out, and we stood in front of the Hulett Police Department office, located next to what looked to be a fifteen-ton military vehicle.

The Cheyenne Nation rested a fist on his hip and stared at the white monstrosity. "What is that?"

I shook my head and pushed open the Hulett Police Department door. It was a small office as police offices go, with a counter and two desks on the other side. An older, smallish man sat at one of them with his hat over his face. He started when I closed the door, but the hat didn't move. "By God, before you say anything, whoever you are, there better be a bleedin' body lying in the street before you wake me all the way up."

"You haven't been all the way woke up since I met you."

He slipped the hat off and looked at me. "How the hell are you, Walt Long-Arm-of-the-Law?"

I spread my palms. "Vacationing."

He stood and placed the straw hat on his head. "In lovely Hulett, Wyoming?" He walked over and, making a face, shook my hand. "During Ham 'N Jam?" He glanced at the Cheyenne Nation and then extended the same hand to him. "Henry Standing Bear—you come over here to show all these lawyers, dentists, and accountants what a real outlaw looks like?"

Henry shook. "How are you, Nutter Butter?"

William Nutter had been the chief of police in Hulett for as far back as anyone could remember. A tough individual with a mind of his own, he kept the town running smoothly; if the man had an enemy in the world, I didn't have an idea who that might be.

"Ready to retire and even more so after this last weekend."

I nodded and threw a thumb over my shoulder. "What, in the name of all that's holy, is that behemoth sitting out there?"

He smiled. "An MRAP, stands for Mine-Resistant Ambush Protected. We got a bunch of that Patriot Act money that's still around and some funding from a local citizen, name of Bob Nance. He wrote up all the paperwork for us. Hell, the federal government's got twelve thousand of the things—we grabbed one before the ban."

"Your town has less than four hundred people in it."

He gestured toward the overcrowded street. "Not today, it doesn't."

Henry parted the venetian blinds and peered at the thing. "What are you going to do with it?"

Nutter shrugged. "I don't know—we've got to figure out

how to start it first." His eyes played around the littered room. "I got the manual around here somewhere, if you guys want to give it a try."

"It's very white."

"It was used by the United Nations."

"What does it weigh?"

"About fifteen tons."

"And how many miles to the gallon does it get?"

"I don't know, maybe three." He leaned on the counter and tugged at his hat like he was saddling up. "We're not allowed to use any town or county money to maintenance the thing, so either Bob needs to come up with some more funding or what it's going to end up being is a big, white lawn ornament." He smiled as Henry continued to stare at the massive vehicle. "She's a beauty, though, isn't she?"

I scrubbed a hand over my face and changed the subject to the one at hand. "So, you want to tell us about the incident this last weekend?"

He shook his head. "No, I'd rather you talk to the investigating officer, who I assume is the one who called you?"

"He did." I studied Nutter, taking in the accumulation of lines on his face, more than I'd remembered from last time.

He moved toward a radio console and, holding up a finger toward us, picked up one of the old-style desk mics. "Woof, woof—hey, Deputy Dog, where are you?"

There was a pause, and then a voice I recognized came over the speaker. "Please don't call me that."

Nutter immediately barked into the mic again. "Woof, woof, woof! Where are you? The Lone Ranger and Tonto are here for a powwow."

There was another pause. "I'm down here in front of the Pondo doing a sobriety test on a guy who thinks riding drunk is the same as stumbling down the sidewalk." There was a voice in the background and more conversation before he came back on. "I'm right here on Main Street—how did I miss them?"

"We came in and parked in the alley."

Nutter relayed the message and then sent us on our way back to the Ponderosa Café and Bar. As we closed the door, he called out, "Don't forget to ask Deputy Dog how he got his name."

"It was stupid."

"It usually is." I leaned back in my chair, sipped my coffee, and studied the former Gillette patrolman and Campbell County deputy, Corbin Dougherty.

"Our K9 guy was a little weird."

"They usually are."

He sighed. "The dog companies were sending us all these samples—you know, shock collars and stuff? So the K9 guy gets to wondering how bad the shock is."

The Cheyenne Nation, who had been gazing out the window, turned back to look at the deputy. "What did he ever do to you?"

He shrugged. "His dog bit me. I mean, he's the K9 guy, so he should have control over his dog, right?" Corbin looked around the packed café and lowered his voice. "I told him he should try one on—you know, get a feeling for the things before he put them on his dog."

"No."

"Yes." He glanced around again. "So, we're in the day room, and this idiot puts the dog collar on. I don't mean just held it there; I mean he buckled the thing on around his neck. So, then he starts barking, real low, like 'woof.'"

I peered at him through the fingers covering my face. "Barking?"

"Honest to God—I guess he figured since it was a *dog* shock collar . . ."

"Let me guess what happened."

"Nothing at first, but he kept barking louder and finally it kicked in, and you've never seen anything like it. I mean, the things have these little prongs on the inside that are supposed to work through the insulation of the dog's fur, but this was bare skin on this idiot's neck."

I tried to keep from laughing, but it was hard. "Then what?"

"It flipped him back over the table and put him on the floor. Honest, it was like he was struck by lightning—like a Taser, only way worse. Well, every time the thing shocks him he yells, so it shocks him again."

"What did you do?"

Corbin paused as a waitress arrived and set our breakfasts in front of us. He watched her go and then continued. "What do you mean what did we do? Nothing. Everybody hates the son of a bitch; that damn dog of his has bitten all of us. So, he's flopping around on the floor, screaming and getting lit up like a Christmas tree, and we've all got our cell phones out taking video."

Henry nodded. "The brotherhood of blue."

Corbin sipped his coffee. "Anyway, one of the other officers posted the thing on YouTube, and it went viral. The *Trib* did a story, and Sandy Sandberg needed a fall guy; I was the one with least seniority."

"So, here you are in Hulett."

"You weren't hiring."

I sipped my own coffee. "I'm always hiring."

The young deputy forked a strawberry. "Besides, it's nice over here, and I met a girl in Sundance."

The Bear and I looked at each other. "There is always a girl."

I remembered the pit bull we'd dropped on the young man last winter. "She like your dog, Deputy?"

He smiled. "More than me."

We started eating in earnest, and the conversation died down. Corbin, the healthiest of us, finished his oatmeal and fruit and straightened his paper placemat before introducing the subject of why we were there. "I hope you don't mind me calling, but I figured after you'd helped out with that mess in Campbell County . . ."

I leaned back in the booth. "This star for hire."

He looked up, a little panicked. "I can't pay you anything, Walt."

"That was a joke."

"Oh." He gathered his napkin from his lap. "Did you stop on your way in and look at the accident site?"

"We did, but it was wet and kind of hard to tell what had happened."

Dougherty glanced around at the crowded café again and whispered, "There was a lot of blood."

"Rain must've washed it away."

He nodded. "Yeah, I mean they had him stabilized down at County Memorial in Sundance, but they moved him to Rapid City. Too small a hospital to keep him here."

"He?"

"The victim—last name Torres, twenty-two years of age, out of Tucson, Arizona. He's got a bunch of priors, mostly drugs along with a few domestics, and an aggravated assault and weapons charge."

"Had he been drinking?"

Corbin shrugged. "A little, according to the doctors, but nothing too bad."

"Current condition?"

"Assorted, along with a whopper of a traumatic brain injury. B-way—" He looked up at me. "That's what they call him, B-way—has got a diffuse axonal injury where the nerve cells are stretched and sheared inside the skull. He was out for six hours and then came to momentarily, but he was acting strange. He's pretty messed up."

"Anybody ask him about the accident when he regained consciousness?"

"I did. I tried to get a statement from him, but he wasn't capable of coherent thought, never mind speech."

"Think he will be?"

Dougherty shook his head. "I really don't know—neither do the doctors, I think. They put him back in an induced coma."

I nodded and then glanced at Henry, who continued to gaze out the windows. "You file a report with DCI's Accident Investigation?"

"I did, and a guy named Novo is coming up tomorrow."

The Bear finally joined the conversation. "Mike Novo?"

"Yeah—you know him?"

Henry smiled. "He is the motorcycle expert in Cheyenne."

I watched Corbin for a moment. "So, what happened?"

"We got a call from Chloe, a local girl who was working one of the tents up here part time. She was headed home when she saw a guy and a motorcycle lying on the side of the road."

"I'm going to need to speak with her."

He nodded. "It was about one in the morning on Saturday night, and with the traffic we get around Sturgis, it must've just happened. I got there right as the EMTs did, and they scooped him up and took him to Sundance. Herb Robinson, who owns the wrecker service, came and got the bike but then hauled it over to the Rapid City Police Department impound yard. I guess Robinson had past problems with bikers who liberate their bikes without paying, and the Rapid cops are the only ones with a fenced yard."

"What do you think happened?"

The patrolman pushed his empty oatmeal bowl away and rested his elbows on the table. "I think somebody hit him."

"Passing him? Rear-ended . . . ?"

"On purpose." He stared at me. "The bike was hit on the side, hard, and forced into the ditch. There's a culvert out there near the turnoff to the Tower—"

"Yep, we saw it when we stopped."

"Right." There was a pause. "What do you think?"

"I think you can jump to conclusions in these situations; there are just too many possibilities. Maybe it was a deer, the other driver was drunk, the kid was on his cell phone. . . ."

Corbin crossed his arms. "He did have a cell phone."

"Was it out?"

"His brains were out. . . . Everything was out."

I gave him another second. "I'll need to check the phone."

"Sure."

Leaning back in my chair, I listened to it squeal and finished my coffee. "So . . . why call us?"

"I guess this kid is a big deal with the Tre Tre Nomads, a motorcycle gang out of the Southwest, and things just got really weird really fast."

"How do you mean?"

"Members of the club were in Sundance already for the rally and strong-armed their way into seeing the kid at the Medical Center, but then he was transferred to Rapid City Regional and I guess they wouldn't let them in the intensive care unit. When I got back up here on Sunday, they were waiting for me at the police station."

"What'd they want?"

"They wanted to know who did it, who hit B-way." He shook his head and swirled the coffee left in his cup. "They said there was no way that he'd just had an accident, and they wanted a name." He leaned in. "I checked, and you know what? They're right. He's never had a traffic accident—everything else under the sun but not even a speeding ticket."

"Well, maybe they're just worried about the kid."

"No, it's more than that. I'm staying at one of the little cabins the city provides on the north end of town, and when I got through on patrol yesterday, one of them was waiting for me there."

"Okay."

"Big guy, kind of the enforcer, I guess."

"Alone?"

"Yeah."

"Okay."

"Wanted to know where we were on all this, what we were doing about it, and I told him that we were doing the best we could, but with the rally we didn't have the manpower to do a thorough investigation without help from DCI, but that they would be here pretty quick."

"And was he satisfied with that?"

"Not really." He studied me. "Can I ask you a question?"

"Shoot."

"What's the one percent mean?" He shoved his empty cup away. "When the enforcer, the strong-arm guy, said I better find out who did it, he said I better or I was going to meet the real one percent."

I nodded, allowing the information to surface in my memory. "The Hollister riot in '47. It was just a little after World War II, and they had this motorcycle rally in California in this little town. A lot more bikers showed up than they had anticipated."

"And there were riots?"

"Not really, but there were a lot of drunk bikers and racing in the streets. Things got out of hand. Hollister had only a nine-man police department, and they panicked and threatened to use tear gas and it got in all the newspapers." Somebody squeezed in near our table as I tried to remember the wording. "I think it was the American Motorcycle Association that came out and said the trouble was caused by the one percent deviants . . ."

". . . that tarnish the public image of both motorcycles and motorcyclists." I looked up to see a man in a leather vest, jeans, and motorcycle boots. "And that the other ninety-nine percent of motorcyclists are good, decent, law-abiding citizens." He slipped off his Oakley sunglasses, revealing what looked like a once-broken nose, and smiled down at Dougherty through a prodigious mustache and goatee. "The AMA came out later and said they never made the statement, but that's bullshit."

I picked up my coffee cup, studied the dregs, and then him, noting the do-rag under his reversed ball cap, his numerous earrings, and enough tattoos to print up a crew of merchant marines. "Hi."

He reluctantly averted his eyes from Corbin to me. "Hi."

"Were you there?"

He looked confused. "Huh?"

"Hollister."

He breathed a laugh. "No, bud, before my time. You?"

"Before mine, too."

He nodded. "Excuse me, but you mind if I continue my conversation with Officer Dougherty here?"

"Yep, I do. We're eating our breakfast, and we don't like being disturbed. Now, if you've got something you'd like to discuss, we'll be through with our meal here in a few minutes and will meet you out front."

He stared at me for a good long time, but I picked up my water glass and just kept drinking as he simmered. "Who the fuck are you?"

I finally set my glass down and stood, my size taking him a little by surprise. He was big—not quite as big as me—but he was younger, probably in his late thirties and built like a strong safety.

His hand dropped to the side toward the small of his back, at which point the Cheyenne Nation also stood, that move immediately getting his attention. As an aging offensive tackle, I was just as glad to have my running back with me.

I leaned in. "How 'bout we make our introductions outside?"

He hard-eyed Henry for a moment and then, curving the corners of his mouth underneath his mustache, looked back at me. "I'll see you out front, bud."

I watched him leave, and we sat back down. I smiled at Corbin. "That him—the Enforcer?"

"Yeah, that's him."

We sat there for a while longer, but it seemed as if the conversation had fled the room, so I stood again. "What do you say we go out front?"

Corbin shook his head. "I think I'll change careers— fireman is looking good."

I grabbed his shoulder. "C'mon, Deputy Dog."

All eyes were on us as we exited the packed restaurant, and I noticed a few people were quickly vacating the area in front of the Ponderosa. I pushed the door open, and as we stepped onto the sidewalk, about a dozen bikers of all shapes and sizes immediately surrounded the three of us.

The Enforcer was seated on a chromed-out bike, a kind of turquoise in color, his legs crossed with a wrist hanging over one of the grips on his handlebars. "Welcome to my office."

"Nice view."

He shrugged as the others stepped back, letting him make his play. He was the alpha, and if he could handle us on his own, he would.

"Now, how can we help you?"

He pointed past me to Dougherty. "I need to talk to him."

"Why? Who are you?"

He stepped around the front of his motorcycle, came in close, and extended his hand. "Brady Post. I guess you could say I'm the spokesman for the Tre Tre Nomads." I took the hand; he tried the old trick of grabbing my fingers, but I slipped the meat of my palm in and gripped him back. My old boss, Lucian Connally, had the strongest grip I'd ever felt, but he'd never been able to break me, so I wasn't concerned as Post began applying pressure. I gave just enough back so that we stayed even. His eyes were a deep blue, almost cobalt, and as he brought himself up close to me, I was surprised that he smelled like Old Spice aftershave. "Who are you?"

"Walt Longmire."

From the flexing of his forearm, I could tell he was putting everything into it, and I had to admit that it was an impressive display. "And what are you, Walt Longmire?"

"Just an interested citizen."

"Yeah? Well, I'm interested in what Officer Dougherty and his department are doing about finding the guy who tried to kill our buddy."

"It's an ongoing investigation, and I'm sure you'll understand that Officer Dougherty cannot make statements that might undermine the department's work." My turn to put everything I had into it. "Anyway, we're not sure there was an attempt on anybody's life. It could've been a simple traffic accident."

He didn't wince but did glance at our hands, which were intertwined in a death match. "I wanna see a report."

"Mr. Post, I'm sure that, as the spokesperson for the Tre Tre Nomads, you've got a lot of responsibility, but in the eyes of the town, the county, and the Wyoming state government, you have no official standing. Any information Officer Dougherty has would be for family members only."

"We are family."

"Blood?"

"More than you want to know, bud."

I did my best to look unimpressed. "I'm sure, but until you can show Officer Dougherty here some ID that corroborates that fact, there really isn't anything we can tell you, either as an individual . . ." I glanced around for effect, "or as a group."

His face was turning red, but I didn't see any reason to tap the leader of the pack on the nose just yet, so I let off and was surprised when he did the same. He let his hand drop, but I noticed he flexed it to get the blood flowing. "We'll be waiting." I started to turn to the left, but the ring of men didn't make way, and it was about then that he called out again, this time to Henry, "Hey, Chief, I didn't get your name."

I turned to see he'd thrown out a hand and that it rested on the chest of the Cheyenne Nation, and all I could think was, Oh, boy, here we go.

The Bear's head turned like a tree swaying, and I tensed, knowing that what was about to happen was going to be scorched-earth massive.

"That's Henry Standing Bear, Heads Man of the Dog Soldier Society, Bear Clan."

I stood there for a second trying to identify where the statement had come from, and then, glancing to my left, I saw

Eddy the Viking, the guy who had spoken with Henry in front of Capt'n Ron's.

It was one of those weird little moments where nobody knew what to do, so we all just stood there like some contemporary Western tableau.

Eddy raised his red cup and saluted the Bear. "I get that right?"

The Cheyenne Nation smiled. "Yes, you did."

I turned and walked between the two nearest bikers and continued on, with Dougherty and Henry following me like a funeral procession. After a few steps, I couldn't help but turn my head and ask, "Is the Viking one of the Tre Tre Nomads?"

Dougherty, happy to be out of the ring of fire, smiled an uneasy grin. "No, that's Crazy Eddy, one of the original Jackpine Gypsies; he lives over in Lead, been a fixture here at the rally for years, or so they tell me." Corbin glanced back at Henry, who was bringing up the rear of our little war party. "You know him?"

The Bear nodded. "It has been a short relationship."

There was a break in the crowd ahead of us that had allowed a real head turner to saunter up the sidewalk directly toward me. Lots of women perfect the sway at some point in their lives, but few get the rumble that this one had in spades. She was probably in her fifties, her dark hair with a sharp strand of silver in the middle swept back from her forehead. Very tall, and dressed in a simple black tank top and jeans, she split the crowd like an icebreaker, and both men and women watched her approach. Her sandals slapped the hot concrete on the sidewalk, as if teaching it a lesson.

I stepped to the side, but she countered, moved in front of me, and looked at me with frighteningly green eyes set in sun-kissed skin, her mouth wide and beautifully shaped, opened as if savoring the moment.

Corbin ran into my back, and Henry was turning to see what it was that might've stopped me dead. You would've had to measure the widening of his eyes with a micrometer, but it was there. He smiled broadly, and the woman did a hair flip that I would've given a 9.5, stepped in front of Henry, and then slapped the Bear's face with a tooth-shattering report.

The effect on the crowd was impressive, everyone freezing in place.

She stood there looking at him for a moment, then curtseyed in a quick dip of those magnificent hips and turned and walked away without a word.

Strangely, it was Dougherty who called out after her. "Lola?"

She kept walking, flailing a hand over a freckled shoulder in absolute dismissal.

I turned to Dougherty. "Lola?"

He cocked his head, watching her go. "Lola."

I turned back to the Cheyenne Nation. "*The* Lola?"

The side of his face still burned a burnished red as he rubbed it and watched her go with the slightest of head shakes and a knowing smile. "*The* Lola."

2

"Lola Wojciechowski?"

He shrugged. "I suppose. I never knew her last name."

I unloaded the trunk, shut the lid, and looked at the Thunderbird. "You named your car after her."

"It was only her first name; besides, it was not a verbal relationship."

The Bear unlocked the door to the cabin we had reserved and turned to me, his expression a little surprised. "It was a long time ago."

"Evidently it wasn't that long ago for her." Entering the doorway, I paused and looked at him. "Henry, you named your car after her, and you love that car." I brushed past him with our suitcases as Dog immediately jumped onto the nearest bed.

Setting a cooler by the door, the Bear stood, stretched, and then walked over to place two of the three volumes of the *Annotated Holmes* on the nightstand. "She did seem upset."

"A little."

He glanced back through the open door with the first book in his hand. "What is our plan?"

"Maybe go back out and examine the accident site. Why?"

"I thought I would take the bikes over to Jamey Gilkey's shop in Sturgis and let him get Rosalie ready for the Jackpine Gypsies Hill Climb tomorrow."

I slipped off my clip holster and .45, placed it on the nightstand beside the books, and sat on the bed next to Dog. "Don't you think you're getting a little old for that stuff?"

"I have done the Climb every year since 1974, when I won."

"All the more reason to stop."

"Lightning could strike twice. It has been a new century, and my luck could change."

"You go ahead then, and I'll stay here. You okay without your phone? I was wondering if you could loan it to me so I can call Cady." I held my hand out.

He handed the device to me. "Did she find a place to live?"

"She got a little carriage house a couple of blocks from the capitol building—Joe and Mary Meyer found it for her."

"It is good to have an in with the state attorney general."

I looked at the phone in my hands. "Yep."

"Emotional qualities are antagonistic to clear reasoning."

"Why don't you and Sherlock Holmes get the hell out of here?"

He shut the door, and I listened as he started up the Thunderbird and pulled away. Dialing the number and holding it to my ear, the phone rang a few times and then switched over to her message. "Hi, I'm not here—you know the drill."

"Hey, Henry."

"You're doing something."

"You've been kidnapped, right? There's no other way you'd be calling on a cell phone." She snorted. "Painting."

"What color?"

"Pistachio, with dark brown trim."

"Sounds interesting."

She huffed. "Don't start."

We had differing ideas about home décor, with my leaning toward off-white everything while she had more provocative tastes. "How's it coming?"

I could imagine her standing on the hardwood floor of the little carriage house, studying the green wall and wielding the roller like a weapon. "I'm not sure."

"Well, Punk, you can always repaint."

"Right, thanks."

"Lola helping?"

"No, thank God. She's asleep in her Pack 'n Play, under the watchful eye of her Nonnie Moretti."

Thankful that Vic's mother, Lena, was taking up the slack, I lay back on the bed and petted Dog. "How's things down at the attorney general's office?"

"Pretty general. Everybody here knows you from afar." Her voice relaxed a little, the tension fading so long as we weren't discussing paint. "They all think you're some kind of big deal."

"Have you been setting them straight?"

"A little—I told them about how you sometimes sleep with your mouth open."

Enjoying her voice, I closed my eyes. "That should do the trick."

"And that you never put the cap back on the toothpaste."

"I'm never going to be able to hold my head up again."

There was silence for a while, so I figured it was okay to ask about the investigation into my son-in-law's death. "Any word from Philadelphia?"

"Still nothing."

"I haven't heard anything from Vic."

"From what Lena tells me, I think she's helping, on a purely unofficial basis, of course."

"Of course." I crossed my boots. "How are the rest of the Morettis?"

"Still stunned. An entire family of police officers for three generations, and Michael is the first to ever be killed in the line of duty." There was another pause, longer this time, and her voice lowered. "Lena is taking it hard. Michael was the baby, you know?"

"Yep, he was." There wasn't anything more to say, so I didn't. That's the thing about comforting—it's almost more important to know when not to talk.

"I'm lonely, Dad."

"I know you are." I breathed a deep breath. "I'm sorry."

"I mean, thank God I've got Lena or I sometimes think I'd go nuts."

There was a knock, and Dog barked, leaping off the bed and standing by the door. I figured it must've been the Bear, having forgotten something, because I couldn't think of anybody else who would know where we were.

I tucked the phone between my shoulder and chin and rolled off the bed. "Hold on, there's somebody here." Lodging my leg between Dog and the door, I opened it to find Lola Wojciechowski pointing a .38 Special, replete with a pink grip, at my face. "Howdy."

She poked the thing at me like it was a stick. "I've got a gun."

Dog barked again, and I thought she was going to drop the weapon. I nudged him back with my leg. "I can see that."

"Dad?" Cady's voice sounded in my ear.

I cocked my head and held the phone. "Hey, I've got to go—"

"Did I just hear somebody say something about a gun?"

"Yep."

"Call me back."

Her concern was touching. "Right." I pulled the thing from my ear, hit the button to end the call, and opened the door the rest of the way to allow her entrance. "C'mon in." Her arm wavered, and she pointed the weapon in the general direction of Dog as I turned back to her. "And don't shoot Dog; it just pisses him off."

She looked uncertain as to what to do with that information but came the rest of the way in as the beast sniffed at her leather-bound crotch. "Hey, you wanna call him off?"

"You want to put the gun away?"

"No."

"Looks like we're at a standoff." I sat back on the bed and gestured toward the chair by the door. "Have a seat."

She swung her purse around behind her. "Where's Bear?"

"Gone." I didn't feel any reason to give out more—I'm like that in armed conversations.

She moved over and sat, pushing Dog's head away with her free hand. "This is not going the way I planned."

"That's the problem with the gun thing—usually it doesn't."

She crossed her legs and leaned forward, resting her elbow on her thigh and keeping the barrel of the .38 on me. "You don't seem too concerned."

I plumped up some pillows and leaned back on the bed, patting it for Dog to join me, which he did; then he sat there, looking at her and panting. I could imagine she got that response all the time. I gestured toward the .45 on the nightstand that she hadn't noticed. "I get a lot of guns pointed at me in my line of work."

She redoubled her aiming effort. "And what do you do?"

Carefully unsnapping the pocket on my shirt, I pulled out my badge wallet and flipped it open for her to see. "Absaroka County sheriff."

"Oh shit."

"Yep." I waited a moment more and then stuffed the hardware back in my shirt. "Now that we're getting to know each other a little better, do you want to put the gun away?"

She thought about it. "No."

I eased back on the bed, took off my hat, and placed it over my face. "Well, I'm taking a nap."

"What?"

I spoke into the crown of the palm leaf. "Sorry, I don't mean to be rude, but I haven't gotten a lot of sleep lately."

"Well, you're not going to get it now."

I tipped my hat up and looked at her. "Look, if you've got something to say, say it or get out of here. Henry's not going to show up any time soon, and I don't have the time to play twenty questions with you." I pulled my hat back down and sat there under it wondering what was going to happen next when I heard a snuffle. I propped my hat up again and could see she was crying. "Oh, please don't do that."

She smeared the tears away with the heel of her hand and looked at me. "I can't help it; I'm upset."

I turned toward her. "Look, Lola . . ."

She re-aimed the .38. "How do you know my name?"

I sighed. "You wouldn't believe how familiar I am with your name—evidently, my granddaughter is named after you."

"Huh?"

"You don't know Henry named his car for you?"

"No."

"Well, he did, and then my daughter for some godforsaken reason named my granddaughter after the car, so we've got vehicles, children, and heaven knows what else running around with your name on them."

She sniffed. "He named the T-bird after me?"

I tried not to let my eyes roll back in my head on that one. "Yep, he's sentimental that way."

"Where is he?"

I pointed at the gun, and she pulled a small purse around, unsnapping it and dumping the revolver inside before closing the bag back up and hanging it on her chair. "There. Now, where is he?"

"Gone to Sturgis."

She started to stand. "Great."

I held out a hand to stop her. "Look, why don't you tell me what's going on? I'm not crazy about you and that .38 leaving here in pursuit of my best friend."

She settled and studied me. "How long have you known Henry?"

"My whole life."

"Can you be more specific?"

"Ever since a water fountain altercation in grade school."

She didn't look as if she believed it to be the truth. "You've known him longer than I have?"

"I guess, but he hasn't named any vehicles Walt."

I watched her weigh her options. "I need some help."

"With what?"

"My son's been hurt."

I had a sinking feeling. "How?"

"He was in a motorcycle accident. Why are you making that face?"

Resting said face in my hands, I asked, "Is your son Bodaway Torres?"

She fumbled with the purse, and I held out my hand to stay her. "Please don't get the gun out again; Corbin Dougherty called me and said that there had been an accident involving a young man and that he thought there might be more to it than just a routine traffic incident."

"They tried to kill him."

"Who did?"

She looked at her hands and then started to get up again. "I need to talk to Henry."

"No, you need to talk to me. Corbin, a traffic analyst from the Division of Criminal Investigation by the name of Mike Novo, and I are going to be heading up the inquiry as to what happened to your son, but we could use your help."

She studied me. "I don't even know you."

"I'm a nice guy." She didn't seem convinced, so I added, "I grow on people."

She bobbed a sandal. "Like a fungus?"

I ignored the remark. "So, how did you and Henry meet?"

She studied me some more and turned to get her bag. "I should go."

I smiled. "Where?"

"To see my son."

I surprised her and stood. "How 'bout Dog and I go with you?"

Fortunately, Lola Wojciechowski drove a dilapidated, slightly dented, faded gold '66 Cadillac DeVille, so there was plenty of room for all of us. I shouted across the expanse as Lola careened through the sloping hills of the Devils Tower landscape, the monument peeking down at us every now and again. "I noticed the Arizona plates. You live down there?"

She shouted back after checking the rearview mirror and the reflection of Dog, dead center. "For quite some time now. My ex has a custom bike shop in Maryvale—Crossbones Custom."

"That would be Mr. Torres?"

She leaned over and, pushing a button in the dash and gesturing toward the yawning glove compartment, handed me the pocketbook containing the .38. "Yeah, Delshay."

I placed the purse in there and carefully closed the compartment. "Motorcycles, I'm assuming?"

"No, Huffy and Schwinn. . . . Of course, motorcycles."

I smiled and looked through the windshield. "Ever heard of a motorcycle club by the name of the Tre Tre Nomads?"

She glanced at me. "No."

I watched the scenery some more as she put her foot into the Caddy, sending us down a straightaway toward Moorcroft at a good ninety miles an hour, passing motorcycles as we went. "You know, I know the HPs that prowl this part of Wyoming during the rallies, and they don't have much of a sense of humor this time of year."

She kept her foot in it a bit longer but then let off.

I placed an arm on the doorsill and adjusted the side mirror so that I could watch behind us. "And point of interest: when law enforcement asks you a question, we generally already know the answer."

She simmered a bit and then pushed a big wave of the black and silver hair from her face. "What do you want to know?"

"Is Bodaway a member of the Tre Tre Nomads?"

"I guess."

I adjusted my sunglasses and stared at her.

"Yes. Yes, he's a member."

"So what are the chances that his accident is gang related?"

"Everybody who knows him loves him."

"That doesn't answer my question. Does he have any known enemies?"

She gestured as another group of maybe thirty motorcycles passed us, headed for Hulett. "He's in a motorcycle gang— everybody is his enemy, including you." Driving the big car with one hand, she threaded her fingers through her hair. "You people . . ." I waited for the rest. "People don't understand these clubs; they think you join them to break heads, take drugs, and generally fuck up society—but the reason you join is because society fucks with you. Do you know what it's like out there on the streets? I'm not talking about Cornhole, Wyoming; I'm talking about a real city with people in it."

I sighed. "I'm not completely unfamiliar with those environs."

"It's family, you know? A tribe—something to help keep the wolves at bay."

"So, why do you need Henry?"

She turned her head as if the answer were obvious. "He's the biggest, baddest wolf I know."

I smiled. "Okay, then who are the leaders of the other packs?"

"I'll have to think about it."

"You haven't already?"

She turned her head to look at me but then returned her attention to the road.

"If you think somebody's responsible for your son's accident, then it would make it a lot easier if you'd let us know of any suspicions you might have—could help us narrow the field."

"The Hells Angels, Mongols, Pagans, Sons of Silence, Outlaws, Bandidos, Warlocks, Vagos. Take your pick."

"Are all those groups represented here in Hulett?"

"Yeah, it's like an asshole convention."

"Weren't you just standing up for all these outlaw motorcycle clubs?"

"Only ours." She gave me a dazzling smile and passed another group of motorcyclists, barely getting back in our lane before scattering another cluster headed the other way. "The rest are pieces of shit."

"Right. Would you mind keeping it under the speed of

sound? I'd like to visit your son, but I'd rather not share a ward with him." She let off the accelerator, but I could tell it wasn't something she was used to doing. "Well, it has to be someone with a car or truck."

"Why is that?"

"I'm no Evel Knievel, but it seems to me it would be hard to run a motorcycle off the road with another motorcycle without ending up in the ditch yourself."

She nodded in agreement. "Hey, you really are a sheriff, aren't you?"

"So, who would be here with a four-wheeled vehicle?"

"Tons of guys; a lot of them bring trucks and vans and tow their bikes."

I watched as a few more motorcyclists passed but then did notice a few vans and SUVs pulling covered trailers. "I thought the idea was to show how tough you are by riding distance."

"You ever ride a Harley a couple thousand miles?"

"Never ridden one a couple hundred feet."

She shook her head. "How does a guy your age ever get to now with never having learned how to ride a motorcycle?"

I philosophized. "Common sense?" I turned to pet Dog. "So, are you a member of the Tre Tre Nomads?"

"No, they don't patch women." She saw the confusion on my face. "When you become a full member of a club, you get the patches to go on your leathers or your kuttes."

"What are kuttes?"

"Short for cut-offs—you know, denim vests or jackets where the sleeves have been cut off."

"Oh." I glanced at her leather ensemble but could see no patches. "So, no female members, huh?"

"No, but you can be somebody's old lady, and that carries a certain standing."

"And whose old lady are you?"

"Delshay Torres, my ex."

"The one that owns the Huffy/Schwinn shop."

"Right. We went our separate ways a few years ago, but I've still got status."

"Bodaway, Delshay . . . Those don't sound like Spanish names."

"Yavapai Apache."

Rapid City Regional Hospital is the largest and most advanced facility in the four-state area, so it doesn't come as much of a surprise that they transferred Bodaway Torres there.

A large man, built like a sumo wrestler, was taking up an entire bench as we entered the waiting room outside the ICU. He stood when he saw Lola. He didn't say anything but gave me a hard look before sitting his prodigious, leather-clad rear back on the bench and folding his massive arms, which just barely reached across his chest.

We continued toward the viewing window down the hall. "One of yours?"

"Big Easy."

"He from New Orleans?"

"No, he's just big and easy—he'd drink my bathwater if I let him."

I made an attempt to change the subject. "You think your son needs a bodyguard?"

"Brady thought they might come back and try to finish the job."

"Brady Post, the guy that says *bud* a lot?"

"You've met."

I nodded. "Momentarily. He seemed like someone who would be hard to get along with."

She shrugged. "If you're not one of us, I'd say yes."

You couldn't see much of the kid behind the glass, but from what you could, I'd have to say he was one of the handsomest young men I'd ever seen. His long black hair was splayed across the pillows, and his face was unmarked by the accident. Bodaway's features looked like they'd been cut with diamonds; he could've been a model for one of those bodice-ripper romance novel covers. "Handsome kid."

"Yes." She stood at the glass, her fingertips touching the cool, smooth surface. "Twenty-eight years old."

"What's the prognosis?"

"Traumatic brain injury, contusion type. We're lucky it wasn't a hematoma type because—"

"I know all about it—my daughter was assaulted in Philadelphia; she had the hematoma injury, and they had to cut part of her skull to allow for the swelling." I studied the young man. "She was out for the better part of a week."

She turned her face and looked up at me. "How is she now?"

"An assistant attorney general down in Cheyenne with an eight-month-old, who is named after you, well, in a way." She continued to stare at me. "Remember, she's the one who named my granddaughter after the car that is named after you?"

"I like her already." She smiled. "Anyway, that gives me hope." Her eyes were drawn back to the unmoving face and the array of EEG electrodes. "They had to shave some of his head; he's not going to like that."

I now noticed where they had removed the hair from his temples. "I don't suppose he was wearing a helmet?"

"No."

I struggled to think of something positive to say, knowing from experience how she was feeling. "It's good that it didn't mess up his face."

"And he's so totally unaware of how good-looking he is." Her hands came off the glass, and she stuffed them in her jeans. "You should see the girls hanging off of him; it's obscene."

"Like mother, like son?"

I wasn't sure, but I was willing to bet that she blushed just a bit. "More like father; he was really handsome—an asshole, but a handsome one." She studied her son a bit more and then, glancing at a fancy gold watch with a turquoise face, stepped away from the glass. "They're going to open the room up for an hour in about ten minutes and that's when I go in there and hold his hand and talk to him. I'd invite you, but they say that too much stimulation can agitate him and raise his blood pressure, so . . ." She reached into a pocket and handed me a set of keys. "I didn't mean to strand you, so just take the Caddy and do whatever you need to do. I'm staying at the Hulett Motel, too, so you can just leave the car there when you're done."

"What about you?"

She nodded toward the Buddha in the waiting room. "Big

Easy or somebody can give me a ride. Just leave it at the motel with the keys in it."

"You're sure?"

She took my hand and forced the keys on me. "I like you, you seem like the real deal." Then she added. "Don't let me down."

When I got back to the hospital parking lot, there was a dog sitting in the driver's seat of the '66 DeVille, which was now parked next to a battered pickup. We'd put the top up before we had gone into the hospital, in an attempt to contain the were-creature I referred to as Dog, and, wagging and smiling, he looked at me through the glass. I was about to unlock the thing when a voice sounded from behind me.

"What do you think you're doing, bud?" I turned to see Brady Post walking across the parking lot toward me. "That's not your car."

I went ahead and unlocked the door of the Cadillac. "Yep, my highly developed powers of deduction tell me that."

He shoved my shoulder, hard, when he got there. "Do you know whose car this is, bud?"

I turned and squared off with him, both of us suddenly aware of the growing growl resounding like a speedboat at idle behind the window of the Caddy. "As a matter of fact, I do."

Post gave Dog a look and then turned his eyes back to me. "Then what the hell are you doing?"

I studied him, getting a read on the way he held himself. Better than the usual barroom brawler, he was steady on both legs, with his weight evenly distributed and his arms hanging relaxed, but with his shoulders turned just a bit to give him the trajectory he'd need to take that first swing with the chrome-plated, three-link belt he held in one hand. I imagined that he wasn't likely to let me up after that if I went down and would use the steel-toed boots to finish the job. "That's really none of your business, Mr. Post."

Dog, a shrewd judge of character, lunged at the glass and snapped his big alligator jaws, and I watched as the biker started. "Gimme the keys, bud."

"No, I don't think I will. Post. Is that your real name, or is it an honorary title they gave you because you're *dumb as a . . . ?*"

He wrapped the chain one more twist in his hand, and all I could think was that I was tired of being hit and tired of hitting. I went through the choreography of violence and saw myself raising an arm to effectively block the chain, then wrapping my hand around his head and bringing it forward to where I would introduce my right fist to his face. If he really was tough, it was possible it might take two shots, or I could just bounce his head off of the pickup in an attempt to save the quarter panel on the gold-toned Cadillac.

All of these things were running through my head when I hit upon a simpler response. Pushing the button on the handle of the Caddy, I swung the door wide.

You would think that, at over 150 pounds, Dog wouldn't be that fast, but I'm pretty sure that DNA strain of his used to run down buffalo and maybe even my ancestors a few thousand years ago.

Say what you want about the Enforcer's intellectual capacities, he knew a life-threatening situation when he encountered one and scrambled for his very existence. He got the lead on Dog, and I reached out to get hold of the beast, but the monster was too fast and was scrambling on his claws and sliding sideways to get around the back of the jacked-up pickup in order to lock his massive jaws into the biker.

Post, realizing that his lead wasn't going to last long, hurdled over the far side of the truck and fell into the bed as Dog leapt up after him, but it was just too high. The biker scrambled backward toward the cab and was getting ready to swing the chain at Dog when I walked over and motioned to get his attention. "You hit my dog with that chain and, in the words of my old boss and mentor, Lucian Connally, I will scatter your chickenshit brains all over this parking lot."

Dog was still throwing his bulk against the side of the truck, and I would've been worried that he might hurt himself, but the thing looked like it had been dragged from a salvage yard. The Enforcer stayed in the middle as Dog, trying to find a way up, circled the truck.

"Call off the fucking dog, bud!"

"Drop the chain."

He did, and I patted my leg. "Dog!"

In the great balancing equations of Dog's mind, there are two things he cannot resist—ham, and me holding open a vehicle door. I'm pretty sure that ham is first and the only reason me holding open a vehicle door is in the running is because it might mean that we are going somewhere to get ham.

The beast looked a little disgruntled, but with one last glance at his prospective lunch, he hopped in the DeVille and sat in the passenger seat as though nothing had been amiss.

I glanced at Post and tipped my hat at the biker as I climbed in after Dog. "Happy motoring, bud."

The Rapid City Police Department's evidence impound lot happens to be wedged in between the city cop headquarters and the Pennington County Jail. Knowing on which side my bread was buttered, I entered the sheriff's office and asked for him.

They asked me who I was, and I told them that I was a sheriff too and that we needed to touch badges so we could recharge. The nice receptionist looked doubtful and then disappeared across the large room just as I heard Irl Engelhardt's voice. "Walt Longmire!"

Venturing across the room, I met the lean man at his doorway, and he invited me in. I stood next to the guest chair in his immaculate office and glanced around at the startling order of the place. "You ever do any work around here?"

He sat on the corner of his desk and folded his arms, palming his chin. "As little as I can get away with. Have a seat, Walt. What are you doing on this side of the Black Hills?"

I continued standing. "Maybe I'm vacationing."

He shook his head. "Try again—I've known you for too many years to count, and I've never heard of you taking even a day off."

"Maybe I'm changing my ways."

"Uh huh." He looked down at the blotter on his desk. "Hey, I heard about your son-in-law."

"Yep."

"I'm sorry."

I nodded. "We all are."

"How's Cady holding up?"

"Surprisingly well—Joe Meyer gave her a job."

"Down in that nest of smiling vipers in Cheyenne?"

"Yep."

"Well, she should be able to fend for herself; she comes from good stock."

"Thanks, Irl."

He laughed and stood. "It's funny, you know. . . . I guess if we didn't all think we were ten feet tall and bulletproof, we wouldn't do this job."

I sighed. "I'm beginning to think I'm about nine two and only bullet resistant."

"What can I do for you, Walt?"

"You've got a motorcycle in your evidence impound lot that has to do with a traffic incident up in Hulett, near Devils Tower."

He nodded and gestured toward the door. "Somebody have one too many and run off the road looking at the scenery?"

"Something like that."

We moved back through the bull pen, out another door, and down a stairwell. "I can't tell you how much of that we get this time of year, and it gets worse as the baby boomers get older. These guys finally get enough money to go out and buy the motorcycle of their dreams—the one they wanted when they were eighteen—but they seem to forget that they're not eighteen anymore and that they haven't been on one of the things for thirty years."

He pushed a heavy door open, and we were back on the

sidewalk where I'd parked. "You mind if I get my dog out of the car and let him have a little walk?"

"No problem."

Sheriff Engelhardt raised an eyebrow as I freed Dog from the Cadillac. "Is this what the stylish Wyoming sheriff is driving these days?"

"Not mine. It belongs to the mother of the accident victim."

Dog bounded up to Irl and nudged him with his muzzle as the sheriff rubbed his head. "A friend?"

"Of Henry's."

"Oh."

The sheriff disengaged himself from Dog and waved at a young deputy in a booth by the gate as we walked into the decidedly urban environment of the vehicle evidence lot. Surrounded by buildings on three sides, the fenced-in area had razor wire circling the top and myriad damaged vehicles lined up in the diagonal parking spots.

"Did you hear about Sturgis last year?"

"Can't say I did."

"Seventy-fifth anniversary. They had over a million bikers."

"Sounds like a good time to spray for them."

He shook his head. "What've you got against motorcycles, Walt?"

We walked past the cars, trucks, and SUVs to a tarped area that held a half-dozen bikes, all of them statuary testaments to the fact that the two-wheeled conveyance wasn't such a great idea. "It's not so much the motorcycles themselves; it's this bogus, outlaw culture that goes along with them—the black leather, chrome death's head crap—that I find tiresome. It's all just fake. I've almost got more respect for the real outlaws than the corporate/consumerist/choreographed version, but not much."

The sheriff pointed toward the closest one. "Well, there's Bodaway's bike."

I studied it. "Doesn't look that bad."

"Glance over here at the other side."

I did, and you could see where something had slammed into the motorcycle, bending all the protruding metal inward. "Wow, somebody meant business."

Engelhardt stooped beside me. "It's an '09 Cross Bones, a model they made a few years, springer front with a softail rear; they bobbed the fenders and put those ape-hanger bars on it to give it a more custom look."

I glanced at him.

"Hey, I know bikes." He stood up. "Who you got coming from Cheyenne?"

"Mike Novo."

He nodded his head. "Well, Mike'll be able to tell a lot more than you and I can." He stared at the bent handlebars, crushed saddlebag, and mashed up floorboard. "Looks like it was broadsided."

I picked at the tufts of grass and dirt lodged between the bent wheels and the deflated tires. "From what I understand he went into the barrow ditch just before a culvert."

He clapped his hands together with a loud smack that startled me. "Bike hit that and sent the kid over the handlebars?"

I reached a finger out and flicked at the crushed side of the motorcycle. "I'd imagine."

"They take him over to Rapid City Regional?"

"Yep."

"How's he look?"

"Not so good—brain trauma." I sighed. "I guess he woke up after six hours, but was incoherent and went unconscious again, maybe for good." I scratched my fingernail across one of the extruding pieces of metal, held the fingernail up to my face, and studied the paint underneath.

Looking back over my shoulder, I studied Lola's Cadillac parked at the curb, the gold reflecting in the broad daylight.

3

In 1938 Clarence "Pappy" Hoel, Sturgis Indian Motorcycle dealership owner, businessman, entrepreneur, and anything-two-wheeled enthusiast, founded the Jackpine Gypsies Motorcycle Club, one of the first sanctioned organizations of that nature in America, and began the Black Hills Classic. The Classic consisted of a single race of a half mile on a dirt track with only nine participants and an audience of about the same number. The vaunted prize: beer money.

Seeking a broader audience for the event, with the philosophy that if you wreck it they will come, the Gypsies elected to include intentional board wall crashes, ramp jumps, and head-on collisions with automobiles. The mayhem worked, and the crowds grew, with only a brief respite during World War II, when activities were curtailed by gas rationing.

In 1961, the craziness that is the rally was elevated to a whole new level of insanity with the addition of the Jackpine Gypsies Hill Climb, where racers from all over the world partake in just what it sounds like: a race to the top of an escarpment that you probably couldn't walk up. Over the years, the competition has escalated to the point where the bikes are modified with such things as extended travel arms and nitro-injected engines that shoot flames from their tailpipes like two-stroke blowtorches.

The first time Henry Standing Bear attempted the hill climb, he was a high school senior and rode on his newly acquired '63 Swedish-built Husqvarna 250 cc with the nifty red and chrome gas tank. The results were: three broken fingers, one shattered radius, a broken tooth, two broken ribs, a punctured lung, and a totaled bike.

He did not win, but that didn't keep him from continuing to try. He finally won in 1974, but one victory was not enough, and he had been trying to win it again ever since.

If I were to catalog the bizarre things my friend the Bear has done in his life, I'm pretty sure it would make the *Sears Wish Book* look like a pamphlet, but the Sturgis Jackpine Gypsics Hill Climb would be listed in the section *A Special Kind of Crazy.*

Henry has unique friends for his more eccentric activities, and I watched in the late afternoon's horizontal light as Jamey Gilkey adjusted the nitro injectors on the newest brand of idiocy, a KTM 450 SX-F named Rosalie that looked more like a four-stroke rocket ship than a motorcycle.

It was the time trials, a preliminary before the big race tomorrow. "Who was Rosalie?"

The Bear adjusted some elbow pads on the outside of his INDIAN DUNES MOTOCROSS, VALENCIA, CALIFORNIA 1975 jersey sporting, of all things, a war-bonnet-wearing, tomahawk-swinging motorcyclist. "A woman I used to date."

"A woman, huh? You usually say girl."

"Rosalie Little Thunder was, by all accounts, a woman."

I turned and watched as one of the riders came unglued, as

they call it, and tumbled back down the hill with his bike cartwheeling on top of him. "What was Lola?"

Henry glanced up and watched as the combination rider/motorcycle crashed in a heap at the bottom of the hill. "That was a bad line." Then he glanced back at me. "When I met her, a girl."

"Well, she's all grown up now, with a son."

"Bodaway." He considered the name, tasting it. "Apache?"

"Yep."

He nodded. "The last I heard of her, she had moved to Arizona."

"Well, she's got a problem, and she thinks you're going to solve it."

"Why me?"

"Because you're some kind of bad motor scooter."

He put on his old open-face helmet and tightened the chin strap. "And what is the problem?"

"In case it slipped your mind, somebody tried to kill her son."

His eyes cut to mine. "You're sure of that?"

"Yep, but there's a twist."

Jamey stepped back as the Bear threw a leg over the motorcycle, straddling it for action. "With Lola, there always is."

I sidestepped around him and stood in front of the motorcycle so he'd have to run over me to escape. "I went to the impound lot in Rapid and took a look at the kid's bike, and it had gold paint on it where it had been broadsided."

His face was impassive as he adjusted his goggles. "So?"

I gestured toward the parking lot behind a chain-link fence, where the Caddy sat, quite prominently. "Lola's car is gold and has damage on the right front fender."

He shook his head. "Have you spoken to her about this?"

"No. When she had me at gunpoint we discussed other things—mostly you."

"Gunpoint?"

"Yep, she showed up at the cabin with a .38, but then things got more conversational and I joined her in going to the hospital, where she was kind enough to loan me her car."

"The one she ran over her son with?"

"Well, we're still not clear on that. I figured I'd ask her about it when I return the Cadillac to the Hulett Motel later this afternoon." I folded my arms and looked at him, still steadfastly in his way. "If you don't mind me saying so, you don't seem all that interested in the case."

"It is a case?"

I shrugged. "As a favor to Corbin, sure."

"In answer to your question, no."

"No, what?"

"No, I do not mind you saying I do not seem all that interested in the case."

A younger rider rapped the throttle on his bike and shouted through his face shield as he pulled up in front of Henry. "You gonna give it another shot, old man?"

The Bear showed his teeth. "'My mind is like a racing engine, tearing itself to pieces because it is not connected up with the work for which it was built.'"

The kid studied us questioningly and then sped away, throwing dirt and gravel.

Lowering the arm that had protected my face, I made a guess. "Obviously not an Arthur Conan Doyle fan."

The Bear watched him go. "Last year's winner." He gave

the KTM a violent kick, racked the throttle a few times, and sat there, looking at me. I waited a moment, then stepped aside, gesturing toward the hill with a touch of dramatic flair and watched as, balancing on the pegs with his old Roger DeCoster boots, he sped off toward the starting gates.

I fanned away the dust and exhaust and turned to look at the bearded man who was standing next to me. "Was it something I said?"

He shook his head and walked back toward his truck with the tools he had gathered, throwing them in before sitting on the tailgate in preparation for the show. "It ain't you; it's Lola. She spins his crank whenever he gets around her." I joined him on the tailgate of the GMC. "I'm pretty sure that if you look up 'drama queen' in the dictionary, the illustration is Lola Wojciechowski."

"Were you around when they met?"

He laughed. "Oh, yeah."

We watched as the Bear spun up to the starting rack and waited for his chance to lodge his back wheel against the massive log they had chained there for a backstop.

"Well?"

"I'm not so sure it's a story I should be telling. Why don't you ask Henry?"

"I have, and he's not talking." I raised an eyebrow, applying pressure.

"You know she was a dancer, right?" He leaned back, his hands splayed on the metal. "I mean, not the Bolshoi Ballet kind."

"Right."

We watched the riders in the lineup perform as they rode

their best for time, the queue slowly moving toward the end where Henry waited. One or two actually made it to the top, but most flipped out, did dramatic U-turns, or just dug into the reddish dirt, burying their bikes and themselves before casually stepping off their mounts, one even kicking his.

"You remember that itty-bitty-titty bar that used to be out on Tilford Road, about halfway between Sturgis and Rapid—the Cattle Kate?"

"The one they used to launder money for the mob?"

"Yeah, that one. Well, there were about a half dozen of these guidos who were giving one of the dancers a hard time—you know, trying to drag her into one of the back rooms. Henry happened to be there saying hey to this monster buddy of his who was a bouncer, Brandon White Buffalo."

The time-trial adjudicators with the clipboards had finally gotten to Henry, and we watched as one of them at the top of the hill raised a green flag. "I know Brandon."

"Well, he had 'em stood off, but they had guns, so Henry backed Brandon's play. There was a lot of shouting and the usual stuff when Henry proposed that they pick out a couple of representatives, one from each group, and then let the two of 'em go out in the parking lot and settle things like real men."

The flagman dropped his arm, and the Bear was off.

"The guidos went along with it, but said it had to be Henry and not Brandon because Brandon is so big, you know?"

Henry sped across the short flat and dug in, the KTM bouncing from one berm to another, chewing up a few sparse patches of sagebrush.

"Big mistake."

"No shit. The mob guys selected this weight lifter that they had with 'em. The guy swings this haymaker at the Bear, who does a double arm block, pivots his elbow into the guy's gut, and then brings the back of his fist up into the guy's face— three seconds, done."

Henry shot up the hill and bounced over the approach rollers that kept the rider from establishing too much speed too quickly. He flew a good twenty feet and then navigated to the side of the devilish curve to dig in and then caught traction, again shooting up the hill through the tufts of prairie grass.

"What did the mob guys do?"

"They didn't know whether to shit or go blind, so they just stood there and then carried the guy back to their car and went back to Jersey, I guess."

Henry was approaching the top but had lost some momentum as the front tire began slowly lifting from the turf.

"So, the dancer was Lola?"

"No, but Lola was there, and I guess she liked the cut of the Bear's jib or something like that."

Both Jamey and I slid off the tailgate, unconsciously drawn to the hill like spectators to a train wreck. The front wheel of the KTM kept rising, even with all of Henry's weight hanging over the handlebars, but he was so close to the precipice that I thought for sure he was going to make it.

"Anyway, they hooked up after that and were together off and on for a while."

The Bear held on till the last second and then flipped over backward.

"Uh oh."

We watched as Henry rolled to the side to get out of the way of the out-of-control motorcycle that missed him only by inches and then cartwheeled down the hill before slamming to the ground. He sat and watched it.

"More off than on."

When I got over to the Hulett Police Department, Chief Nutter was inside the MRAP, trying to figure out how to start it. "We're going to drive it through town."

I stood below, looking up into the cab at him. "Why on earth?"

"Gape and awe—we're going to show these bikers what they're up against if they start anything." He gave me a thumbs-up like a fighter pilot and held the tough-guy look for as long as he could but then broke up laughing. "Gas station is on the other side of town, and if we don't put fuel in the damn thing, it's going to be useless."

"Bill, you don't want my opinion on that." I stepped on the running board and glanced around at all the hi-tech. "Why don't you bring the gas over here?"

"Do you know how much fuel this thing holds?" He glanced around the cab, looking for a gauge he could recognize. "Hell, I don't know how much fuel the thing holds. You think it's gas or diesel?"

"You better hope it's diesel, if you're aiming to get even a mile to the gallon." I took a look down the crowded street. "I'm trying to find Corbin."

"Last I heard he was settling a dispute at the campground, but he should be back any time." He gestured toward the dash. "Hey, you were in the military; you should know how to start this thing."

"Not really." I glanced around the interior at all the monitors and switches. "The stuff we had in Vietnam was decidedly less advanced, but I'll go hog wild and venture an opinion: Does it have a key?"

"No, just had a padlock and a chain holding the doors closed, which are hydraulic like in *Star Trek*. Took us forever to figure out how to open and close 'em."

"Then there's a switch."

"No, there's not."

"It probably doesn't look like any switch you've ever seen, and there's probably a coil preheating mechanism." I started climbing up. "Get over in the passenger seat and let me take a gander."

He did as I said and turned to look at me as I scanned the dash. "What do you need Deputy Dog for?"

Spotting the less-than-obvious switch, I glanced at it to see if, as in most diesels, you just turned it in the opposite direction to preheat, but there was nothing. Finally spotting a safety toggle to the left, I hit it and watched as a red light came on beside the ignition along with a spiral coil that lit, then flickered and went out. "He supposedly has the Torres kid's cell phone, and I'd like the name of the woman who found Bodaway after the accident."

"Bodaway?"

"The kid that was in the wreck. That's his name—Apache."

"Oh."

I hit the starter, and the gigantic engine in the MRAP rattled to a lopsided cant, sounding a lot like *Steamboat*, an old B-25 I'd flown in years ago. Reaching over and tapping the fuel gauge—a habit I'd picked up from my old Doolittle Raider boss who had piloted the vintage bomber—I glanced at Chief Nutter. "How far is it to the gas station?"

"About a mile."

"You might make it."

"Well, let's go then."

I laughed. "I'm not driving this thing."

"Then who is? You're the one who was a jarhead and all." He nodded toward the crowded street. "I'm likely to run over a building or something."

I sighed and hit the push button to engage the drive, assuming *R* was reverse. "All right then, let's bring the mountain to Mohammed."

He shook his head. "You sure do know a lot of biblical quotes for a fellow that doesn't go much for churchin'."

I started easing the fifteen-ton behemoth backward, attempting to see if there was anything behind me on the street. "That's not the Bible—it's Francis Bacon, from an old Turkish proverb."

He shook his head some more and looked at me. "Hey, you're good with names; what should we call it?"

"How about the Pequod?"

He thought about it but changed the subject. "I'm going to turn the red and blues on. You know, to let 'em know we're cops." He reached overhead and flipped another toggle. "I know where that is, because I was the one who had 'em installed." He held out a piece of paper with a diagram. "Shows the lights right here. There's also a PA system if you want to announce our presence with a sense of authority."

Having successfully backed the MRAP, I was looking point-blank at the quarter mile of Hulett's main and only thoroughfare, the direction we would be heading before taking a left and pulling into the Dakota Gas Company like happy motorists. "I don't suppose there's a siren, just to let people know that this thing actually moves, is there?"

"There could'a been, but I didn't order that."

I nodded, straightened my hat, and pressed the *D* button. Hitting the gas, I was appalled at how fast the gigantic vehicle moved and immediately adjusted the weight of my foot on the accelerator. "Wow."

"Dual turbos and an overdrive." He giggled. "I opted for those, too."

We went down the hill at a reasonable speed, and it was interesting to see the crowd's reaction to the bright white colossus, most just standing with their mouths agape, figuring they were being invaded.

I paused at the only intersection in town, but I needn't have bothered since the Gape and Awe portion of the exercise appeared to be holding sway. There were about eight bikers on one side and a pickup truck, sedan, and a few more bikes on the other, but they were all stopped, probably afraid that we were going to open fire. I glanced around, half expecting to see a turret and .50. "Is this thing armed?"

Bill had broken out what I assumed were the copious manuals for the vehicle and was now studying the door in search of a window crank. "How do you think the windows work?"

"They probably don't; that would compromise the Ambush Protected part of the MRAP title."

"How the hell are you supposed to yell at everybody?"

I pulled forward through the intersection. "That's what the PA system would be for."

"Oh, we gotta find that—"

"Oh, no we don't."

He studied the manual some more. "In answer to your question, no it doesn't have any guns on it. Hell, it's just a big truck that's hard to blow up, but you'd think we were trying to bring a tank in here when I was fighting with the county commissioners about the thing. There's this one old hippie on the board from Sundance, and she's sure we're trying to militarize the police department. Hell, there's only two of us, so I'm not so sure how much militarization we could summon up."

"What was the name of the guy that underwrote this thing for you?"

"Bob Nance—one of those computer whizzes from out of California—a specialist in acoustic something or other. He's got a place up at the golf course. Comes out here in the summers to play and pretend he's a cowboy. 'Course, I never met a cowboy with a log mansion on the ninth green."

Traveling at a majestic five miles an hour, we were approaching the Ponderosa Café at midtown, where I could see Corbin Dougherty leaning on his vehicle as he talked to a group of bikers, all of them pausing in their conversation to watch the rolling fortress pass by. "Hell, there's Deputy Dog. You wanna stop, and I'll figure out how to open the door?"

I kept moving. "Why don't we spare ourselves the embarrassment? I'll get the information I need from him on the walk back."

Bill looked a little unnerved. "You're not going to drive it back for me?"

"Wasn't planning on it. Anyway, you're going to need the practice."

"What if I run over somebody?"

"You'll hardly feel it." I made the left, careful to avoid Lola's Cadillac parked next to the sidewalk adjacent to the motel, where I'd left it earlier, the keys in the ignition as she'd requested. We crossed the Belle Fourche bridge, and I was just glad the thing held. Amazingly enough, the MRAP had turn signals, and I clicked the stem down, indicating an impending left. The oncoming bikers had already stopped, never having encountered a great white whale like this one.

I spun the wheel, goosed the accelerator, and the big truck leapt across the lanes and roared into the Dakota Gas Company lot, where I figured out pretty quick that it wasn't going to fit under the awning. "Oh, ye whale, now what?"

"There's a big-rig island in the back; just circle around there."

I did as instructed and pulled up to the diesel pump with the green handle, then hit the *N* button and subsequently the *P*. "There you are, Captain my Captain—she's yours from here on out."

He reached around behind him, then began patting all his pockets with his hands. "Um, I appear to have left my wallet back at the office. You wouldn't happen to have some cash on you, would you?"

"How's the bike?" We were sitting in the Ponderosa Bar behind the Ponderosa Café. Actually, we were sitting at a picnic table in the alley behind the Ponderosa Bar behind the Ponderosa Café, because it was the only place where there were a couple of seats together, and we were soon to have guests. "Irreparable, I hope?"

The Bear rewrapped the gauze and Ace bandage around his hand after readjusting the nonstick pad that covered the burn he'd received from the KTM as it had attempted to squash him like a bug. "I bent a few things, but we'll be ready for tomorrow."

"Why?"

Exasperated, which I could tell only from a slight change in the angle of his head, he turned and looked at me. "You act as if I am the only one who does crazy things."

"Name one crazy thing I do."

"It is pinned to your shirt."

I sipped my Rainier. "Actually, it's in a natty leather wallet in my pocket."

"You know what I mean."

It was a velvety evening in the Black Hills, and the slight breeze carried the scent of the pines and the clear high-country air or maybe it was the lumberyard on the other side of the river. "That's different; it's my job."

He raised an eyebrow and savored his Snowden cabernet. "Why is that different? I am thinking it might actually be worse."

"Why?"

"Mine is driven by passion, yours by wages."

I gave him the eyebrow back. "Civic duty, if you please."

"Even worse—insanity as a duty?"

"The insane part of my work is accidental, an improvisational by-product, whereas you are actually courting crazy."

"Not true. I am, like you, participating in actions which may or may not lead to certain results which you deem as crazy."

"No, you choose to do these things."

He gestured with the wineglass. "And you did not choose to wear that badge in the natty leather wallet?"

I considered it and then raised my bottle in a toast as he joined me. "Touché."

"What are you guys toasting?"

I looked up at the smiling man with the blue sweatshirt and mop of silver hair. "Well, if it isn't No Go Novo." I scooted over and made room for the traffic expert for the Division of Criminal Investigation. He sat, and I noticed that he'd already fortified himself with a beer from the bar, a prudent action seeing as how we hadn't spotted a waitress in twenty minutes.

The investigator glanced around, pushing the hair from his face. "Kind of crowded around here."

"'Tis the season."

Mike nodded to Henry. "You make your time trial over in Sturgis?"

The Bear smiled. "Nine-tenths of it."

"Uh oh."

I shrugged. "He's in the front third."

Mike seemed impressed. "Well, that means they think you'll actually make it; the guys they throw in the back third are doomed."

Henry nodded. "I know, I have been there."

"What time is the race tomorrow?"

"Eight."

"In the morning?" He drank from his beer. "I'm not through throwing up by then."

Spotting a waitress rounding one of the other tables, I flagged her down and turned back to my comrades. "I'm getting another; you guys want something?" Agreeing that we might not have another opportunity, I ordered a double round and then turned back to Mike. "Did you have a look at Bodaway's bike?"

"No, but I saw the incident location."

"And?"

He took a couple of sips of his beer, encouraged by the hope of another. "It rained, of course, and there's been no end of traffic on that road—"

"Yeah, yeah, yeah."

He smiled. "There are about three different types of gyroscopic instability on a motorcycle. The ones that happen at high speed are weave and wobble, both occurring at more than eighty miles per hour and on dry pavement. Weave is a snakelike oscillation of the motorcycle around its center of mass. Usually confined to the rear of the bike, it doesn't have much of an effect on the steering but does generally cause the bike to weave from side to side along the path of travel."

"And wobble?"

"Wobble is uncorrected weave, where it begins to affect the frame of the bike and then the steering axis. The transition from weave to wobble is about .02 seconds, and I don't even think the great Henry Standing Bear has reflexes that quick." He smiled at the Cheyenne Nation. "Once the wobble sets in, the motion becomes so severe that the rider loses control and the bike is slammed to the pavement, resulting in a totaled bike and a dead rider."

"Factors?"

He palmed a chin and looked at me through the silver curtain, partially hiding eyes that had seen more vehicular mayhem than I would ever want to. "Weight distribution, center of aerodynamic pressure, tire inflation, tire size, tread shape and wear, and rider weight."

"He's not a large man."

"And the bike?"

I paused for a second and then recited what Sheriff Engelhardt had said to me at the impound lot. "'09 Harley Cross Bones, springer front with a softail rear, and I have no idea what I just said."

"Big bike."

"It looked big to me, but that just makes it a larger death trap. Can't you just slow down?" I finished my beer as the other drinks arrived. "Um, does anybody have any money?"

They both looked at me. "The gas station over here doesn't take credit cards, and I had to use all my walking-around money to fill up Chief Nutter's MRAP."

Mike studied me, pretty sure this was the most elaborate way of getting out of paying a check he'd ever heard. "A what?"

The Cheyenne Nation handed me a fifty, which I transferred to the waitress. "Keep the tip."

Henry shook his head as I handed him his two glasses of wine and Mike his beer backups.

"So, can't you just slow down?"

"It happens too fast, and at that speed most riders make the mistake of slamming on their brakes instead of redistributing their weight by transferring it from the saddle to the pegs. And add-on accessory boxes can change both the weight distribution and the aerodynamics." Mike glanced at me. "You saw the bike?"

"I did, and I saw the kid, too."

Sticking to the subject at hand, he asked about the motorcycle. "Was it stock?"

"How the heck should I know?"

"You say it had the springer forks?" I looked at him blankly. "Did the front have a set of springs, kind of vintage looking?"

"Yep."

"Those models can get out of tune and cause problems."

"There's something else . . ."

"Were there any saddlebags on it, big ones?"

"Um, no—but there was gold paint."

He looked at me. "What color is the bike?"

"Black."

"You think somebody hit him?"

"I can't be sure, but I think you'd better take a look at the bike and then the car I've got on loan."

"Well, when I get down to Rapid, I'll . . ."

I pulled the phone from my pocket and handed it to him as he gave me a questioning look. "When did you start carrying a cell phone?"

I pointed at Henry. "It's his. I took pictures; well, Irl Engelhardt did." I gestured toward the device. "I barely know how to take a photo."

"It's pretty easy to operate; you just hit the little icon that looks like a camera. Here, see?" He showed me and began swiping through the photos, finally glancing at the Bear. "You mind if I send these to my email so I can look at them on my computer?"

The Cheyenne Nation tipped his wine. "Feel free. I just own the thing."

Mike smiled and began pushing buttons. "By the way, Walt, you described the bike magnificently—it almost sounded like you knew what you were talking about."

"Thanks." As the investigator worked, I glanced at the Bear. "Why would Lola hit her own kid?"

Henry shrugged. "You have a child; you know how it is." His face tightened in a slight smile, and I looked past him where I could see a table of women who were openly staring at him. I sometimes forgot the effect that the Bear had on the opposite sex, but then, when I saw any of them around him, I remembered.

"Seriously."

"Walt, you have to remember that my interaction with this woman is almost thirty years old; I have no idea what her relationship with her son is like, and with someone like Lola, I am not remotely willing to guess."

Novo handed Henry his phone and then turned back to me as the Cheyenne Nation checked for messages.

"You said there were three specific types of gyroscopic instability on a motorcycle."

Mike smiled. "I did, and though the third usually doesn't leave marks on the pavement, we were lucky that the kid was riding in the emergency lane, and the pavement was remarkably fresh."

"Wait—he was riding on the edge of the road?"

He nodded. "Just on the other side of the rumble strip."

"Where he ran off the road."

"No, he was riding there for quite a ways, and here's the thing: there was an instability, but it was a low-speed phenomenon called flutter, which is when the front tire and steering assembly experience rapid oscillation—think of an unsupported castor on a shopping cart. It happens only one way, when the rider's hands are not on the handlebars."

Henry and I looked at each other and then back to Mike. "So, you're saying that he was riding on the edge of the road with his hands doing something other than steering?"

Mike nodded again. "Yes, and if flutter is the case, then that means there must've been something on the rear of that bike."

"Like the heavy saddlebags you mentioned?"

"Or . . ."

"Or what?"

"From the photos you took, I could see that there was a seat pad on the Harley."

The Cheyenne Nation carefully set his wineglass on the uneven surface of the old picnic table, his voice rumbling in his chest. "Then someone was on the back of the motorcycle."

4

The Bear decided to stay at the Pondo, as the locals called the bar, and talk with Jamey and some of the other hill climbers who had arrived as our little party was breaking up, but I was worried about Dog back at the motel cabin. I thought the quiet by the river might be a chance for him to get out, and evidently he thought so, too.

I walked along after him in the thin fog that rolled off the water as he sniffed at the high stalks of grass and the cattails that had sprung up near the edge. "Don't get any wise ideas— I'm not sharing my bed with a wet dog."

He ignored me and trotted on along the bank to where I could see someone in the mist. I was about to call Dog off, but he seemed to know who it was. After another step, I recognized her profile, and I joined them. "Hello, Lola."

She didn't look at me but petted Dog's wide head. "Hi, Sheriff."

"Did you get your keys?"

"No."

"I put them under the floor mat on the driver's side."

"You don't have to do that; nobody outside of the Tre Tre Nomads would touch that car."

I stopped and turned to look at the river, the fog rolling tendrils from the surface, the water reflecting the high clouds just starting to disappear in the dusk. "I guess it's the lawman in me, but I can't leave the keys in the ignition of a car, especially in a town with thousands of bikers in it."

She glanced at me.

"Although, I am sure ninety-nine percent of them are good, law-abiding citizens." I looked around. "I'm amazed you found a quiet spot."

She took out a cigarette and lit it, taking a deep drag. "Might be the only one."

"You mind if I ask you a question?"

Her voice took on an officious tone. "Where were you on the night of January sixteenth?"

"Something like that."

She stared at me. "You're serious?"

"I am. Where were you the night of your son's accident?"

She took another drag on her cigarette. "Who wants to know?"

"You wanted an investigator; this is called investigating."

"Me?"

"Everyone's a suspect until we find out who did it."

"So, you do think somebody did it?"

Dog was getting too close to the water, so I patted my leg. "You're not answering my question."

She studied me for a moment more. "The Dime Horseshoe Bar in Sundance for the Burnout."

"The what?"

"They put up a big platform on the street, and then guys ride their bikes up onto it and do these epic burnouts—you know, locking up the front brake and spinning the rear? Lots of smoke, lots of beer and leather—an All-American spectacle."

"Were you driving your car?"

It took her a few seconds to answer. "No."

"Then who was?"

"What are you saying?"

"Without laboratory analysis I can't be absolutely sure, but it looks to me as if somebody hit your son with your car. There was gold paint on the Harley and there appears to be damage to the right front fender of the Cadillac."

"There's damage all over my car; it's a beater."

"It's a flake gold beater, a pretty unusual paint job." I folded my arms and studied her. "I'll ask again: Who was driving your car?"

"And I'll say how the hell should I know? Everybody borrows it." She smoked some more. "The thing was sitting where it is now that day with the keys in it, so I literally have no idea."

"Who usually borrows it?"

"Everybody—everybody in the club anyway." She stopped talking and looked up at me.

"I think your exact words were, no one outside the Tre Tre Nomads would touch that car."

"It couldn't be someone from our club."

"You're sure of that?" She didn't seem so, all of a sudden. "How many club members are there here?"

"A couple dozen maybe?"

"Can you get me a list?"

"No, I can't do that." She took another drag on the cigarette. "It would be like dropping a dime on them—ratting them out, you know?"

I smiled my everybody's-an-outlaw-until-the-outlaws-show-up smile. "Well, I don't have the time to go around and ask fifty thousand bikers if they happen to be members of the Tre Tre Nomads."

"I can point them out to you."

"And then what? I ask them if they happened to borrow your car on the night your son was run over? No, I think it would be a lot easier if you just asked around among your friends."

"They're not my friends."

"No, the exact term you used was family."

She said nothing, and we both watched as a tandem of motorcycles thundered across the bridge above.

"Just tell them that somebody used the car and didn't fill it up and that you want some gas money, or tell them that somebody left something in the car and you want to give it back to them."

"Like what?"

"I don't know—money."

"They're not going to buy that."

"Well, then think of something. You're an enterprising woman."

Finishing her cigarette, she turned back toward the river and flicked it into the water, where it disappeared in the mist but for a brief sizzle. "Thanks for your help."

She turned to go, but I called out to her. "Look, I'm willing to do this, but if you want to know what happened to your son, I'm going to need your assistance."

She lodged a hand on her hip. "Junior detective, huh?"

"Something like that."

"I'll think about it."

"Don't think too long; after Henry's race tomorrow, we're out of here."

She cocked her head. "Maybe I'll just ask Henry."

"You're welcome to, but I'd advise against it."

"And why's that?"

I gestured toward the river and, more important, the bridge. "Lot of water, huh?"

She studied me for a moment more and then swiveled on a heel and walked away.

When I got back to the cabin, I was surprised to see one of the two Hulett police cars preparing to back out from the spot in front of our door. Dog and I came around the left rear just as the reverse lights came on, so I tapped the quarter panel and Dougherty jerked to a stop.

I leaned on the sill. "How come you're not driving the new and improved MRAP?"

"He's calling it the Pequod; even ordered up decals to put the name on the side. Now where did he get that name from?"

"Heck if I know, troop. Better than the *Andrea Doria*." I checked on Dog, who was sniffing the squad car's tires. "What's up?"

He handed me a bulky manila envelope through the window. "This is the cell phone that was on Bodaway, or, more exactly, lying in the grass where the incident took place. Sorry it's taken so long to get it to you, but I've been kind of busy."

I stuffed the envelope under my arm. "Anything else?"

"The preliminary accident report along with the testimony of the witness."

"Witness?"

"After the fact." He reached up and tapped the package. "Local girl by the name of Chloe Nance; she's the one that found him."

"Nance. Why does that name sound familiar?" The thought struck as the words left my lips. "Related to Bob Nance, the guy that underwrote the Pequod?"

"Yeah, that's him. He's underwritten about half the county." He gestured toward the manila bundle again. "Look, the phone is dead, and I haven't had time to find a charger to fit it."

I pulled the device out and studied it and was pretty sure it was similar to Henry's. "I'll find a way to get it to talk, even if I have to use a rubber hose."

I started to back away so that he could get going when he called after me, "So, what the hell is a Pequod?"

"You mean other than the ship in *Moby Dick*?"

"Yeah."

"A Native tribe in Connecticut, although it's spelled differently now, with a *T* instead of a *D*. By the early twentieth century, there were only a little over fifty of them left."

"Are they still around?"

"One of the richest tribes in the country—casinos. Good night, troop."

"Good night, Sheriff." He backed the cruiser the rest of the way out and crunched gravel as he left.

Dog and I made our way to the cabin door, and I was surprised to find it ajar when I was pretty sure I'd closed it. Figuring it might've been Henry, I gave pause but then slipped my .45 from the small of my back just in case. Training it through the opening, I pushed the door wide.

"I thought for sure that cop was going to come in here, and that would've been bad." He was sitting on the guest chair, leaning backward against the wall with the television on mute. In one hand he had a beer and in the other a 9mm semiautomatic. "Hope you don't mind, but I made myself at home."

I kept the Colt on Brady Post, the Tre Tre Nomad enforcer, and stepped inside, sticking a leg out to restrain the growling beast behind me. "I don't mind, but I think he does."

"Keep a handle on that dog or I'll shoot him."

"You do, and he won't be the last one to get shot here tonight."

The biker lowered the Glock and stuffed it in the front of his pants. "I figured you and I ought to get introduced; besides, the ice machine is broken up at the Pioneer."

I waited a second and then lowered my weapon. "I thought we had been."

"Not formally." He reached into his pocket again and tossed something onto the bed near me.

It was a nifty leather wallet not unlike the one in my shirt pocket, but unlike mine, his read DEPARTMENT OF THE TREASURY.

"ATF?"

"Special Agent Post at your service. I don't usually break cover to the locals, or anybody for that matter, but you seem pretty capable and I could use some help—sure didn't throw any kind of scare into you at the hospital parking lot earlier today."

"Generally, I'm too stupid to be scared."

"Oh, I doubt that."

Holstering my Colt, I picked up his badge and ID card. "So, which one is it, alcohol, tobacco, or firearms?"

"Firearms—the Nomads are responsible for about thirty percent of the illegal guns showing up in the Southwest these days, mostly imported from their chapters in Mexico."

I sat on the bed and called Dog over. He still growled at Post but recognized that the dynamic had changed. "So, the enforcer for this particular chapter happens to be a federal agent?"

He set the beer bottle on the nightstand, crossed the room, and closed the door. "Sorry, can't be too careful these days." He crossed back and sat, reaching a hand out to Dog, who pulled back a lip, giving his interpretation of the night of the long knives. "Whoa . . . easy there."

"He'll warm up to you; just ignore him." I folded my fingers in my lap and looked at the man, younger than I'd thought underneath the Buffalo Bill facial hair. "So, what's the deal with the kid, Bodaway?"

"A major pain in my ass is what it is." He picked up his drink and took a long draw. "Bodaway is involved in the gun trafficking—he's the conduit to all the other clubs."

"Gangs."

"Whatever. Anyway, all cats being gray in the dark, the kid is getting weapons to all the other gangs and I've been working on his source, but so far, nada."

"I thought you said it was the connections in Mexico that were coming up with the guns."

"Until recently. We were able to motivate the *Federales* with all the Fast and Furious fallout, and when that source dried up, we thought we had them, but now they seem to be getting them from here in the U.S."

"So you're just shadowing Bodaway to find the source?"

"That and some information on some other things—been deep undercover for more than nine months now."

"Like what information?"

"I'm not at liberty to say."

"Lola have anything to do with it?"

He shook his head. "I don't think so, but who the hell knows with her."

"Any sign that she's involved up to now?"

"No, but she loves the little asshole and would do anything for him—including getting you and your Indian buddy involved."

"Cheyenne." The three of us looked up to see Henry standing in the doorway, leaning on the jamb with his arms folded, neither of us having heard the door itself open. "If you please."

"Henry Standing Bear, meet Special Agent Brady Post." I turned to look at him as Dog sidled over to the Cheyenne Nation. "Is that your real name?"

"No."

"Do you want to tell us what your real name is?"

"No."

I shrugged and turned back to the Bear, gesturing toward the tattooed man in the chair. "ATF."

Post interrupted. "Why don't you just tell everybody?"

"My bet is that he heard everything anyway."

Henry nodded and closed the door behind him. "I heard about the guns and the fact that you have been in deep cover for the last nine months. Amazing that you have risen as far as you have in that short amount of time."

Post gestured with a thumb toward the accessories on the back of his denim vest. "Fully patched."

"So, what is it you want from us?"

"Well, I thought it would be nice if we weren't working at cross-purposes." He turned back to me, picked up his beer, and rolled it between his hands. "Look, I know you're investigating the accident at local request, and I'm assuming also because of Lola Wojciechowski?"

I shrugged again. "It's still debatable as to whether we're going to take the case."

Henry smiled. "We?"

Post sipped his beer and studied me for a while before slowly smiling. "That why you've got a manila envelope under your arm that says Bodaway Torres?"

Amazingly enough, Torres's phone fit the Bear's charger. Henry plugged it in and set it on the nightstand between the beds. I studied the small screen as he stripped off his motorcycle gear. "Isn't it supposed to do something?"

"It is probably so dead that there is no power to the screen yet."

"How long does that take?"

He climbed in his bed in his underwear and a T-shirt. "You know, I think I am going to buy you one of those things one of these days."

A dim red light appeared on the screen inside a graphic of a depleted battery. "It's charging."

He flipped off the reading light on his side. "It will take almost an hour to fully charge; are you going to watch it the entire time?"

"Technology fascinates me."

He grunted and rolled over, and I could see the road-rash scrapes on his back through the thin shirt. "You do not have to keep me informed as to the progress. Good night."

"Good night." Dog rested his head on the bed and looked at me. I patted the spread, and he was up in an instant, occupying a full half of the surface area. "Hey, Henry?"

"What?"

"Why don't you want to help this woman?"

"She is a manipulator, and I do not think she has done anything in the last thirty years besides sharpen her skills." He waited a moment before adding, "Not all fair maidens are worthy of rescue, Walt."

"Maybe she is this time."

He studied me over his shoulder and then, reaching out, turned off my light. "I never make exceptions. An exception disproves the rule."

I sighed, stood, and undressed, hanging my clothes on the chair by the desk. I went to the bathroom, brushed my teeth, and then stood there looking at myself, trying to figure out what to do next. Corbin Dougherty needed my help, Lola Wojciechowski needed my help, maybe even Bodaway Torres needed my help. On the other hand, Special Agent Brady Post didn't need my help, and Henry Standing Bear didn't appear to want to be involved with anything that included *the* Lola.

Sometimes it was like that, I suppose; some people become so important in your life that they're almost like a trademark, but then they're gone. Sometimes they might reappear, but they're nothing at all like what you've assembled in your mind since their departure; sometimes you can't even stand them anymore, because they break up the legend and nothing dies harder than a good, personal legend.

I looked at the crumbling giant in the mirror, nowhere near as young as he used to be. Maybe if I were thirty or even forty I might think about hanging around Hulett, but I'm not. Plus, it was the Bear's call since he knew Lola, and the Bear was softly snoring in the next room, blissfully unconcerned.

So tomorrow I'd watch him attempt another hill, and then we'd load up and go home. It was that simple—that, or I wanted it to be.

By the time I got back to the bed, Dog was taking up a full two-thirds, and I was relegated to the one-third left, clutching the mattress like a mountaineer in a hanging bivouac. I had just closed my eyes when I heard a buzz.

Flipping the light back on, I looked at Bodaway's phone, but it was dark. Then I noticed it was Henry's cell lying next to it that was making noise.

The Bear hadn't moved, so I picked it up and stared at the screen, confirming the fact that I was in deep trouble. I hit the button and took my medicine.

"So, you're not dead?"

I kept my voice low in an attempt to not wake the Cheyenne Nation. "Nope, I, uh . . . escaped with my life. Just now."

"You know, if you had called me back I would've been worried." Her voice took on a fake Western tone, emblematic of every bad cowboy movie made in the '40s. "The last time we encountered the good sheriff he was at gunpoint. . . ." Her voice slipped to serious. "So, who's pointing a gun at you this time?"

"People are always pointing guns at me."

"Daddy?"

"Lola."

There was a pause. "You don't mean *the* Lola."

"I do."

"Henry's Lola?"

"The one my granddaughter is named after."

"Don't start." Another pause. "I assume she's gorgeous?"

"In a rough, roadhouse kind of way."

"Oh, my."

"Yep, her son was hurt in a motorcycle accident over here."

Another pause. "Umm, so how are she and Henry?"

"They're not."

She laughed that lovely, melodious laugh that reminded me so much of her mother. "Then don't you get involved."

"I wasn't planning on it."

"Planning has nothing to do with it."

"Right." I smiled and held the phone close, knowing full well that part of it was that she was my daughter, but also just from the sheer joy of knowing her. "Did you call just to give advice to the lovelorn?"

"No, I called to make sure you didn't have any bullets in you."

"I'm bullet-free. So, how's *my* Lola?"

"Sleeping, finally. She's a night owl. Was I like that?"

I glanced at the time on the phone. "You still are."

"Yeah, I guess so. Hey, I thought I'd better give you a heads-up. Lena said that Vic is planning on flying into Rapid City tomorrow and surprising you guys."

I dropped my voice even lower. "I hope she gets in early. Henry's talking about skipping the Show and Shine and just heading home after the hill climb tomorrow."

"He's not going to show Lucie this year?"

"I guess not, so hopefully Vic will get here early." I smiled into the receiver. "Is my undersheriff's imminent arrival the reason you warned me about Lola?"

"No, I warned you because you're stupid when it comes to females of all shapes and sizes when they are in distress."

"That's the second time I've been cautioned about that tonight." I tried to touch on the next subject as lightly as possible. "So, there's still nothing going on with the investigation in Philadelphia?"

"No, and she says she misses Wyoming, but I think she misses you." I wasn't quite sure what to say to that, so I just remained quiet and listened as her tone changed yet again. "Hey, when are you coming down here to see the new digs?"

"Probably next week. I told Ruby that I was taking a few days off to go spend time with my family."

She yawned. "Good. We miss you, too, you know?"

"I do. Get some sleep, Punk; that little one'll be up soon enough."

"Roger that. Love you."

"Love you, too. Over."

She giggled. "Over."

I turned the thing off and laid it on the nightstand just as the other phone there began vibrating. Evidently, it had summoned enough energy to work. Curious as to who was trying to contact the young man, I picked it up. It had buzzed twice, which I had learned means a text message, and I stared at it for a moment, checking the date and time to see if it was old, but the date was today and the time, two minutes ago.

MEET ME AT THE NINTH GREEN

The sender's name had not come up, but the number was a 310 area code. I just lay there looking at the message, making sure it said what I thought it said. I hesitated, looking at the time of morning and thinking about whether I really wanted to continue being involved with this case, but then went ahead and did what I knew I was going to do—and sent back two letters in return.

OK

I guess it all comes down to the fact that I hate mysteries, and I wanted to know who had attempted a vehicular homicide on Bodaway Torres. I quietly dressed, went to the door, and looked back at Dog. He raised his head and looked back at me, but then lowered it and didn't make another move.

So much for backup.

I closed the door behind me, fingered the Cheyenne Nation's keys that I'd taken from the nightstand, and walked around the cabin just in time to interrupt two scruffy-looking guys attempting to unlock Lucie, the Bear's Indian motorcycle, from the trailer.

The nearest one tilted his Viking helmet back, smiled, and waved as I approached. "How you doin'?"

"Good. You?"

"Oh, we're having trouble with these locks." He noted that I'd stopped and was watching him. "Um . . . this yours?"

"Might as well be."

The other scruff, who was holding a tire iron, stepped back. "Then you're saying we shouldn't be doing this?"

"If I were the real owner you never would've heard him, and they would've found your bodies in the Belle Fourche River tomorrow morning."

The one with the tire iron palmed it a few times, attempting to send a message via Morse code. "He a tough guy, like you?"

"Tougher."

"Well, how 'bout we see how tough you are."

I sighed and looked down at the more reasonable of the two. "Look, Eddy, I'm old and tired and if you piss me off bad enough I'm going to have to pull this .45 I've got at the small of my back and shoot you just to show your friend how tough I am."

He studied me as his buddy started sidling to the left back of the trailer. "We know each other?"

"That Indian belongs to Henry Standing Bear, Heads Man of the Dog Soldier Society, Bear Clan."

"Oh, shit."

"Oh, shit is right."

"How come I'm the one that gets shot?"

I gestured toward his buddy, now coming around the back, supposedly out of my line of sight. "He looks too stupid to learn from it, but you know, I just might be changing my mind." I slipped the Colt from my back and turned to look at number two. He froze when he saw the semiautomatic hanging at my thigh. "Go home, or wherever it is you go; nothing good ever happens this late at night, and the two of you are liable to get killed."

Tire iron's mouth unfroze. "Is that a real Colt?"

"Yep, it is." I gestured with my sidearm. "Go. Home."

"I hear they jam a lot."

"Not this one." I raised the weapon. "I said, go home."

They left, mumbling to each other, something about life not being fair. Figuring I'd pushed my luck borrowing the real Lola's Cadillac all day the day before, I slipped behind the wheel of Henry's Lola and started her up. Dodging through the remaining motorcyclists who appeared to be impervious to both exhaustion and alcohol, I made my way across town toward the only golf course I knew existed in Hulett.

The Devils Tower Club sits on a private mesa above the town, which gave me the first indication as to who might be attempting to contact Bodaway. I turned the vintage bird and trailer in a broad arc, lined up in the diagonal parking at the center of the lot, and killed the engine. To my right was what I assumed to be the clubhouse, a beautiful if predictable structure of stone and massive logs.

There were no other vehicles, just a few carts parked near the building. I quietly got out of the T-bird and walked over to a large, hand-engraved map to look for the ninth green. It was a red moon that shone across the clipped fairway and I struck off, careful to stay on the cart path in the shade of the conifers.

I climbed a rise, and when I got to the top I could see someone standing under a tree by a water hazard, and I listened as the frogs croaked at each other. A trail cut through the trees so that I would come up behind whoever it was. I stopped about fifty yards away and studied the figure long enough to know that it was female.

I got a little closer and noticed she was wearing a set of earbuds, her head bobbing to the music—so much for stealth. I stepped to the side and raised a hand, trying not to scare her.

"Howdy." I needn't have bothered with that, either—she screamed loud enough to be heard by Mount Rushmore. I held up my hands in surrender. "Hey, it's okay."

She had an arm in a sling but managed to yank the earbuds out to scream at me some more. "Who the hell are you?"

"Sorry—my name is Walt Longmire."

"You scared the shit out of me."

I folded my arms over my chest to show her I didn't mean any harm, meanwhile studying the extraordinarily beautiful young woman. "Sorry."

"Where's Bodaway?"

It seemed like an odd question. "As far as I know he's still in a hospital room at Rapid City Regional."

"He's still in the hospital?"

I stared at her. "Well, yes. I was under the impression that you were a witness to the accident."

"Who told you that?"

"Corbin Dougherty, the officer here in Hulett."

"And who are you again?"

"Absaroka County Sheriff Walt Longmire."

She didn't seem impressed and swiped a long lock of blonde from her face. "And where the hell is that?"

"About two hours from here."

"Wyoming?"

"Yep." I studied her in return. "You're not up too much on Wyoming geography, are you?"

"I'm from California, and I don't give a shit."

"Fair enough."

"Excuse me, but do you know who I am?"

"I was under the assumption that you are Chloe Nance."

"Yeah, but do you know who I *am*?"

One of the great trials in law enforcement is the "do you know who I am" question, which pops up every now and again. Usually it's a county or city councilman from somewhere else or a state representative, but I didn't think she fit the bill. "Um . . . Bob Nance's daughter?"

"Well, that's one thing, and do you know who he is?"

"Not really." I took a step past her and looked out at the picturesque scenery, only partially marred by little flags and golf-ball washers. "Look, Miss Nance, are you a witness to Bodaway Torres's accident?"

She tried to fold her own arms but then remembered the sling. "Why should I talk to you about it?"

"I'm assisting the investigating officer."

She sighed and looked away. "My father says I'm not supposed to say anything to anybody, that it'll just lead to trouble with those people."

"Well, seeing as how you're an eyewitness to what may or may not have been an attempted homicide, I can get a subpoena and we can have this conversation down at the Hulett police headquarters or the Crook County sheriff's office."

"I found him, okay? I didn't witness anything."

"On the side of the road."

"Yeah."

"Was he alone?"

"Yeah."

I turned and looked at the young woman. "Can you give me an indication as to what kind of condition he was in?"

"What do you mean?"

"Was he conscious, unconscious?"

"He was unconscious."

"Did he have anything with him on the motorcycle that you saw lying around—saddlebags or anything like that?"

She took a long time to answer. "No."

I looked pointedly at her injured arm. "Was there anybody else on the motorcycle with him?"

"No."

I gave her the long pause I'd learned from Lucian—the one that crept like an epoch-eating glacier—just to let her know I had my suspicions. "Then I guess I've got only one more question."

"Yeah?"

"When did you get his cell phone number?"

A voice sounded from behind me. "I think you've answered enough of the sheriff's questions, Chloe."

I turned to see a fireplug of a man with a shaved head standing behind us, aiming what looked to be a sporting-clay over-and-under shotgun mostly at me. "Mr. Nance?"

He strolled up a little closer, and I could see two men standing behind him in matching black polo shirts. "You're supposed to follow that with 'I presume.'"

I shrugged. "It's late, and the guy who does my Sherlock Holmes is asleep."

Next to big-game hunter Omar Rhoades's log palace back in the home county, and Versailles, Bob Nance's ranch house was just about the most extravagant place I'd ever visited.

"Will you still be needing us, Mr. Nance?" The muscle in the black shirts continued to glance at me. "We can stick around if you need us."

Nance, with his back to the three of us, was mixing two drinks. "That's fine, Mr. Frick. I think we'll be okay."

I watched as they left and turned back as Nance handed me one of the drinks. "Is the other one's name Frack?"

He ignored my joke. "Vintage '66, thirty years in cask 559, and bottled on June eighteenth of 1996 at the Laphroaig distillery." He handed me a tumbler, neat, and then adjusted the flames on the river-rock fireplace with a remote. "I know it's summer, but I like the ambiance—a little like Dick Nixon in that regard." He lifted his glass. "I hope you enjoy it."

"I have to tell you this is the most civilized stickup in which I've ever taken part."

He sat in an overstuffed leather chair, throwing his polished boots onto a matching ottoman. "We strive to please."

I took a sip of the amber liquid and was pretty sure that it was the finest stuff my palate would ever touch, and that if I wasn't careful I'd be asleep by the time I finished it. The room was lined with bookshelves, and there was a gigantic burled-wood billiards table at the center, with red felt where he had laid the Krieghoff K-80 Pro Sporter. "Nice place—almost as nice as mine."

"Is yours log?"

I nodded. "Yep, and I believe my whole house would fit in this one room."

He smiled and glanced up at the timbers, a good forty feet in the air. "It's kind of over-the-top, but you know how it is when you think you're building your last one."

"I haven't even finished my first."

"Well, the ex got the other three—one in Palo Alto, one in Grosse Pointe, and one in Paradise Valley—so I guess I felt entitled." He took another sip of his scotch and studied me. "So, how can I help you, Sheriff?"

"Your daughter is a pretty girl."

"Yes, she is, and you can see why I'm a little protective of her, especially since it's rally week." He put his scotch on a massive Indian drum, which had been turned into a coffee table. "I heard her try the old 'do you know who I am' on you."

"It was done pretty well."

"She's an actress."

"You don't say."

"Or was till she got into trouble." He gestured toward a few framed one sheets near the fireplace. "You mean to say you haven't seen *Barasharktapus* or *Pagan Women of Planet X*?"

I walked over to the posters, which were far worse than anything anybody could've imagined. "I've let my subscription to the Metropolitan Opera lapse, I'm afraid."

"Crap, all of 'em, and this is her father talking. . . . But she tries, you know?"

"Must be a difficult business."

"Four years at NYU and then two more at UCLA and a stint at the Guildhall School of Music & Drama. I tell you, I sat through more crappy, esoteric one-act plays with people in black leotards than you can shake a stick at."

"I can shake a lot of sticks at crappy, esoteric one-acts."

"I wish I had. Anyway, what's going on, Sheriff, and why am I talking to you instead of the sheriff of Crook County or Chief Nutter?"

"I'm assisting the Hulett police with an investigation concerning a young man who we believe was forced off the road."

"And what does that have to do with my daughter?"

I walked toward the pool table and glanced at the stairwell where Chloe Nance had disappeared. "From what I am made to understand, your daughter was a possible witness to the incident."

"She wasn't a witness—she just found that young man on the side of the road, after the fact, and did what any decent human being would do and tried to help."

I pulled the mobile from my pocket and touched the screen, then turned it so that Nance could read it. "Is that your daughter's cell phone number?"

He got up and came over and stared at the screen for only an instant. "Yes."

"You're sure?"

"I pay for the damn thing once a month, so I know the number."

I placed it back in my shirt pocket. "How do you suppose your daughter has Bodaway Torres's number if they'd never met before the accident?"

Nance leaned against the pool table and fingered the adjustable comb on the Monte Carlo Turkish walnut stock of the shotgun that probably cost as much as my truck. "You shoot, Sheriff?"

"Trap?" I shook my head. "Not so much lately."

"It's a sport known for its congeniality, like golf." He set his glass on the bumper and picked up the 12 gauge, swinging the 30-inch barrels around toward the flying mounts of two pheasants above the fireplace. "I've learned that it's the relationships in life that really matter, Sheriff Longmire, whether it's with your family, your business associates, or your community."

"Like the MRAP?"

He nodded. "The MRAP for the local police and why I give so much to so many charities and organizations." He lowered the shotgun and looked out the windows. "I mentioned some trouble concerning my daughter."

I waited and said nothing.

"She had a little substance abuse problem in L.A." He handed me the Krieghoff. "We've got a little benefit shoot tomorrow evening, and I'd like you to come up and take part as my guest."

I held the expensive beauty and thumbed the top-tang push-button safety, locked in the off position. "So, you're thinking that she might've met Bodaway previously and was attempting to obtain drugs?"

"It wouldn't be the first time. I've been running interference for about eight months now."

"We're still going to need to have her come in and make an official statement."

He smiled and took the over-and-under back, throwing it over one shoulder like he knew what he was doing. "That's fine, Sheriff. I'd just rather she not make it on the ninth green after midnight."

5

I watched as the Cheyenne Nation held the bike steady while Jamey, who was whistling a Beatles tune, made the final adjustments on the KTM. We all turned at the sound of a racer's engine just in time to see another of the hill climbers flip over backward and have his motorcycle land on top of him, man and machine intertwined as they slammed back down the slope.

"This is a really dumb sport."

The Bear pulled on his helmet and tightened up the chin strap. "Well, not all of us are lucky enough to go shooting sporting clays with the millionaires up on snob knob."

We watched as the EMTs scraped the kid off the hill and loaded him into a van, another in a bunch that had gotten carted off to Rapid City Regional.

"Wasn't my idea."

He pulled on his gloves and took in a crowd that was much larger than the previous day's seated on the makeshift bleachers. "Any idea where all his money comes from?"

"Nope, but I figure I'll ask Corbin and get the story."

As I finished speaking, the youngster who'd razzed the Bear just the previous day pulled up and rapped his throttle a few times, shouting to be heard over his own noise. "You up for it today, old man?"

Henry ignored him, so I answered. "Hey, Evel Knievel, why don't you go find a canyon to fall into?"

He smirked, and this time I was quick enough to get my arm up to protect my face as he spun out toward the starting gate and sprayed all three of us with a rich coating of South Dakota dirt.

The Bear dusted himself off. "Do you think he knows who Evel Knievel is?"

"I don't know." I watched as the kid took his place in line, waiting to back up against the buttress log and make his run. "But I really wouldn't mind seeing him bust his ass all the way down that hill."

"He had the fastest time trial yesterday."

I glanced at the Bear. "What, he got his training wheels off?"

He scanned the competitive field. "They all look young, do they not?"

"To us? Yep, they do."

He twisted his head, stretching the muscles in his neck, and all I could think was that if he didn't climb the hill, he could always take a pickax and destroy it. "I am thinking this might be my last run."

"Well, think about staying for the Show and Shine. Vic may be flying into Rapid City."

He studied the hill, and I wasn't sure if he'd heard me.

He had been here at sunup, slowly climbing the course on foot, studying the terrain, and getting a read that you couldn't get even from the closeness of a motorcycle. He'd taken his time and stooped to look at the rocky knobs, the tufts of prairie grass, and, most important, the ruts and berms left by the other racers. There would be no surprises for Henry Standing Bear on the run this morning, and if he lost, he would be satisfied in the knowledge that he had done everything humanly possible to win and more. "Or not."

I sighed. "I'm headed over to the peanut gallery where I can join the throngs in safety." I could see the third-row spot that Corbin and Lola had saved for Jamey and me. "Looks like your old flame wants to see you in action."

"She would probably not mind seeing me bust my ass all the way down that hill."

"Or that." I patted him on the shoulder. "I'll see you in the winner's circle."

He gave a curt nod and then kicked the dirt bike to life, circling toward the starting line as Jamey ambled along with me.

"That kid posted a 14.01—that's faster than Henry's ever been able to climb that hill and nobody's ever broke 14."

I noticed that the Bear had pulled up at a respectful distance to watch the other riders try their luck. "Why do you think he does it?"

The biker shrugged. "You'd know better than me, dude."

We went through the gate in the chain-link fence and moved over to our seats as the EMT van pulled away. "Not about this. I've never understood it."

"If it was anybody else, I'd say they were trying to recapture their youth, but not him. I think it's just the challenge." He looked back and smiled through his bushed-out beard. "I don't think he's used to partial success, Walt."

"You're probably right about that." The others made way,

but Jamey motioned toward his truck in the pits. "My tools are all out over there, so I think I'll watch from the tailgate in the cheap seats."

Lola watched him go and then turned, studying me through a large pair of Italian movie-star sunglasses. "I don't think he likes me."

I turned back to the hill. "There seem to be an awful lot of people who don't particularly care for your company."

She adjusted the glasses and studied Henry. "And here I've always thought of myself as such a likable person."

I turned toward Corbin. "What are you doing out of uniform, troop?"

He shrugged. "I go on at noon, so I thought I'd get out of town for a few hours before the real rally starts."

We watched as the smart-aleck kid backed into the log and made ready to make his run. There was a lot of screaming and yelling as the crowd began cheering for the odds-on favorite. The flag on the hill dropped, and he rooster-tailed it, rocketing through the short straightaway and then timing the loop-de-loops. He got a little sideways but was able to pull it out just before the prairie grass got hold of him and bounced him like a pinball. He started to stall but then gassed it and flew over the top with a flourishing cross up. The kid was good, you have to admit.

"Hey, I met a patron of the Hulett Police Department last night."

"Who's that?"

"Bob Nance."

Dougherty looked genuinely surprised. "Where in the world did you see him?"

I leaned forward and looked toward the hill where the

young rider had posted a 14 flat, and then glanced at Lola for her response, but there didn't seem to be one. "On the ninth green with a very expensive shotgun in his hands."

"You were at his house?"

"Eventually." I turned a little toward Lola. "Hey, do you know if your son was associated with a young woman by the name of Chloe Nance?"

The corner of her lip nearest me curled up just a bit. *"Associated?"*

"For lack of a better term."

"Chloe Nance?"

"Yep."

"Never heard of her." She turned toward me, but it was difficult to read her expression through the glasses. "But like I told you, he had lots of *associates.*"

Corbin interrupted the interrogation. "Wait, you met Bob and Chloe?"

"Yep. Last night after you dropped off Bodaway's phone, I plugged it in and a text came from Chloe wanting him to meet her at the golf course. I got dressed and went up there and met her father, too."

We all watched as another rider made an emergency dismount and did a comic bow as his bike catapulted back down the hill. Corbin checked his wristwatch, probably estimating the time it would take to get back to Hulett and his shift. "She's a pain in the ass, but the old man's all right."

"Sure, he just bought you guys a million-dollar truck."

Lola broke in. "Hey, don't knock people that buy you things."

We watched as Henry got closer to the starting point. "How did he make all his money, anyway?"

"He worked for the automobile industry—developed some kind of ceramic stuff they use on exhaust manifolds and still holds the patent. He's rich about ten feet up a bull's ass."

"So it would appear." The Cheyenne Nation was having a brief conversation with the officials—it seemed as though there was a problem up top. "Any idea how Chloe could've been involved with Bodaway?"

"Nope."

I turned to Lola. "You?"

"Me what?"

"Any idea why this young woman might've gotten in touch with your son?"

I got the curve at the corner of the lips again. "I told you, he's popular."

"Your son wasn't dealing in anything illegal, was he?"

I got the full sunglasses this time, and it was like looking at two identical versions of myself. "Like what?"

"Drugs?"

"What makes you say that?"

"The young woman's father mentioned that his daughter had a substance abuse problem, and I was just wondering if that might've been a connection."

"There isn't."

"You seem pretty sure of that." I waited and then continued. "He's had a few run-ins with the law."

"Nothing involving drugs."

"No, but . . ."

"But what? He's an Indian kid, a biker with a few brushes with asshole cops and so he must be bad news, huh?"

"That's not what I said."

"But it's what you were thinking."

I smiled and started getting the feeling that Henry was right to keep Lola at arm's length. "You know, I can hardly do enough thinking for myself, so if you'd like to do some of mine for me, feel free."

She studied me for a good long time and then stood. "I'm taking a walk. I'll see you later." She sauntered away toward the pits.

"Do you think it was something I said?"

"Absolutely."

I nodded and watched as the Cheyenne Nation backed up against the starting log and looked at that hill the way I'm sure his ancestors had studied the Seventh Cavalry. There was a war about to happen, and I wasn't going to miss it because Lola Wojciechowski was having a fit of pique.

I've seen some pretty amazing feats of derring-do, but I could tell this was going to be special. We watched as the Bear leaned up over the handlebars and made ready, the official at the top raising the green flag.

It wasn't a complete hush, but there was a stillness in the crowd. All the old Jackpine Gypsies knew Henry and respected him for his one triumph and the years he'd spent attempting to replicate it. They knew he was a tough competitor, but there is a time when you stop doing certain things, and I think that the Bear was there and everybody knew it.

The flag fell, and the Cheyenne Nation was off.

The reason the loop-de-loops are there at the beginning of

the course is to keep the riders from gaining too much momentum, allowing it to carry them halfway up the hill, but the
Bear was having none of it and the KTM's motor screamed as
he shot off the log like a clean-hit baseball from a gigantic
wooden bat.

I'm pretty sure his front wheel never touched the ground
till he hit that first hill, but I can guarantee nothing touched
the second. He landed on the downslope at a much higher rate
of speed than the other riders had, and the front wheel levi-
tated again as his right hand peeled back the throttle and he
blew up the hillside in a direct path, ignoring the routes that
the others had taken.

There was a reason why no one else had tried the more
direct route: there was a concave area dug into the hillside
that, if you took it head-on, was likely to shoot you back out
into open space where a fall the rest of the way down the hill
was certain.

The Bear hit the indentation but then kicked to the right,
taking a slight berm that shot him back toward the middle. I
was wondering what the next part of his plan would be when
he threw the handlebars to the side and leapt up the center
third of the hill at a ferocious diagonal.

I wasn't even aware that I'd been drawn to my feet but then
noticed that the hundreds around me were standing, too.

Henry couldn't keep going in that direction or he'd go out
of bounds, so he slammed into another hillock, teetering for
only a second, and used the force of impact to ricochet back up
the hill with the same momentum he'd started with. Unlike
all the other racers, he didn't pause at the sandy precipice but
took another diagonal that flew both the KTM and him over

the heads of the scrambling officials in one final blast, like a Saturn V rocket headed for the ghostly shape of the moon in the blue South Dakota sky.

13:59.

Henry and Jamey were seated on the tailgate of Jamey's truck and passed a bottle of champagne back and forth, each smoking a cigar as Lola and I approached through the crowd that surrounded them. KOTA Territory News was interviewing the Bear, and it looked like all of Sturgis was trying to have a word with him.

We waited at a respectful distance, and when the crowd began to thin, she sidled up to him and they looked at each other. I wasn't close enough to hear what she said, but I guess it was pretty important because he reached out a hand and stopped her when she started to walk away. He stood and said something to her, and she said something back. He stood there for a moment more and then let his arm drop.

Whatever it was she said, I'd never seen a look like that on the Bear's face.

She gave him one last hard stare and then turned and walked away.

I'd been in enough wars and a few relationships to realize when a bomb had been dropped, so in deference, I stood back a moment before leaning over the side of the pickup bed. "Pretty good trick for an old Indian."

He turned but didn't smile. "Not bad at all."

He handed me the trophy, and I looked for his name on the plaque, but it wasn't there. "When do they engrave it?"

"This afternoon." He thought about it, staring at the crinkled leather of his old motocross pants. "I suppose if we stay for the Show and Shine, I could go to the ceremony this evening and pick it up."

"If you win the Show and Shine, you might get two trophies out of it."

"And leave them in a dumpster here in Sturgis."

I handed him back the trophy and studied him. "You okay?"

"Yes."

"You don't seem like it."

"I have some things on my mind."

"Has Lola finally leveraged you into this investigation?"

He barked a short laugh with no humor in it and then carried his gaze back toward the hill he'd finally conquered. "It is beginning to look like that might be the case."

"Well, congratulations."

"For what?"

"Winning."

"Is that what I'm doing?" He stood, still holding the half-full bottle of cheap champagne, and, puffing on his cigar, walked toward the hill.

I studied him for a good long time and then figured if he wanted to really talk he'd get around to it on his own. I glanced over at Jamey, who was quietly packing up his tools and trying his best to appear uninterested. "When is the Show and Shine?"

He stopped working and smiled. "Noon, over in Sturgis near the Bucket of Blood Saloon."

"Then I guess we'd better get going."

I helped Jamey load up the tools, paraphernalia, and the

KTM, and we strapped it down on the trailer as Henry continued to study the hill.

Maybe it didn't have anything to do with Lola. Maybe it was just what happens when you finally get something you want and it turns out not to be what you wanted after all. You spend most of the time in life running after things that aren't that important, and the pursuit becomes more desirable than the prize.

I started out toward where the Bear stood but stopped. "I'm thinking he needs some time."

The biker joined me. "Maybe so. You got somewhere you have to be?"

"A friend of ours is flying into the Rapid City airport this morning, and I was thinking I should pick her up, but it's supposed to be a surprise, so maybe I'm not."

"Not what?"

"Supposed to pick her up."

"Oh." He glanced at Henry and then back at me. "You can borrow my truck, but is there anybody you can call to ask whether or not she's really coming?"

"Well, I could call the person in question, but that's going to blow the surprise, too."

He shrugged. "If it was me I'd call; life has enough surprises as it is."

I fished Bodaway Torres's cell phone from my pocket; it was evidence, but there was no reason why it couldn't be useful.

I punched in Vic's cell phone number and listened as it rang. After a moment she answered. "Who the fuck is this?"

"It's me."

"What's me doing with a strange cell phone?"

"It belongs to a young man named Bodaway Torres. He wasn't using it; he's in the hospital."

"You put him there?"

"No."

"You just stole his phone."

"I borrowed it—it's evidence."

She snorted a laugh. "This is getting better and better."

"Where are you?"

"I'm in Philadelphia." She sniffed. "Why?"

"A little bird told me you might be surprising us and flying into Rapid City."

There was a pause. "You know, that little bird has a problem keeping things to herself."

"Yep, it's not her strong suit." I smiled. "So, where are you?"

"About twenty feet behind you." I turned and looked. "I bet you turned and looked just now."

I turned back around. "I did not."

"I'm getting my bag at the luggage carousel at Rapid City Regional Airport, which looks remarkably like a Mayan shopping mall with nothing in it. I heard you rode with Henry, so I figured I'd rent a car."

"You don't have to—Jamey says I can borrow his truck."

"What is it?"

I studied the vehicle. "It looks to be a late seventies—"

"I'll rent a car."

"Right."

"Where do I meet you?"

"I think we're headed for the Bucket of Blood Saloon in Sturgis for the motorcycle show."

"Did Henry bring Lucie?"

"He did."

"Cool—he owes me a ride. I'll meet you there."

She hung up, and I shook my head; life as we know it was about to get interesting. I looked at the phone and then tapped Jamey on the shoulder. "Hey, do you know anything about these phones?"

He shrugged. "A little—why?"

"Can you track the previous calls on this thing?"

The Bucket of Blood Saloon during Sturgis is a marvelous place to get puked on, but then, during the rally, pretty much all of the town met that qualification.

Jamey knew the owner of the Bucket and was able to get Henry the prime corner spot for Lucie. The 1940 Indian Four was designed when the Indian Motorcycle Company of Springfield, Massachusetts, absorbed the assets of the Ace Motorcycle Corporation. Into the thirties, even though there was low demand for luxury motorcycles, Indian continued to develop and refine the inline four cylinder until the thing was capable of more than a hundred miles an hour, an unheard-of speed at that time.

With its large, decorative fenders, it looked like a jukebox on wheels, but its pedigree was so great that in 2006 it graced the 39-cent stamp and was part of the Smithsonian Motorcycle Collection at the National Museum of American History.

The Bear's was nicer.

Adding to its worth was the matching factory sidecar,

which I thought resembled a chrome-trimmed prow of a boat. "Who in the heck would ride in that thing?"

Jamey studied the vintage contraption. "I guess it's as safe as riding the motorcycle."

"My point exactly. You know, Pete Conrad died on a motorcycle."

"Who's Pete Conrad?"

"The third man to walk on the moon." I sipped my canned iced tea and looked up and down Sturgis's crowded Main Street for what might pass as a rental car. "Where's Henry?"

"Inside having a drink."

I pulled out my pocket watch and frowned, placing it back in my jeans. "A little early for that, isn't it?"

"He didn't look like it was open for discussion."

"Oh, boy."

About a half block down I could see a neon-orange coupe moseying its way through the throng. Every once in a while, when someone was a little slow getting out of the way, the driver revved the engine, causing the offender to hop a little quicker.

When she got closer, I could see she was holding her badge out the window. I walked over and leaned on the passenger-side door. "What is this?"

My undersheriff smiled her crocodile smile, the one that showed no innocence. "Hemi Challenger; it was the only thing the rental guy had left, so we made a deal."

"I bet you did." I glanced around. "Where are you going to park this thing?"

She raced the motor again. "Anywhere I want."

I gestured toward the beer garden outside the Bucket of Blood. "We're over there where the red umbrellas are."

Pulling out, she barely missed another mass of bikers. "See you in a few."

I hopped back up onto the curb to keep my boots from being run over.

Jamey was waiting as I slid between some of the other classic bikes. "Who's that?"

I watched as the Great Pumpkin made a right and then a U-turn to dodge into a parking spot across the street. "A force of nature." I glanced toward the bar and saw that Lola was headed inside. "When my undersheriff gets here, bring her over, will you?"

"You bet."

Fighting the current on the sidewalk, I tacked my way toward the corner entrance of the bar and finally pushed through the swinging saloon-style doors. The Cheyenne Nation was seated at the last stool of the bar, up against the wall with a motorcycle boot propped up on the adjacent seat. Throwing back a shot and looking over the crowd, he puffed his cigar.

We were in trouble.

We were all in trouble.

I hadn't seen that particular look in decades, and I had been hopeful that I'd never see it again. The Bear was looking for a fight, and odds were, he'd find one.

Lola was rounding the table beside the bar where the bikers were four deep and making a lot of noise. I thought I better get over there quick but was given pause by the fact that I might be interrupting a personal conversation.

There was a high-top table by the window that had just

been vacated, so I grabbed it and waited for Vic and Jamey to arrive. As I sat, a dark-haired young woman in a skintight Sturgis tank top paused and asked if I wanted a drink other than the can of iced tea in my hands.

"No, thanks."

"You gotta have a drink if you're gonna sit."

I pulled out my pocket watch and acquiesced. "Give me a Rainier, a dirty martini, and a Jack and Coke."

"Bud, Bud Light, and Coors."

I sighed. "Coors."

Satisfied with that, she turned and walked away.

Lola had pulled up an arm's length from the Cheyenne Nation and stood there talking with him as he clinched the cigar in the corner of his mouth, both the cigar and the Indian smoldering.

I felt someone lift my hat and turned in time to see my undersheriff place it on her head. She surveyed the place, raising her voice to be heard above the raucous music that blared from everywhere. "Bucket of Blood, huh?"

I half-yelled back, "That's what they call it."

"Bucket of pig shit, looks like to me."

"Maybe." I kicked a stool out and Jamey ushered Vic onto her seat. The waitress arrived with the drinks, and I palmed her a twenty. "Keep the change."

Vic, looking adorable in jeans and a plaid shirt tied at the waist, tipped my hat back on her head. "You making friends already?"

"Trying."

"Looks like they've got hot and cold running venereal diseases in here. You didn't catch anything while I was gone, did you?" Jamey pushed the martini toward Vic, and she sipped it, watching Henry and Lola. "You go over there?"

"Not yet."

Vic studied the couple in question. "That's her, huh?"

"Yep."

Her eyes narrowed like a gunfighter's. "Looks like ten miles of bad road, if you ask me."

"A bit bumpy, yes."

"So, what does she want from Henry?"

"To look into who might've hurt her son."

She took a swallow of the cloudy martini, rife with olive brine. "I thought she wanted you to do that."

"It would appear that she doesn't think I'm up to the job alone."

"Hmm . . . she doesn't know you very well, does she?" Vic watched as Lola continued to talk at Henry. "How's that conversation been going for her?"

"Not so well as near as I can tell, but she's upsetting him and I'm not sure what to do about it."

"Henry upset, huh?" She set the martini glass down and spread her hands across the lacquered surface of the table, and I noticed her fingernails matched the rental, casting further doubt on her having acquired the muscle car by accident. "I know this isn't my usual response in these types of situations." She smiled. "But stay the fuck out of it."

Jamey nodded, backing up Vic. "I was thinking the same thing."

It was about then that one of the bikers at a table adjacent to the conversationalists said something to the Bear.

Vic turned her head, and we all watched as the Cheyenne

Nation said something back. The bikers looked at each other, and the talker laughed and said something again.

Henry responded, but this time his answer was shorter.

The biker reached out and slapped the Bear's boot, indicating, I think, that he should move it and let Lola have a seat.

"Oh, no."

The Cheyenne Nation removed the cigar from his mouth and stubbed it out in the shot glass.

Both Jamey and Vic were already standing. "We'd better . . ."

Henry slowly rose from the stool like a bird of prey.

There were five of them, but it didn't matter.

6

Sturgis is in Meade County, South Dakota, and not so surprisingly, its jail was full. Pennington County, where I had been just the previous day, had not been and was receiving, so here I was once again in the sheriff's guest chair.

"Four of them are in the hospital."

"He's responsible for only three of the five. She's the one who hit the guy with the popcorn maker."

Vic turned toward me from the other chair. "Bad road—I told you."

Irl Engelhardt closed the file and smiled at the two of us. "That's four. What happened to number five?"

Vic smiled back at him. "He ran."

The sheriff studied us some more. "The brains of the outfit, huh?"

"So it would appear."

"They're pressing charges."

Vic laughed. "Five on one, and they're pressing charges?"

"Four on one."

"Whatever."

He leaned back in his chair. "I might be able to talk them

out of it, but somebody's going to have to pay the damages at the Bucket."

I interrupted before things got out of hand. "I'm sure Henry won't have a problem with that; he's a business owner and knows how these things work."

Engelhardt placed the file in his lap and rubbed his nose; finally letting his hand drop, he sat there looking very tired. I had a feeling that it was what I looked like most of the time from this side of the desk. "Walt—"

"I know what you're going to say, Irl, and I apologize. I know this is a busy week for you."

"The busiest."

"Yep, well, I promise it won't happen again. Things just got out of hand."

He was nodding his head. "All right, go get your friend, but tell him I told you that if we have any more shenanigans like this I'm going to have to lock him up for real."

"Thanks, Irl. Where is he?"

The Pennington County sheriff tapped a few keys on his desk phone. "Brenda?"

"Yes, Sheriff."

"Where have we got Defending Champion Henry Standing Bear?"

There was a rustling of papers from the desk outside Irl's office. "Medical. He was complaining of headaches, and the staff thought he might have a concussion, so they shipped him over to Rapid City Regional."

"Thanks, Brenda." He tapped the button again. "You know where that is?"

We stood. "Um, yep."

He reopened the file in his lap. "What do you want me to do with the woman?" He looked back up at us. "Wojciechowski?"

"Have you got anything like solitary confinement? It might be the only way to keep the world safe." Vic followed me toward the door and closed it behind us as we made a speedy retreat.

"I'm glad I made it back before all the excitement was over with." As we crossed the bull pen and made our way down the steps, she shook her head. "You've got to admit, as fights go it was pretty impressive."

"On one side it was."

We stepped through the glass doors onto the sidewalk as she raised the key fob and unlocked the Dodge. I opened the door and struggled to fit. "How do people get in these things, anyway?" I watched as she pulled a parking ticket from under the windshield wiper and tossed it into the back. She climbed in and hit the ignition. "I'm guessing you're not going to pay that?"

Vic made a face, slammed the selector in gear, and, after laying a good twenty feet of rubber as we sped off toward the hospital, weaved through traffic like she was in a Friedkin film. "I'm on the fucking job."

I fastened my seat belt as quickly as I could. "Who did you say were your driving instructors—the Blue Angels?"

I pointed the way, she turned a corner, and I felt the car go slightly airborne as we went over some railroad tracks. "I like driving fast—I like doing things fast." She gave me a side-glance. "Most things, that is." I indicated a right-hand turn, and she flat tracked the Dodge around another corner, expertly correcting the drift. Rocketing into the hospital parking lot, she slipped into a diagonal spot and cut the engine. "So, you miss me?"

I still had both hands braced against the dash. "Can I open my eyes now?"

"Pussy."

I shook my head and got out of the car, happy to be on solid boot leather. "C'mon, the ER is this way."

She caught up as we weaved our way through the parked cars, and I swallowed. "Where are we on Michael's case?"

She took a deep breath and then shot it out through her shapely nostrils. "Zip-nada. The woman who witnessed the incident from the building across the street couldn't identify her own husband in a lineup, and it looks like we've ground to a halt." She stepped in front of me and stopped me in my tracks. "I've got the files."

I chewed the skin on the inside of my cheek. "The originals?"

"Yes."

"Katz and Gowder gave them to you?"

At the mention of the Philadelphia police detectives, she stiffened a bit, and I had my answer before she spoke. "*Gave* is a relative term."

"Vic—"

"He's my little brother, Walt, and he's dead."

I stuffed my hands in my jeans and stared at the parking lot's painted lines. "I'm sure that they—"

"You're the best, and I need the best; this is personal."

"I know."

"It's what you do."

"I know."

She tilted her head back and squinted up at me. "You'd do it for any citizen on the street, so why not for me?"

"You're right."

"What?"

Taking a deep breath, I repeated myself. "I said you're right." She looked as if she wasn't quite sure what to say next, so I helped. "Copy the files and give them to me, and I'll go through them." I waited a moment. "It's personal for me, too. He was my son-in-law."

Her eyes clouded, and she reached out and grabbed my shirtfront, pulling herself in and muffling her voice against my chest. "Thanks."

Just then, a sheriff's deputy hustled from the ER. Moving toward his unit at a clip, he was rapidly followed by another. They jumped in and backed out, barely missing us.

"What's up?"

The deputy looked a little anxious, but I think he recognized me from my visit to their headquarters the previous day. He called out as he slapped the car into drive. "Fugitive at large."

"Who?"

I barely caught his voice as they peeled away. "Some damn Indian."

Vic's face pulled back from my chest as she watched them go. "Uh-oh."

Boy howdy.

"So, why are we searching in the one place he supposedly escaped from?"

The fact that I'd gotten lost twice in the labyrinth of Rapid City Regional did nothing to lessen the assurance of my next statement. "I've got a hunch."

"About?"

"Bodaway Torres is in the ICU here, and I think Henry might've decided to look in on him. Lola's been hitting him pretty hard, and I'm thinking it's had an effect."

I finally found the ICU at the end of yet another hall, and I could see the giant Lola had introduced me to still sitting in his chair. I waved at the man with the dark sunglasses, but he didn't move. "Hey, Big Easy."

Vic murmured. "What, he's from New Orleans?"

"Yep, um, I'm not sure. It's complicated." We stopped, and I looked past him toward the nurse's station, but the one woman there was ignoring us and I brought my eyes back to the large man. "Easy, I'm looking for . . ."

I leaned in closer and examined him, Vic joining me. "What the fuck, he's asleep?"

I took one of the giant's hands, lifting it and then letting it drop. "Out cold."

"He's a sound sleeper."

I examined a dent in the drywall behind him, about where the biker's head would've been if he'd been standing. "Might be more than that." I felt the man's pulse, just to be sure he was alive, and then glanced in his nostrils, where I could see blood, and at his face, where the beginnings of two black eyes were hidden beneath the sunglasses. "He's unconscious, but he's all right."

My undersheriff made a face. "Have I told you lately how scary your friends are?"

I moved past him toward the observation window around the corner. "You're one of my friends."

She followed after me. "Case in point."

The Cheyenne Nation was standing there with his arms folded, the torn motocross jersey still hanging from his shoulder with a few bloodstains here and there—fresh from the Indian Wars.

I stood beside him and looked in at Bodaway, nothing having changed. The Bear didn't say anything, but there was a look of sadness on his face.

Vic came up and stood with me. "Handsome."

I nodded, glanced at Henry again, and then looked back at the young man. There's something profoundly sad in the striking down of a young person in his prime, an injustice that offends beyond all others. I've had numerous engagements with the Reaper, but it's outside the lines when he takes the young—just plain cheating.

I studied Torres's profile, the strength of the jaw, the powerful nose, and the black, black hair. I stood there for a long while, not trusting what might come out of my mouth next.

My undersheriff turned, leaned her back against the glass, and looked at the two of us. "So, what happened?"

"Um . . . he was riding out near Devils Tower and somebody ran him off the road. Mike Novo did a preliminary and said it was possible that he wasn't going particularly fast but that he had some weight on the back, either saddlebags full of something heavy, or possibly a passenger."

Her eyes drifted over to the Bear and then back to me. "No witnesses?"

"No, but there was a young woman named Chloe Nance

who found him, and I'm thinking there might be a connection there. According to her father, she has a substance abuse problem and Bodaway here might've been supplying."

"You think it was drugs on the back of the bike?"

I shook my head. "His mother says no, and besides, they wouldn't weigh enough to be a factor, but he is under investigation by the ATF for illegal gun sales."

"The Alcohol, Tobacco, and Firearms ATF?"

I glanced around to make sure that Big Easy was still out. "None other. I got a visit last night from Brady Post, one of the chief enforcers for the Tre Tre Nomads; he's fully patched and undercover with these guys." I paused. "And then there's the paint issue."

She folded her arms. "The paint issue?"

"Irl let me in to the impound lot at the sheriff's department, and I found gold paint on the side of the Harley Bodaway here was riding."

"Gold."

"Lola Wojciechowski drives a '66 Cadillac DeVille, gold in color."

There was a predictable pause. "You think she ran over her own son?"

I glanced at Henry. "The more you get to know her, the more it seems like a possibility, but then again it appears that the vehicle is something of a staff car for the entire Tre Tre Nomad gang."

"So, somebody in his own gang ran over him?"

"Possibly." I pulled out the cell phone, handed it to Vic, and gestured toward the young man in the bed. "This is Bodaway's phone. Can you pull up his previous calls?"

She took it and began pushing buttons at an alarming rate. "Made or received?"

"It can do both?"

She shook her head. "You are such a Neanderthal."

Henry cleared his throat, and I turned to look at him. "You okay?"

"Yes."

"You want to talk?"

"No."

"Okay."

I started to look at Vic but then turned back. "You ever going to want to talk?"

"No."

"Okay."

Vic showed me the phone and started counting. "Seventeen calls from the Nance household, a couple from the 310 area code, thirty-two from Lola Wojciechowski, nine from a number with a Phoenix area code but no ID, and twenty-one from a place called The Chop Shop, with a few from a pizza place, the last two both here in Rapid City." She looked at the phone screen. "I say we start with the pizza place. I'm famished."

I looked back at the Bear. "You need a getaway car, and we've got one."

Studying the Cheyenne Nation just as I had, Vic pushed off the glass window. "And a driver, but you'll have to hunker down in the back, seeing as how you're on the lam and all."

• • •

Piesano's Pacchia is a joint up on Canyon Lake Drive, reputed to make the best pizza in the Hills, and when the Philadelphian concurred, I feigned a heart attack and slumped in my half of the booth.

"No, really, this is good pizza." She chewed and postulated. "Not as good as my uncle's, but it's good."

I sipped my iced tea and glanced outside where a large man with long, dark hair sat on the hood of an orange muscle car with his back to us.

The waitress, a cute little blonde, came over, refilled my tea, and offered Vic more wine, but my undersheriff showed restraint. Vic waited until the waitress departed and then set down the rules. "Okay, I'm going to ask a few questions, but I don't want you to do anything but answer the questions one at a time. No embellishments."

I turned back to her. "Okay."

"How old is Bodaway Torres?"

"Thirty-two."

She nodded. "How long ago did Henry know Lola?"

"A little over thirty years ago."

There was a pause as she thought about how to proceed, deciding on her usual course: straight forward and full speed ahead. "Asking the question as a crass white woman, would you say that Bodaway bears more than a passing resemblance to Henry fucking Standing Bear?"

I sighed. "The thought more than crossed my mind when I saw the two of them together."

She turned her head and watched him. "Have you ever seen him this upset about something before?"

"I've known him my whole life, so a few times, yes, but not many."

She turned the tarnished gold eyes back to me. "You are now free to embellish."

"I don't know."

"Walt . . ."

"I grant you, there is a resemblance."

"They look exactly alike." She shook her head. "If you were to go to the Henry Standing Bear Store and they were out of Henry Standing Bears, they would offer you a slightly more diminutive Bodaway Torres."

"Why would she wait this long to tell him?"

She sipped her soda and postulated. "I don't know; she's nuts?"

"There's that." I slouched in the corner of the booth and poked my boots out the end. "Working on the supposition that you're right and there is a connection, maybe she didn't have any intention of telling him, but then this happened and she truly is desperate."

She shook her head at me.

"What?"

"You are such a goofball for women." She set her glass down and leaned in across the table. "I know this is going to come as a surprise, but there are women out there who are capable of doing anything as horrible as a man can do and worse."

A large shadow suddenly darkened our table. "What are you two talking about?"

Vic scooted over so that Henry could have a seat, since there was more room on her side. "Um, nothing."

I gestured toward the half a pie. "Want some pizza?"

"I am not hungry."

"I would offer you something to drink, but that led to your being a fugitive."

"But I like pizza." He picked up a slice and took a bite, grabbed Vic's wineglass to spite me, and took a sip.

Vic and I looked at each other. "So, what are the chances?"

He took another bite and chewed, obviously hungrier than he had thought. "I do not know."

Vic leaned forward, looking at him and maybe making an aesthetic analysis. "He looks like you."

"Yes."

"Has Lola ever said anything to you?"

"No, I have not heard from her in over thirty years."

Vic ventured a question. "Um, not to put too delicate a point on this, but can you remember the last time you and Lola . . ." He turned to look at her. "I mean a date, time of year?"

"No." He stared at her. "I did not keep a diary."

"Gimme my wine back."

He handed it to her. "I am saying it is improbable. I am not saying it is impossible."

She sipped. "I'd like to see a photo of the Delshay Torres of record."

I looked up at a clock on the wall and noted the time. "If we get back to Hulett before Chief Nutter closes up shop, we can ask him to take a look on the National Crime Information Center database. They've probably got a photo of him."

Vic watched the Bear. "You really don't think he's yours?"

"I do not know." He pulled his own phone from his pocket.

"I have received a text from Jamey saying he has Dog in his truck and is wondering where you would like him deposited."

"If he doesn't mind Dog-sitting, he can just hang onto him till we get back. Dog doesn't like being in the motel room alone."

"I will text him." He did and then returned the phone to his pocket. "What do we do now?"

"We were thinking that was your call."

He nodded and reached for Vic's wine again, and this time I could see where the skin had been stripped from his knuckles. "Why would the ATF be so interested in the distribution of guns?"

Vic barked a laugh. "Because it's illegal, and because their jurisdiction is alcohol, tobacco, and—let's see, what's the last one? Oh, yeah—firearms."

The Cheyenne Nation shook his head. "When we met Agent Post in the motel room, it seemed like more than that." He glanced at me. "Almost a year of undercover work to infiltrate one of the most violent biker gangs around just to locate some random hardware?"

"What are you thinking?"

He shrugged and then turned his head, watching the sun start to make its own escape behind the Black Hills. "Something that would fit on a motorcycle."

"So, smaller than a bread box?" They both looked at me. "It's a box you put bread in." They continued to look at me. "So, do you want to go get what may or may not be the mother of your child out of jail?"

"No."

"Okay." I pulled out Bodaway's phone and looked at it

again. "You said seventeen calls from Chloe Nance, a couple from the 310 area code, thirty-two from Mom, nine from a number with a Phoenix area code but no ID, twenty-one from The Chop Shop, and three from this pizza place." I sipped my tea and glanced at the waitress behind the counter. "So, let's start with the easiest." I gestured to get her attention. "Miss, could I get some more iced tea?"

She hurried over. "Sorry, I was folding napkins."

I watched as she filled my glass and then looked at Henry. "Would you like something?"

"No, I am fine."

She studied him, and I asked, "Miss, we're looking for my friend here's son and was wondering if you'd seen him. Bodaway Torres?" I quickly added. "B-way?"

She smiled a dazzling grin toward Henry. "I was just thinking he looked like you." She stuck out her hand. "I'm Tiffany. I'm sure he's told you about me?"

The Bear matched her grin for grin, enveloping her hand in his. "Tiffany, of course he has."

"You tell that dirty bird I'm mad at him; he hasn't called or anything for days."

I redirected the conversation. "He's been kind of tied up lately. As a matter of fact, we've been having trouble tracking him down ourselves. You wouldn't happen to know who he's been running with these days?"

She thought about it. "There's that guy with the do-rag and the tattoos."

"Tall with a goatee?"

She nodded. "And the broken nose, yeah."

I glanced at the others. "Brady Post."

"Yeah, that's him. I remember him saying his name."

"Anybody else?"

She stepped back, and the smile died; I guess I was pushing a little too hard. She looked at Henry. "You are his dad, right?"

The Bear broadened his grin, displaying stunning white ivories against his sun-bronzed skin. "Far as we know."

She relaxed and punched his shoulder, but withdrew her hand and wiped it on her jeans, just now realizing his jersey was torn and had blood on it. "Um, there's Billy ThE Kiddo. That's the only other person I ever saw him with."

"Billy the Kiddo?"

"No Billy ThE with a capital E. You've never heard of him? He's got his own TV show—*Billy ThE Kiddo's Chopper Off?* It was huge till he punched some producer and they canceled it. Word is he's in negotiation with another cable network, and they're gonna have another series based on him." She shrugged. "At least that's what they say. He's originally from here and has a custom motorcycle place just down the street called The Chop Shop."

"The Chop Shop." I shook my head. "Do you have an address?"

"Oh, you can't miss it." She glanced at Henry again. "You tell B-way to text me, okay?"

We decided to call Sheriff Engelhardt to ask him to check on Torres Senior, and after the Cheyenne Nation apologized, Irl agreed to message a photo of the man as soon as they found one. As a precautionary measure, I had him look up Billy ThE Kiddo, just so we'd know what we were up against.

"Kiddo? That's his real last name? Shit, I'd get a nickname, too." Vic parked the Challenger across the street from The Chop Shop, which was housed in a remodeled corner gas station still replete with old-fashioned pumps albeit modern neon.

The Pennington County sheriff read to me over the speakerphone. "Oh, he is a real piece of work, Walt." I glanced at the face on the screen and then held the phone for the others to see. Irl continued, "Behold Billy ThE Kiddo, six foot two, two hundred and twenty-seven pounds. Over a dozen cases of aggravated assault, two domestic violence charges, one assault with a deadly weapon charge, and once even choked a K9 unit dog unconscious in Orange County, California."

Vic studied the mug shot. "He's got a mullet."

Irl laughed. "It's a nice one, isn't it? I doubt he hears much with that party going on in the back of his head. He can build bikes though. Started over in Sturgis at those build-offs and somebody from Hollywood saw him and figured he was a genuine American outlaw and gave him his own reality show. He was living out there in Los Angeles, but something happened and he's back here with a couple of those motorcycle places set up like franchises."

Henry turned the phone his way and looked at the photo, and at the multitude of tattoos and piercings. "I do not think he is the president of Rotary."

"Originally from Rapid City and a good family; it's undisclosed exactly where the poor little lamb went astray."

Vic opened the glove box, took out her Glock, checked the magazine, and slapped it back in the 9mm.

Irl interrupted. "Excuse me, but was that the sound of a

semiautomatic pistol's magazine being expertly reintroduced between the weapon's grips?"

I made a face at my undersheriff. "Nope, just the glove box."

"Walt?"

"No trouble, I promise."

He continued, "We've had a number of zoning problems with this jaybird and a few charges for dumping harmful chemicals into the local water system. You want me to send a few guys around to back you up?"

"No, we're just going to ask him a few questions about the kid that got hurt. I guess they knew each other."

"All right, but don't shoot anybody."

I assured him. "Right."

"Vic?" Evidently he was not assured.

"What?"

"What are we not doing today?"

She climbed out, flipping the seat forward and allowing me egress as she took the phone and began making squelch noises with her mouth. "Schweeesclerbleee, swurchscwerch, scweee . . . can't hear you, Irl, you're breaking up. Schweeesclerbleee, swurchscwerch, scweee scwch scwch." She made a few more noises into the phone, then hung up and handed it back to me.

"I just want you to know, I'm never falling for that one again."

She curtseyed as she stuffed the Glock in the back of her jeans. "Sure you will."

As we walked across the street toward The Chop Shop, the music of air wrenches drifted out to meet us, along with the sound of an acetylene torch turning metals into liquids.

It was one of those vintage gas stations with a rounded

glass-block front and vaulted canopies that covered the old pumps and stretched out toward the street. The building was painted black, and there were a multitude of outrageous-looking motorcycles to match lined up everywhere, in different stages of disrepair and assembly. Through a door in the work area were a few young ladies in skimpy outfits and smoking cigarettes, loafing in what must've been the office.

One of them looked up as we walked into the bays. "Hi. Welcome to Billy ThE Kiddo's Chop Shop. Can I help you?"

I smiled. "Do you have to say that every time somebody comes in?"

"Pretty much."

"Is Henry McCarty, aka William H. Bonney, around?"

She pushed off the edge of the desk and abandoned her companion. "I luh?"

"Billy ThE Kiddo."

"You got a bike problem?"

She was talking to me, but she was looking at Henry, not that I blamed her.

Henry saved us by speaking up. "I have got a shovelhead rebuild that I am doing, and I am past the wrist-pin alignment and the pistons are ready to go in. Now I know the ring gaps should never be in line with each other or placed on a thrust area of the bore. The major thrust area is the rear of the cylinder wall and the next minor thrust area is the front, but will the oil ring expander come in contact with the cylinder bore or the oil ring scraper rail gaps?"

You could see the struggle as she thought about bullshitting the Bear but then thought better of it. "Um . . . maybe you should talk to Billy."

The Cheyenne Nation showed some teeth. "That would be nice. Thank you."

The dishwater blonde threw a thumb over her shoulder toward the bay where all the noise was coming from. "He's welding, so shield your eyes."

She left us, and we ambled toward the back where a very lithe-looking individual was crouched down working on the gas tank of a bike that looked as though it had undergone a great deal of modification. It also looked like a death trap.

As we waited, I glanced around the shop and noticed a very heavy security door led to the back and had to admit that it was an impressive operation—a little grimy but impressive.

"What do you want?"

I turned around and discovered that The Chop Shop's chief cook and bottle washer was holding the brass nozzle of the torch away from his work and had nudged the dark glasses up onto his rooster-like platinum hair.

"We're looking for Mr. Kiddo?"

"Billy—people call me Billy ThE." He stood, closed off the acetylene, and turned to face us, and I'm not sure if I'd ever seen that much defined muscle on one person before. He had the easy smile of someone who was used to getting what he wanted, and I was betting we were seeing a good seven thousand dollars' worth of dental work; then there were the diamond earrings, which probably cost a couple thousand more. He hung the nozzle on the rack with the tanks, pulled a red shop rag from his back pocket, and wiped off his long, tattooed fingers. "Well, you found him. Now what?"

"Do you happen to know a young man by the name of Bodaway Torres?"

"Yeah, I know B-way. What about him."

"Do you mind telling us what your dealings with him might've been?"

He studied the three of us. "You guys cops?"

I gestured toward Vic and myself. "Two out of three."

He tossed the rag onto a nearby tool rack and then turned back to scrutinize us. "Well, two out of three of you can go fuck yourselves."

The Bear glanced at us and then back to ThE. "Does that mean that I get to stay and ask questions?"

Kiddo smiled and even went so far as to crack his knuckles like some cartoon badass. "It means you get to stay, and I can stick my boot so far up your ass I'll be using your mouth as an ankle bracelet."

The Bear smiled, and I watched as he seemed to grow and swell, or maybe the room was just becoming smaller. "Really."

Kiddo's grin grew wider as he reached over to the same bench and picked up a disc metal cutter. "You know, I hate it when people don't take my threats seriously."

"Maybe you should get better writers or work on some better threats."

ThE took a step forward with the cutter and punched the trigger so that he had to speak over the dangerous whine of the thing. "You ever try to pick up your teeth without fingers?"

The Bear looked at me. "That wasn't bad."

"I'd give it an eight."

Henry turned back to Kiddo. "No, but when we were kids waiting on the bus in front of the Jimtown Bar in Lame Deer, we used to pass the time picking up teeth in the parking lot after the weekend fights."

I nodded toward the Cheyenne Nation and half-yelled over the whine. "That was better—it had a personal quality and didn't sound like a line from a crappy Chuck Norris movie."

Billy ThE stood there with the cutter, and I swear he was thinking of using it on us just as Vic pulled the 9mm from the back of her jeans, letting it rest alongside her thigh. "So, you're the kind of asshole that brings power tools to gunfights?"

7

"He says you threatened him."

I held the phone to my ear and tried to remember how I'd gotten involved in this mess but then recalled it was a damsel in distress who was more like a dame. "He started it with a metal cutter."

"He said Ms. Moretti was brandishing a gun."

I glanced at my impromptu posse leaning on the fender of the screaming-orange Dodge, one watching the horizon and the other checking her nails. "Define brandishing."

"Walt."

"Okay, she brandished it a little bit." I sighed. "Look, Irl, it isn't like we got anything out of him."

"You got a restraining order, harassment, and a charge of cease and desist. He learned a lot of litigious lessons out there in California, and, pending court action, you're not going to be able to go within a hundred feet of him."

"What's he hiding?"

"Heck if I have any idea, but he's all lawyered up now, so it's going to be a lot harder to find out."

I sighed and began pacing back and forth. "Anything interesting from his sordid past?"

"Other than the things I've already mentioned?" The sheriff sighed and then chuckled. "A couple of years ago, he was back on a visit and attempted to shoot his next-door neighbor with a .40 for mowing his lawn on a Sunday afternoon."

My response was slightly incredulous. "He's religious?"

"About football."

"Oh."

"Came charging out of the house but must not be much of a shot with that Glock 22, because he fired the thing twice before killing it."

"The lawn mower, I'm assuming we're talking about."

"Yes."

"Is lawn implement destruction a felony here in South Dakota?"

"Nothing runs like a Deere or smells like a John." Engelhardt laughed outright. "He bought the old guy another one, but Billy can be hell on wheels. He trashed a bar in Deadwood a few months back—stuck some guy's head in a toilet." I listened as he rustled some papers. "Don't be fooled; he can be charming as hell in court—shows up in a coat and tie, all Hollywood businessman, and makes jokes about not being able to grow up. You'd be amazed how many middle-aged jurors want to get free work on their bikes around here."

"So, no serious time inside, then?"

"No, he's pretty careful about that kind of thing. I mean, it's all just assault and battery type stuff, like I told you." There was silence over the phone. "Why are you so interested?"

"Bodaway Torres called his shop twenty-one times in the last week."

"Maybe he was having bike problems."

"Maybe."

There was another pause. "All right, then, but would you keep me informed so I don't have to find these things out via APB?"

"Roger that." I hit the off button and walked back toward the Dodge. "We are free agents once again, but Irl says ThE is lawyered up and that we need to leave him alone."

"They say that genius is an infinite capacity for taking pains. It is a very bad definition, but it does apply to detective work." The Bear turned and looked at Vic. "Arthur Conan Doyle." He shrugged and looked back at me. "All we wanted to do was talk."

"I guess he's got nothing to say."

Vic stared at the Cheyenne Nation and then at me. "Neither of you want to hear what I have to say next."

The Bear scratched the side of his face. "Then do not say it."

She continued to thwart him by looking at me. "There was this guy I know who taught me that when an investigation grinds to a halt, you go back to the beginning and start over."

I thought about it. "You know, I hate that guy who taught you that." I leaned on the fender with her. "That was me, right?"

Henry interrupted. "And where, pray tell, is the beginning of this case?"

We both looked at her as she smiled.

Following the gold Caddy on the highway, Vic and I watched as the two heads turned toward each other, their hair whipping in the wind. "What do you suppose they're talking about?"

"Probably the two thousand dollars of bail money she owes him."

"I imagine she'll tell him to put it on her tab."

Vic wound her way through the Black Hills, her foot in the Challenger, causing it to bellow as we raced along behind the Cadillac. "That tab is getting to be pretty big." She glanced at me, sideways. "So, you think he's Henry's kid?"

"No."

"Why?"

"Because he says he isn't."

"Boy, I want you on my side in a paternity suit." She nodded toward the car ahead of us. "Of course, she says he is."

"Well, like I said, Lola Wojciechowski's turning out to be less and less a credible entity."

"Momma's baby, Poppa's maybe."

"I just don't think it would've taken her thirty years to get in touch with him about it."

My undersheriff cocked her head. "She's tough."

"She's had to be." I studied the car and could see Lola was putting a little distance between her and us. "I'm beginning not to trust her any farther than I can throw her."

"So, it's solely about justice for the kid?"

I took a deep breath. "As far as I'm concerned, but I'm not sure about Henry."

"Did you talk to the doctors?"

"No."

"I did."

I turned and looked at her again. "Oh, now why don't I like the sound of that?"

"That kid's never coming back, Walt."

I nodded my head and turned to watch the road being gobbled up by the muscle car. "Never?"

"Not one chance in a thousand."

"That's not what his mother thinks."

"Yeah, the doctors told me about that, too. The one I talked with said he explains the situation to her, but then she keeps coming back with all kinds of scenarios, not a one of them with any medical credibility." She watched me as I continued to study the rapidly passing outskirts of Rapid City. "I suppose you didn't want to hear that, huh?"

I settled into the bucket seat, evidently larger than a bucket. "Not really—makes me sad."

"I'm sorry, Walt. I just don't want you pinning your efforts on bringing that kid back."

I nodded, glancing at the speedometer and noticing we were approaching a hundred. "Um, you think we're going a little fast?"

She gestured with a hand toward the windshield. "You want me to keep up with Maria Andretti here or what?" We banked another turn and started climbing an extended hill just as a siren sounded from a long way behind us. I watched as Vic glanced up into the rearview mirror. "Company."

Swinging around, I could see the flashing lights of a black South Dakota Highway Patrol car gaining on us. "Well, hell." It was about then that I heard the bellow increase and the Challenger felt as if it were shooting out from under me. "What are you doing?"

She gestured through the windshield again. "She's out on bail; you think they're going to let her get away with doing a hundred on an interstate highway?"

"Probably not—"

"I'll bait and switch—give this highwayman a run for his money; besides, if he catches us, I'm sure you can talk our way out of it."

"I don't suppose we could just pull over and talk to him?"

She glanced at the speedometer. "Maybe before we went past a hundred and twenty."

I reached out and clamped a hand on the dash.

Lola and Henry's pace now seemed sedate as we blew past. Vic waved in the rearview and then checked on the HP's progress. "He's still gaining on us." She glanced at me, smiling just enough to reveal the slightly oversized canine tooth, increasing her lupine features. "He's gamer."

Just before we topped the hill, I glanced back to see the trooper pass the Cadillac as if it were dragging an anchor. "Mission accomplished—we are now his sole and exclusive target."

The Challenger became very light in the tires as we weaved between the cars on the road and leveled off, starting down the hill. "What's the next town?"

"Sturgis."

"Is there a main artery leading out?"

"Alternate 14, which heads toward Deadwood and Boulder Canyon Road."

The speedometer was now tipping one hundred and sixty as she blithely steered the Dodge into the emergency lane to pass two semis running in tandem. "This first exit. Here?"

I swallowed and tried to work up enough spit to speak. "No, the second one."

Rocketing past the trucks and the startled driver of a minivan, she tipped the wheel, and the muscle car leapt back into the open lane like an animal on the hunt. "Cool, ho-daddy."

I turned to see if the trooper was a member of the Joie Chitwood Danger Angels, but so far he hadn't caught up, possibly slowed down by the eighteen-wheelers. "Take the next exit and then left under the underpass and out of town, but there's going to be some traffic with it being rally week."

"I like traffic—it's cover." She spotted the exit up ahead and, predictably, there was a lineup of cars and trucks with trailers hauling motorcycles backed up almost onto the thoroughfare. "You said left, right?"

"Yep, left."

Slicing down the emergency lane, she decelerated and tipped the wheel just enough to get the rear end of the Challenger to break traction and begin a sickeningly slow slide to the right as the two back wheels attempted to catch up with the front.

I looked straight ahead at the intersection that was rapidly approaching, aware that the light was red and that traffic was streaming by in front of us.

Vic casually countered the drift just enough to keep the Dodge in play and, slowing her speed, continued turning to the right, glancing up at the overpass where the highway patrolman was sliding across the bridge with his antilock brakes fully locked. "Gotcha."

A truck driver, pulling across the intersection, suddenly looked up the ramp in time to see us rapidly approaching slideways. He slammed on his brakes as Vic threw the Dodge across the opposing lanes, beat out a sedan, and put her foot into the more than seven hundred horsepower, slinging us forward as she took the emergency lane again, shooting past more cars, then roaring back onto the road and weaving her way through the lanes of traffic.

I could still hear the whine of the HP's siren and turned to see that he had made a U-turn farther down the road in order to take the Boulder Canyon exit in the opposite direction. "He's still back there."

"Where does this road go?"

I glanced out the side window, the pines compressed by the speed like the opening credits of a movie not formatted to real life. "Deadwood."

"Anything between?"

"Some small secondary roads in Boulder Creek and Oak Ridge."

We leapt across a bridge and made a hard right, following the geometry of a curve not designed for almost ninety miles an hour. "Is that Boulder Creek we just went over?"

"I suppose—we were going too fast for me to read the sign."

She dipped her head forward, indicating the road beyond. "He's going to radio ahead, and they'll be waiting for us at the cutoff in Deadwood."

"I'd say that's probably true." A sign that read BOULDER CREEK COUNTRY CLUB flashed by. "Take the next road on the right."

"What?"

"Do it."

She pressured the brakes and broadsided through the turn onto the tiny road. "Apple Spring Boulevard—really?"

"It's not on the maps, but there's a dirt road that connects with Crook Mountain and leads back up to Whitewood and

Route 34 that'll get us back to Hulett. Tim Berg told me about it a while ago."

She bellowed up the two-lane past the assorted houses, slowed at the end of the pavement, and stopped just before she cut the engine. "The human pencil holder?"

Vic referred to Tim's propensity of sticking pencils and pens in his prodigious beard and then losing them. "And the Butte County sheriff, yes."

She rolled down her window, and we listened to the highway patrolman's approach. There was only a small break in the pines, but after a moment the black sedan flashed by. She raised a fist and smiled at me. "Let's hear it for the Philadelphia Police Academy Tactical Driving School."

I cleared my throat and attempted to settle my stomach by stepping out of the car. "No offense, but I don't ever want to do that again."

Vic slipped out the other side and looked at me over the hood. "You getting sensitive in your old age?"

I ignored her and leaned on the grille, feeling the heat from the Hemi engine as it ticked and cooled.

She joined me, crossing her arms and bumping her shoulder into my side. "What's up?"

"I don't mean to sound like a child . . ." I shook my head, clearing it with the scent of ponderosa pines, Black Hill spruce, quaking aspens, paper birch, bur oak, and green ash in this island of trees surrounded by a sea of grass. "But I really don't want to be here."

"Then go home."

"I can't."

"Because of the kid?"

"Yep." I stubbed the toe of a boot in the pine needles on the ground. "It was all up for grabs until I saw him, and now it seems like it's something I have to do."

Vic laughed. "And this is a revelation?"

"Not exactly, but I'm fighting the feeling that I'm some kind of windup toy that, when faced with a criminal enigma, falls into a mechanical response in order to solve the mystery."

"You just answered your own question." She laughed. "Walt, however it is you look at what you do, whether it's a job, a duty, or—when I watch you do it—an art, you're very good at it, and for my money you're doing it for all the right reasons." She swung around and stood in front of me. "You're not doing it for that woman, you're not doing it out of some bullshit sense of duty or some philosophical construct called justice; you're doing it for that kid who can't speak for himself. I swear you're like this detective for the disenfranchised. Everybody that nobody gives a shit about, the people out there on the fringes—those are the people you speak for and that's why I love you."

I stared at her.

"That last part was just me."

I continued to stare at her.

"And if you don't say or do something right now, I'm going to kick you in the nuts."

I leaned forward and gently kissed her on the top of her head.

It might've gone further, but then two more highway patrolmen howled by like internal combustion bandits on Boulder Canyon Highway, one after the other.

She looked at the pine needles I had disturbed, then turned

back to me, and I could tell the spell was broken. "Speaking of cases that have ground to a stop . . ."

I nodded and thought about the man who might've been responsible for Michael's death. "I've got feelers with the FBI."

"McGroder?"

"Yep. He's got contacts over at State and the NSA, and they are looking for anything on Bidarte. Some of the leads say he's near the border in that Copper Canyon area, but others say he's in Mexico City."

"When do we leave?"

I took a deep breath. "It's not that easy."

"No? The asshole killed my little brother."

"We don't know that for sure."

She shrugged, unconsciously hugging her abdomen. "That's okay; there are plenty of other reasons to kill the son of a bitch."

I reached out, draped an arm over her shoulder, and pulled her in close. "Yep, I just want to make sure which one it is before we go hunting for him."

"You're so law abiding."

"I try." I looked up the dirt and gravel road leading to the top of a ridge and turning to the left. "So, you ready to go four-wheeling?"

She shrugged. "Fuck it—it's a rental."

The Challenger did pretty well, but there were a few spots where we could hear the low-slung undercarriage dragging on the rocks and catching on the sagebrush. "I don't think this is what this thing was made for."

We topped the ridge and barely missed the trunk of one of the aforementioned pine trees. "You could be right."

"I think it's only about a quarter mile or so to the paved road, so we might make it."

There was a small wallow and then a turn, and I could see the gravel lot and turnaround where the pavement started up again. I could also see the Pennington County sheriff sitting on the grille guard of his shiny black Tahoe, and replacing his worn-out chewing gum with another stick.

"Been chewing that gum long?"

"Three sticks. I figured you would've showed up by now."

I shut the door on the Dodge. "We were enjoying the environs."

"I bet." He pulled himself off the hood and stretched his back.

"Where's the Highway Patrol?"

"I don't know, probably out patrolling the highway." He smiled at Vic as she closed her door, and then walked around the front and extended his hand to her. "We meet again?"

"Always a pleasure."

He turned back to me. "Just because I know where you are doesn't mean they know where you are. We got to the roadblock in Deadwood, and they said this pumpkin latte hadn't showed, so I started thinking."

"And here you are."

"And here I am." He waited a moment and then asked. "Explanation?"

I shrugged. "Which part?"

"What's so interesting about this kid over in my hospital?"

"I'm not sure, but I'm thinking it must have something to do with guns or drugs."

Engelhardt breathed a sigh. "Usually does."

"The problem is, how do you haul enough of something on a motorcycle to make it worth killing somebody for?"

"How do you know it was something on the bike and not just something personal?"

"Mike Novo ran the scene, and he says it was weight or possibly somebody else on the bike."

"Mike would know. Who found him, anyway?"

"A young woman by the name of Chloe Nance."

"Bob Nance's daughter?"

"Yep."

"He's kind of a big dog around these parts. Is that the only connection, the daughter finding the Torres kid?"

"Maybe not. I came into possession of Bodaway's phone, and she had called him a number of times before the incident."

"Chloe." He tilted his head. "She had a drug problem herself."

Vic sat on the front of the Challenger. "Hell, heroin is a hundred and ten dollars a gram, with crack cocaine at six hundred; methamphetamine is sixteen hundred dollars an ounce, and LSD three thousand a gram. In a single set of saddlebags the kid could've been carrying millions."

I shook my head. "Funny enough, he doesn't have any dealings with drugs on his rap sheet."

My undersheriff seemed incredulous. "Nothing?"

"Nope."

Irl listened as another siren rose in the distance and then quieted. "What was the other thing you mentioned?"

"Guns—he's got a record of gun running."

Engelhardt made a face. "I don't hardly think you could carry enough guns on a motorcycle to make it worth attempting to take somebody's life. Any history of dealings in antiquarian weapons? I mean, he wasn't carrying around Jesse James's pistols or something?"

"No, just street stuff."

"Then I think you're going to have to stick with drugs. Who knows, maybe he's broadening his horizons—Lord knows the money's better." He tipped his hat back and studied the two of us. "Now, maybe you can tell me why it is you were going a hundred and fifty miles an hour on my highway?"

Vic smiled, webbing her fingers together and cracking her knuckles. "One seventy."

Irl looked at the Challenger with renewed respect. "This big dude'll do that, huh?"

Vic ran her hand over the hood as if petting an oversized cat. "Advertised at just under two hundred."

I interrupted. "Lola was driving over the speed limit by a somewhat wide margin, and my undersheriff decided to provide a decoy to keep her from going back to slam."

"I see."

"You're not going to arrest us, are you?"

He sighed. "No, I'm just trying to think of how to get you out of here. I could call in the situation, but I'd just as soon not owe them a favor."

Vic pushed off the Dodge and stood. "Trade cars with us;

then, if they pull you over, you can say you found the ditched car and are impounding it."

He shook his head at her. "Boy, if you want to know how to break a law, ask a cop." He laughed. "How do I get my car back?"

"We'll drive it to Rapid tomorrow and pick up the Dodge; by that time the heat will have simmered down."

"That's all fine and well for you, young lady, but what about me? I'm going to get pulled over by every highway patrolman between here and my impound."

"And then they'll owe you a favor for pulling you over and wasting your time."

He turned to me. "She's got an answer for everything, huh?"

"Welcome to my world."

"Well, speaking of favors." He hitched his thumbs into his duty belt. "Walt . . ."

"Yep, I know."

"Do you? Like I said before, this is the biggest week of my year, and instead of paying notice to the things that require my attention, I am continuing to babysit you and your staff. Now, I appreciate you taking care of the investigation for those fellows up in Hulett with this hit-and-run, but it's not in my county, not my state, and not my problem."

"I'm aware of that, Irl."

After a second, he smiled with one corner of his mouth. "You goin' all cowboy on us?"

I shook my head. "No. None of this was planned. We'll try and be a little more circumspect."

"I'd appreciate it, at least for the next week." He tossed the Tahoe keys to Vic and then pointed at her. "Not one scratch, young lady."

She crossed her heart. "Hope to die."

"Where are the keys to this ridiculous conveyance?"

"In it."

He paused. "You had this planned out all along?"

She smiled again. "You bet your ass."

He shook his head and walked around, calling out before climbing the rest of the way into the car, "I'll be heading south on Crook City Road, so you head north and in White-wood you can jump on 34 to Belle Fourche; then it turns into 24 in your godforsaken state and takes you straight into Hulett." He started to duck his head but came back up with one last warning. "Keep 'er under the speed of sound, would you?"

As we drove through the bucolic beauty of western South Dakota, Vic caught me glancing at the clock on the dash of the souped-up Tahoe. "What, you've got an appointment?"

"I was invited to a benefit trap shooting competition up at the Hulett golf course."

"By who?"

"None other than Bob Nance."

Vic navigated the sweeping turns of the Bear Lodge National Forest. "Oh, la de da."

I pulled my hat off, rested it on my lap, and leaned back in my seat. "I'm thinking it's something I should do."

"I assume you can bring a guest?" She glanced at me. "So,

are we doing this because we're good citizens or because we want to give the daughter a look?"

"Well, there's something going on; I'm just not sure what. I mean, what was she doing out on the road at that time of night, and why was she calling him so many times?"

"Did you ask her?"

"Surprisingly, I did."

"And the answer?"

"Noncommittal, but her father mentioned that he'd been running interference on a potential relationship for almost a year now."

"A year?"

"Eight months."

"So, this isn't just some met-him-in-a-bar-and-took-him-home and-clean-his-plugs-and-blow-out-his-lines kind of thing."

I turned my hat over and looked at the band with the letters of my name faded gray. "I guess not."

"You said this Bodaway character was from Arizona?"

"Tucson area."

"And she's from here?"

"Well, I guess lately Los Angeles—aspiring actress."

"And Daddy was here?"

"I suppose." I was starting to see what she was getting at. "So, how did California and Arizona hook up, and, more important, how did Big Dog break it up from Hulett?" She stepped on the accelerator. "And it's been going on for eight months? That's a lot of driving time in that three-way."

"Yep."

"Well then, let's go shooting."

A few minutes later she made the left heading up the plateau to the Golf Club at Devils Tower clubhouse and the packed parking lot overshadowed by the massive MRAP, now fully decorated with the emblems of the Hulett Police Department and the name PEQUOD on the rear.

"What is that?"

"Oh, just a little gift from Bob Nance to the local constabulary."

"We need one of those."

"No, we don't."

The construction I'd seen the other night was now a series of platforms arranged at the edge of the cliffs looking back toward the snaking Belle Fourche River and the town. We got a few strange looks as Vic parked the Pennington County sheriff's vehicle in the NO PARKING area—the wrong county and the wrong state.

She shut the car door and came around to meet me in the front. "So, we're going to assume that Henry's all right?"

"He's a big boy and can take care of himself."

"Uh-huh." Vic scanned the assembled crowd and checked out the high and low towers on each end of the elaborate decking. "What the hell is all this, anyway?"

"The original discipline back in the 1900s was called 'trap' for the cages they used to hold the pigeons in before releasing them."

"And blowing them out of the sky."

"Um, yep. With fluctuating sensibilities, the sport switched over to clay pigeons."

"The ashtrays?"

I nodded. "They are even biodegradable these days. Anyway, the sport evolved further, taking the name 'skeet,' which, oddly enough, came from Gertrude Hurlbutt in Dayton, Montana, who won a hundred dollar magazine contest with the word that's derived from the Scandinavian for 'shoot.'"

She stopped and, shaking her head, studied me. "I am consistently stunned by the shit in your head."

I looked for a place to check in. "They used to do it in a circle, but that proved awkward for spectators."

"I bet."

"The typical course spans one hundred and eighty degrees and has ten to fifteen different shooting stations." I spotted an event table to the right and began angling that way like a pulling guard, with Vic following closely. "And now we have sporting clays, which started in England and spread here in the '70s. They are laid out to simulate the unpredictability of live-quarry shooting with different trajectories, angles, elevations, speeds, and distances, usually on a trail."

We got to the table, and Vic studied the elaborate setup, which looked almost like a cliff dwelling. "So, golf with shotguns."

"I guess." I stood at the table and waited until the man I'd met the previous night finished up with the shooter in front of me. He shifted a piece of paper to his cohort, Frack, as I glanced around for Nance. "Mr. Frick."

"Sheriff."

"I was invited by Mr. Nance to participate in the tournament."

He sighed and ducked his suntanned face into the popped collar of his black polo shirt. "What's your name again?"

"Longmire, Walt Longmire."

He studied the sheet, flipped a few pages, and then looked

back up at me again, this time with a smirk. "You're not on the list."

"Is Mr. Nance around?"

He looked over his shoulder. "He's probably at the shooter's table getting ready to compete."

"Well, is there any way to ask him?"

"Not me; he gets real serious when he's shooting." He glanced past me at my undersheriff as she watched the participants approaching the different stations. "All the shooters have registered, including the alternates—so there isn't any room anyway."

I nodded, just as happy not to compete. "Okay, but if you could let him know I'm here and that I tried, I'd appreciate it."

He nodded and glanced at his friend. "Frick and Frack, huh? I've heard that my whole life; do you know where it comes from?"

"They were a pair of Swiss skaters who came to the U.S. back in 1937; they were in the Ice Follies shows and became a household phrase."

He stared at me. "Before my time, pops." I nodded and we started to surge our way back through the crowd as he called after us, "Hey, I said there weren't any spots in the men's bracket, but we had somebody drop out in the women's, so do you think your friend would like to shoot?"

Vic looked at him and then tilted her head back—showing off the elongated canine tooth. "Fuck yeah."

8

Not for the first time in our collective lives, we needed a shotgun.

Lucky for us Chief Nutter was shooting in the second round, and even more fortunately, he was a small man and had extra equipment, including a lovely 332 Remington that had been cut down an inch, making it a perfect fit for the Terror. While the first-round shooters peppered the air with pellets and the hillside with broken pottery, Vic tried on Nutter Butter's old shooting vest, which, with a little adjustment, fit like a dream.

"I need my shooting gloves."

"Where are they?"

She looked at me as if I were the raw recruit who'd just been brought up from stupid. "They're on the seat of the Tahoe with my Flyers hat. Could you get that for me, too?"

"Anything else?"

She examined the beautiful over-and-under. "Lessons?"

When I got there, Dougherty was studying the SUV as if it had dropped out of the sky. "What are you doing with Irl Engelhardt's car?"

"It's a long story." I tossed the gloves in the orange and

black hat. "You stuck doing crowd control or can you watch the competition?"

"I can't. I've got to move around and keep people from getting into trouble. Hey, I saw your dog down at the Ponderosa Café with Henry and Lola." He cocked his head. "The conversation seemed pretty intense."

"I bet." I started back. "Well, you might want to try to see some of the tournament—Vic's shooting." When I got back to the competition, there was a group around my undersheriff, all of them giving her advice.

Vic nodded and smiled the way she did when she wasn't listening. I arrived with her equipment, and she pulled her Broad Street Bullies hat down low, just above her space-age Oakley Radarlock sunglasses.

She thanked everybody for the pointers, hooked her arm in mine, and looked at the late afternoon sun. "Okay, what the hell am I supposed to do—hit the little ashtrays?"

"Yep, and make a visual connection with the target—keep a good line with it, don't start low when you're shooting high. The better you get set up, the more efficient you become."

"Got it."

"Attack the target line but don't rush."

"Got it."

"Stay loose and lead fast. Those ashtrays are moving pretty quick."

"Got it."

"Have fun."

She nodded, pulling the gloves on and wrapping the Velcro around her wrists. "I always have fun with a gun in my hands."

I followed her back to where Chief Nutter was polishing the proffered weapon. "Where'd you get that antique, Bill?"

"Oh, my wife bought it for me before we got divorced—she got the house and I kept my guns. No harm no foul." He looked at the sheen sparkling off the stock. "It ain't nothin' too fancy, just a working man's gun, but she's true and shoots straight with no idiosyncrasies, which is more than I can say about my ex-wife." He handed the shotgun to Vic.

Vic held it like a baby, smiled at the old chief, and then turned toward the assembled competitors with a predator's eye. "Who am I up against?"

"Some of the best shooters in all of the upper Midwest." He pointed at a blonde woman with a straw cowboy hat. "Connie Evans, two-time national champion from Sioux Falls." He gestured to a dark-haired woman. "Patricia Frontain out of Chicago, teaches at the National Sporting Clay Association. And that cool drink of water on the end is Annemarie Potter, who can out-shoot most of the men here." He tiptoed to see the others. "Raye Lankford, all-Midwest, and Kelly McBride on the end down there won it all last year."

I nudged her shoulder. "Scared?"

She barked a laugh. "Hell with that; I'm used to targets that shoot back."

Carefully watching how and what the other women were doing, she joined them with the Remington's butt cupped in her hands, which were laced at her crotch.

There seemed to be an unstated pecking order, with Evans going first. She was good, very good, catching the targets on a perfect line, graceful and balanced. The Frontain woman was faster but clipped one of the clays in a double and you could feel the others sensing a weakness. The tall woman, Potter, was a natural but didn't keep a good line with the target, and I could see that she could be beaten—so did Vic. Lankford was a short blonde whose shooting was flawless, but she didn't seem as bloodthirsty as the rest, and that lack of competitiveness might be her downfall later in the shoot. McBride shot like Evans and was a problem.

Like a nervous groom, I watched as Vic stepped up to the station and carefully raised the over-and-under.

The puller lifted the remote that would signal the high and low houses and spoke in a loud voice: "Ready?"

All the other shooters had barked their command, almost as if the added impetus might help them in destroying their nemeses, but Vic was loose and draped around her weapon like a gunfighter. Although the place was almost silent, I had to listen carefully to hear the word drifting out like a sigh of foregone conclusion. "Pull."

Firing points at one and six launched the two targets like miniature flying saucers, and they'd no sooner gotten to their separate trajectories than they both disappeared in two sequential blasts that almost sounded as one.

The chief leaned over to me. "That was her taking her time?"

"I guess."

He whistled quietly. "Shee-it."

Evans, McBride, and Vic graduated to the next level. The other shooters were talking, but Vic, with the Remington on her shoulders, stood looking into the distance like a major league pitcher throwing a shutout.

• • •

Bob Nance was in the finals of the men's competition but had made time to come over to where Chief Nutter and I were standing. Now leaning on the steel divider that separated the contestants from the hoi polloi, he squinted at me. "You bring a ringer to my tournament?"

"It's her first time."

"You're kidding."

"Nope, but she's got experience with shooting things. Four brothers who . . ." I paused and then started over. "Three brothers who are active-duty police officers, and a father who's the chief of detectives north back in Philadelphia."

He looked at me out of one eye. "What's she doing in Wyoming?"

"I ask myself that a lot of the time." I waited a moment and changed the subject. "Where's your daughter?"

He shook his head as he glanced around at the circumstance, if not the pomp. "She's bored silly by this stuff, but then she's bored silly by most of the things that I enjoy."

"I'm sorry to hear that." I waited again. "Hey, how long has your daughter been in county?"

He thought about it. "It's August, so I guess it's been about two months."

"Before that she was in Los Angeles?"

"Yes." His eyes stayed with mine. "Why?"

"You mentioned the other night that you'd been running interference on this relationship between your daughter and Torres for eight months."

He continued to look at me. "So?"

"You said she's only been here for two months, so I guess they knew each other in L.A. or Tucson?"

He glanced at Chief Nutter and then back to me. "And why do you care, Sheriff?"

"I'm just trying to get a clearer picture of the relationship between Chloe and Bodaway in hopes that it might shine some light on the accident that may end up costing the young man his life."

He crossed his arms over the Krieghoff K-80. "Are you accusing Chloe?"

"Nope."

He glanced at Chief Nutter again to register his disapproval at being interrogated in this manner and then spoke slowly as if I might not understand English. "I have business dealings in Phoenix. I stay at the Biltmore, but my daughter, who used to stay there with me, said it was too stodgy, so she set herself up at the W, which evidently doesn't monitor the individuals who frequent their poolside bar." He took a breath. "That's where they met and established a long-distance relationship, which I have been attempting to end for eight months."

"I see."

"Good, I'm glad you see."

"And where were you the night that Bodaway Torres was run off the road?"

His eyes clinched down like the bore on the gun he held. "You know, Sheriff, I invited you here because I thought it might be fun, but you're proving to be tiresome."

I smiled. "Oh, just give me a chance; I can get a lot more mundane."

He studied me for a long while and then moved back among the other shooters.

"I don't think he likes me."

Chief Nutter turned and rested the small of his back against the steel bar. "Is that your method, to go around pissing off all the people you're investigating?"

"Go with your strengths, I always say."

"I know he's a little on his high horse."

"And I know he bought you a truck."

The chief was silent for a moment and then leaned over into my line of sight. "You got something you want to say?"

"He hates that kid lying in a hospital bed in Rapid, and when I'm looking for somebody who might've done a victim harm, I generally look for a suspect who doesn't particularly care for that victim."

"And if I told you Bob Nance didn't have anything to do with injuring that boy, you'd believe me, right? Because the night Bodaway Torres was hurt, Nance was drinking with me at the clubhouse over there." I stared at him, and he looked at the power broker. "So, I guess that means I'm one of the bad guys now, huh?"

I watched as the other women in Vic's round began to shoot. "Not necessarily."

"Well, I'll tell you, I truly wish I had the finely tuned instrumentation that enables you to tell the difference between right and wrong, Sheriff."

"Speaking of high horses."

He smiled—it was slow, but he smiled. "He's divorced, too. Sometimes when I finish a shift, it's just easier to come up here than sit down in town with all the people I arrest for DUIs. Last week when that kid got tagged, Bob was here with a bunch of friends, playing cards into the wee hours."

"Good enough." I folded my arms over my chest. "Speaking of Bodaway, did I mention that both Mike Novo and I found gold paint on the young man's bike—the same gold paint that's on his mother's convertible?"

He made a face. "Jeez, Lola ran over her own kid?"

"Think she's capable of it?"

"Yes. Well, no. Well, I'm not sure, to be absolutely honest. I don't know her that well."

The Evans woman stepped up, preparing for the targets that would be pitched from the opposite towers, both high and low. She shot, annihilating the first clay but barely clipping her second.

I tipped my hat a little forward so that I could see better. "The car was parked at the Hulett Motel that night with the keys in it, so I suppose anybody could've been driving it."

"You ask her?"

"I did."

"And?"

"She says it wasn't her."

"You believe her?"

I chuckled. "Well, I'm not sure, to be absolutely honest."

Vic stepped up to the fifth station, which was made out of redwood and dug into the hillside, the 12 gauge broken down and cradled in the crook of her arm. She tightened her gloves, adjusted her hat, and then loaded the Remington with the two rounds one of the pullers handed her.

The chief unconsciously straightened his own hat. "She gets two clean hits, and she'll advance." He turned and grinned at me. "And then she'll shoot against the men's finalists, who I'm pretty sure are going to end up being your buddy Bob Nance and that surgeon from Billings."

"Well, that should be interesting."

The puller looked at Vic. "Ready?"

Once again, you could barely hear her voice, and it was epic watching her raise the thirty-inch barrels like a cobra rising to strike. "Pull."

The target flew in a flat trajectory, different from the ones launched before, so Vic had to re-aim, but the result was devastating, the clay pigeon exploding. Something must've happened in the release of the second bird, though, and it was already speeding in the opposite direction when Vic sighted it. She waited just a split second.

Nutter was clutching the steel bar. "She's waiting too long, it's going to be too far for . . ."

At that second my undersheriff jerked back with the blast of the shotgun, and the clay target burst apart at the very edge of the Remington's range.

The crowd erupted, and she turned and bowed, slinging the shotgun on her shoulder, whereupon they roared some more. She popped the two empty shells and gave them to a puller and then walked straight toward us. Handing Nutter the 12 gauge, she smiled through the carnival-glass optics of her glasses with millions of tiny rainbows dancing. "I like this game."

He laughed. "It shows."

She pulled the earplugs. "I think I could get good at it."

I nodded toward the blonde woman. "Looks like you and Evans are going to be representing the gentler sex in the next round."

She turned her face, scanning the other shooters. "Who's next?"

"Bob Nance and Frank Carlton, that older hotshot over there with the khaki hat. The chief here says he's some kind of five-time national champion."

"They miss anything yet?"

"Nope."

"Well then, we're all even."

Nance sauntered over and, leaning on the railing, studied my undersheriff. "Bob Nance."

"Vic Moretti."

I thought he was attempting to get a little edge. "Hey, you're pretty good."

"Thanks."

He smirked. "You're pulling just a bit when you fire."

"'There is no hunting like the hunting of man, and those who have hunted armed men long enough and liked it, never care for anything else thereafter.'"

Unsettled at being interrupted, he caught himself. "Excuse me?"

Vic's smile narrowed, and her jaw muscles bunched just a bit. "You come over here to mind-fuck me, Bob? Because if you did you're going to end up getting fucked yourself." She gestured toward the elaborate walkways and towers. "This golfing with guns is fun, but I've been trying to hit shit that was shooting at me since I was in my twenties, so if, indeed, you are trying to mind-fuck me—go fuck yourself, because I fuck back."

He stood there for a stunned moment and then, at a loss for anything else to do, turned and looked at me. I grinned. "She does and not gently."

He stood there for a moment more and then, without another word, turned and walked away.

"Hemingway—that's where the quote came from."

Nutter laughed. "Bullshit that you know that."

I glanced at the chief. "She's got a T-shirt from the Philadelphia Warrants Department with that quote on it."

Vic grinned. "I love that shirt—it's one of my favorites."

My undersheriff's partner came over and extended a hand toward me, the late-in-the-sky sun playing off her curly blonde hair and Pacific-colored eyes. "Cornelia Evans."

"Nice to meet you." I turned toward Bill. "This is Chief Nutter, and I assume you've already met my undersheriff, Victoria Moretti?"

She leaned in closer to the Terror. "Hey, generally we split and do mixed doubles for the finals; is that okay? You know, Sadie Hawkins. You can pick first."

My undersheriff looked baffled. "Huh?"

I translated, gesturing toward Nance and Carlton. "Ladies' choice."

"Oh." She smiled and glanced at the two men. "I'll take the old guy, the surgeon."

"Carlton's good, but he's getting a little long in the tooth. Are you sure you don't want Bob?"

"No, he's a prick." She made the statement as if it were the time of day.

It took Evans a few seconds to regain her composure. "Okay then." She stuck her hand out. "Good luck."

"Thanks." They shook, and Evans continued on her way toward the two men to deliver the news.

After a brief conversation, the older gentleman came over to meet his new partner, and in a soft, Southern accent murmured, "Well, hello young lady; how should we go about vanquishing these upstarts?" Vic smiled as they shook hands, and he glanced at me. "Walt Longmire, the much-vaunted sheriff of Absaroka County, Wyoming."

"You and I have a connection, Dr. Carlton."

"And what might that be?"

"Back in the late eighties you had a patient in Billings, a young girl of Japanese descent, who was in an automobile accident and had to be helicoptered down to Children's Hospital in Denver."

He clutched his chin like it was a knuckleball and took a second to think. "*Amaterasu*, shining over heaven. As I recall it was a difficult case, and the helicopter didn't make it to Denver." He didn't say anything more, and I could see that he was unsure about asking.

"It didn't, but she did. Came into my office a while back at Christmas—she lives in San Francisco. Maybe we'll have a beer sometime, and I'll tell you the whole story."

"I would enjoy that." He turned back, smiled at Vic, and gestured toward the course. "In the meantime, young lady, we have work to do."

It was decided that the two teams would face off at station four and shoot with random pulls just to make things a little more interesting. If needed, the two teams would go into a second round or even a third if things stayed tight.

Nance and Evans were going to shoot first, and, evidently,

Bob wasn't into the whole ladies-first thing since he strode up to the platform and lifted his shotgun into a median position.

He barked the call. "Pull!"

It was a tough one, the first target being the high house and coming from the left. He nailed it and then drew down on the one that had just taken flight from the low house and his right. The thunder of the 12 gauge echoed against the Black Hills, and the second clay exploded.

Chief Nutter nodded. "Bob's good—there's not too much doubt about that."

"Yep, but let's see if the surgeon can carve him up."

Carlton looked every bit the national champion as he raised the barrels and focused in on the upcoming targets. If you were doing diagrams on how to shoot skeet, you could've done worse than the figure the older man presented—classic was the only word for it.

The first clay came out of the high house again, and Carlton smashed it. Then the next came from the same direction but at a lower trajectory; the surgeon quickly adjusted and shattered that one as well.

He cocked his head as he turned back toward the crowd, and I noted that there was more applause for him than there had been for Nance—evidently the doctor was a fan favorite.

Evans shot well but barely clipped her first clay with an overenthusiastic shot; she then tagged the second.

Vic carefully placed the plugs back in her ears and stepped up onto the station without a shred of self-consciousness. The trigger hand sat at her side like a coiled spring, her slender fingers flicking every so often, and she carefully loaded the Remington.

The puller regarded her. "Ready?"

My undersheriff's hand relaxed and came up in a graceful arc, snapping the shotgun together and in place, her soft voice once again like a pin dropping. "Pull."

The two clays came from the low tower to her right simultaneously, and Vic peppered them with 12-gauge shot.

Carlton shook his head as he stepped up; he hit his first target but cleanly missed his second shot. I could see him apologizing to Vic as he stepped from the stand.

I watched as Nance coached Evans, but the two-time national champion missed one and we were tied.

There was a brief conversation at the stand, and the pullers and judges got together with Nance and Evans as Vic and Carlton stepped over to where we were.

I smiled at her. "How you feel, deadeye?"

The Terror pushed her cap back and pulled her earplugs. "I'm cool, but I could use a drink."

Nance approached with a couple of judges; Evans was not with them. He leaned on the rail again. "Frank, Connie's graciously elected to step down, and if you're willing to do the same, Miss Moretti and I can go head-to-head Tour Pro style."

The older man stepped to the side. "I'm afraid all I'm doing is holding my partner back, so I'm happy to acquiesce."

Nance smiled and glanced at Vic. "Tour Pro style then?"

"Fuck yeah." Vic bared her teeth, especially the extended canine. "What's that, anyway?"

Nance didn't say anything but turned away toward the range.

Carlton watched him go and then shook his head. "You shoot multiple times. They'll place a row of rounds in front of you and as you fire, you break the shotgun down and fire again, sometimes as many as a dozen rounds instead of the two."

She studied me. "Like tactical with pop-ups?"

"Pretty much."

She snapped a finger and pointed before walking away. "Hendrick's—stirred, not shaken."

Chief Nutter and Carlton both looked at me. "Dirty martini, her favorite. Olives with the juice and onions."

Carlton nodded. "Fighting scurvy, is she?"

Nutter watched Vic's nether parts as she stalked toward the shooting stand. "Somehow, I don't think scurvy would stand a chance."

Gentlemanliness be damned again, Nance strode to the platform and stood, blocking Vic's way as my undersheriff casually placed the butt of the Remington in her cupped hands again, the barrels lying easily against her shoulder.

It was easy to see why Nance chose this form of shooting for his finale. He handled the mechanics of reloading impressively and didn't miss a single shot until the last set, where he missed the lower clay completely but then caught it with the second shot—scoring an eleven and a half.

There were cheers from the crowd. Like him or not, it was damn fine shooting.

I didn't see how Vic was going to be able to do it.

The Terror ignored Nance's smirk, stepped to the station, and stretched her neck to one side and then the other as I'd seen her do at hundreds of weapons qualification shoots down at the academy in Douglas.

Nance moved to the far side of the narrow table but then

stopped and stood there, just barely in Vic's line of sight. I waited for the attendants or judges to make him move, but they didn't.

Vic's hand dropped again and twitched once.

The puller seemed hesitant but then asked, "Ready?"

She gave the barely perceptible nod and then brought her hand up in the elegant arc again, slipping two of the shells from the table, loading the shotgun, and raising the barrels in one infinitely supple move. Her head dropped like a mongoose ready to strike, and her lips pursed. "Pull."

Like a machine-fed shotgun, she adjusted her aim, dropping the barrels and reloading after each twin pieces of destruction, moving down the course like a ballerina working the barre. The closer to her opponent she came, the wider his eyes grew. Science was meeting art, and art was kicking science's ass.

I've seen some shooting in my life, but I don't recall ever seeing an exhibition like the one Vic was giving just now. There was a rhythm to her that was otherworldly, a matching of flesh and metal resulting in a series of explosions that echoed off the hills like a paradiddle of percussive beats. You could feel the crowd leaning forward as her momentum grew until two of the next-to-last targets dove with the wind. There was the briefest of pauses as she dipped the barrel, but the Terror's aim was true and the clays exploded as if she'd reached out with a talon and crushed them one by one.

I'd like to think that Nance jarred the table by accident. Vic's last two shells fell over and, like a ship hitting an iceberg or a dirigible bursting into flames or two locomotives slamming into each other on an elevated trestle, they rolled off the edge of the table in agonizingly slow motion.

The crowd buzzed, but without pause, Vic cracked open the Remington with one hand and stooped but could catch only one shell, which she slipped into the breech, slamming the 12 gauge erect. The first target sailed, having been caught by the wind again, but the other launched in a direct trajectory, and I'm sure the Terror was smiling that subtle little smile that made only one wrinkle at the corner of her perfect mouth as they crossed paths just above the bead sight on the Remington.

She blew both of them out of the sky with the single shot.

9

As I slipped the champion into the bed in our room at the Hulett Motel, she slurred her words just a touch, having succumbed to her fifth dirty martini. "Get in here wi'me."

I sat beside her. "I can't. I have to go find Dog."

She clutched my arm. "He can climb in'ere, too."

I glanced at the smallish bed. "I don't think there's room."

She stuck her tongue in my ear. "You can have som'ma my room."

"I just want to make sure he and Henry are all right, considering the company they're keeping."

Releasing me just a little, she turned her head and smiled at the monstrous loving cup on the nightstand that barely left room for the lamp. "You seen my trophy?"

I pulled away a little and nodded. "Yep, I have."

"I won that."

"I know you did."

"'Ma helluva shot."

"Yep, you are."

"Get in'ere."

I stood, her hand still holding my wrist. "I'll be right back."

She ran her tongue along the web of my thumb and curled her legs. "Promise?"

"Yep."

Her eyes strayed to the nightstand again. "Y'see my trophy?"

"Yep."

"I won that."

I pulled my hand loose and retreated, not quite sure if I could turn my back on her just yet. "I'll be back."

"Promise?"

"Yep."

She slumped into her pillow with a smile, her eyes closing. "'Kay."

Slipping the door shut behind me, I stepped out into the cool, clear air of night. It had been quite a party up at the Golf Club at Devils Tower clubhouse.

And as far as I knew, it was still going on.

Nance had taken the loss better than I'd thought him capable, and the bar had been open to all. I'd had a beer, but the Terror, flushed with victory, had imbibed like a sailor on shore leave; actually, she put them to epic shame.

I made the corner of the motel in time to see the two miscreants who'd attempted to steal Rosalie, Henry's motorcycle, now attempting to find the hood release on Lola, which was parked next to the Pennington County sheriff's Tahoe. "You know, you guys need to find another line of work. Honestly."

Eddy the Viking was the first to speak. "We were just wanting to look at the engine. It's got the 430 Interceptor motor in it, right?"

I shrugged. "I guess. I'm not much of a car guy, but the man who owns it is, and if he catches you monkeys fooling around with his vehicle, he's likely to kick your asses so long you'll be wearing them as hats."

They looked at me blankly.

"Your asses."

They still stared at me.

"As hats."

They didn't move.

"Never mind." I walked past them, deciding that I'd rather take in the air than drive the two blocks with the trailer in tow. I pointed at Irl Engelhardt's cruiser. "Get out of here before I lock the two of you in the back of that thing with the radio tuned to the rap station in Rapid at high volume."

I crossed the motorcycle-ridden street, passed the art gallery at the corner, and, cutting through a beer garden to the alley behind the Ponderosa, tried my best to get there without getting anything spilled on me.

I sidestepped around a row of bikes and could see a large crowd. There was a lot of yelling, which even conquered a really bad garage-band rendition of "What's Your Name." As I got closer and could see over the rabble, I caught a glimpse of a tattooed, platinum-haired man in one of those blue service-station jackets, who was pushing someone hard enough to collapse his rib cage.

Figuring there were enough people around so I really didn't have to get involved, I slid along the side in hopes of making it to the Ponderosa.

As I took another step, I could see between the two guys in front of me that the pugilist who was losing the battle was none other than Patrolman Corbin Dougherty. Frozen for a split second, I watched the rookie's eyes get wide as the biker kept after him.

It was pretty much every police officer's nightmare—to be surrounded in unsure territory with no backup and facing a much greater physical opponent. There were two equalizers, however—that piece of metal on his shirt and the even bigger piece of metal in the holster at his side. The first one having failed, I watched as he began reaching for the second.

There was a crate of some kind behind me, so I stepped up and pushed off it between the two guys in front of me. I rolled my right fist like a cudgel and brought it down in a full swing with all my body weight into a blow that came from above, striking the antagonist in the side of the head like a falling tree limb.

The guy looked like he had a hard head, so I didn't figure it would kill him, but it might've come close. He dropped like a poleaxed steer, pausing for only a second at his knees and then falling the rest of the way onto the gravel surface of the alley, face first.

I landed somewhat clumsily but then righted and turned a full circle just to make sure that no one was going to rush me in retaliation, even going so far as to look for a little reinforcement from Brady Post, the ATF agent, but he wasn't there. Everybody looked a little stunned, but none of them appeared to be ready to make a move, so I turned and focused on the patrolman. Dougherty sat there with his opponent lying between his legs as I held my left hand out, quietly flexing the feeling back into my rapidly swelling right. "Fight's over."

He took my hand, and I pulled him up as he wiped some

blood from the corner of his mouth with the back of a wrist. "I'd say."

Quickly dusting him off, I turned to look at the assembled pack of onlookers who were just now getting their bearings, their challenger still doing his best impression of a biker-skin rug. "Break it up and get out of here before we run all of you in."

One of the ones in the back shouted, "You some kind of cop or something?"

I zeroed him out as he tried to duck behind another guy, and I held up my badge wallet, letting it fall open to display my own piece of trusty metal. "Absaroka County sheriff. Beat it. Now."

There was more mumbling and a few veiled threats, but they moved off, leaving the tattooed man still lying facedown and showing no signs of getting up. So much for the camaraderie of the road. He was breathing, but I stooped anyway and felt the pulse at the flames inked at his neck, satisfied that he was still among us.

I looked back up at Dougherty. "What happened?"

He shook his head. "I was walking down the alley, and he ran his shoulder into me, so I turned around and said something. It just got stupid from there."

I nodded, thinking something about the cold-cocked fighter looked vaguely familiar; I pulled him over by the shoulder, revealing the somewhat warped head of Billy ThE Kiddo. "Oh, hell."

"You two know each other?"

"We met earlier today." I glanced around for some help as I checked him for any weapons. "I don't suppose you could call in some backup to help you get him to the jail?"

"Why can't you?"

I stood, convinced that Billy wasn't carrying. "Because he's got a restraining order against me."

The patrolman glanced at the man at our feet. "I can see why." He pulled the mic from his shoulder and called it in, then turned to look at me. "Get out of here."

I started off. "You bet."

He called out as I hurried away, "And thanks!"

The Pondo was crowded, but I saw two of my favorite life-forms seated on a bench in the far right-hand corner. I threaded my way through the throng and was glad to see that Lola wasn't there.

Finally reaching the elevated cable spool that served as a table, I slid onto a stool opposite the Cheyenne Nation and my faithful companion, who smiled and wagged his massive tail. The Bear looked up from what I assumed was a sparkling water with a lime slice and then at the half-filled wineglass in front of Dog. "I am attempting to get your dog drunk, but he is not cooperating."

I caught the eye of a waitress, gestured toward a Rainier at an adjacent table, and then turned back to the two of them. I reached over and ruffled the hair behind Dog's ear. "He's generally smarter than we are."

"I heard Vic won the shooting competition."

"She did."

"Is that what took you so long?"

"Well, that and we were running interference with the highway patrol for you and Lola."

"So, that is what took so long."

"That . . . and a few other things." I glanced back toward the alley. "Do you think it's a hundred yards between here and that beer garden on the corner?"

He studied the swollen knuckles on my right hand. "Why?"

"Nothing." I turned back, tucked my fist under the table, and studied him, taking in his lackluster demeanor. "What's up?"

He brushed his hair away from his face and taking a piece of paper from his shirt pocket, tossed it on the table between us.

"What's this?"

He said nothing but sipped his sparkling water and eyed me as I picked it up and unfolded it.

At the top were the printed words DNA Genetic Ancestry, University of Arizona. I read down and could see that the registry listed Native American first, Plains Indian second, and Northern Cheyenne third, to be specific. "Yours?"

He set the glass back down. "Bodaway's."

I stared at him. "I thought you were sure."

"So did I."

"I thought he was Southwest—Apache."

"So did I."

Reading the rest of the sheet, I could see that the breakdown of the young man's heredity and genealogy matched Henry's very closely except for the part that was Polish or Mazovia by way of Kujawy. The date of the testing center's findings was less than a month earlier. "She did this in anticipation of meeting you here?"

"So it would appear."

I flipped the piece of paper back on the table as the waitress came over and set the Rainier down. "Buck fifty."

I handed her two and waved her away. "It's just a piece of paper that says you and he share a genetic ancestry, but it isn't absolute proof that he's yours."

"No, we would need a blood test for that."

I spun the paper around and looked at the registered blood type, O—the same as Henry but still a pretty common type. "Does she want you to take a test?"

"No."

"You should. Do it and then you'll know—till then she's messing with your head."

He sipped his water and, leaning over, nudged Dog with his shoulder, whereupon the beast reciprocated by licking the side of the Bear's head. "What if he is mine?"

"Then you have a son."

He smiled. "Is that the way it works, Grandpa?"

"No, well yep. . . . But it's worse than that, Henry. Vic talked to the doctors at Rapid and their considered opinion is that Bodaway's injuries are serious enough that they don't think he's coming back."

His big hand covered the bottom of his face, and he mumbled through his fingers, his eyes still on me. "No chance?"

"They seemed to indicate none."

He breathed a laugh that would've frozen sagebrush. "That would be about right. I would have had a son for thirty years, and the weekend I was to first meet him he would go into a coma with no hope of awakening."

"Do a blood test."

He let his hand fall to his lap. "I am not much of a test taker these days."

"So, what are you going to do?"

He looked away. "Go by my feelings."

"Just so you know, that's usually what you warn me not to do."

"Am I usually right?"

"Only ninety-nine percent of the time."

"So, we have an obvious fact."

We talked for another twenty minutes until I felt the pressure of a revolver muzzle pressed into my right ear and heard a very angry voice. "Did you hit me?"

Fortunately, Henry's first move was to grab Dog's collar or else the hundred-and-fifty-pound brute would've launched off the bench to sink his teeth into the arm of the individual I figured was holding the .38 in my ear. Instead, Dog pulled back his lips in a promise.

I raised the beer and took a sip, attempting my best Leo Gordon. "Have a seat, Kiddo, and I'll buy you a beer."

He nudged the two-inch barrel farther into my ear canal with his left hand and repeated the question. "Did you hit me, motherfucker?"

Setting the Rainier down, I slowly turned, and he traced the muzzle across my cheek until it now rested on the bridge of my nose. His face was red, and all I could think was how did he get away from Dougherty and where did he get the sidearm after I'd checked him. "Why, yes, I did."

If it was possible, his face grew even redder, and I was calculating what my next tactical move would be. The saloon was crowded, and I didn't want anyone else to be hurt, which meant I would have to kick him at the same time I grabbed the revolver, shoving it upward, flipping it, and pushing it into his body so that if he did pull the trigger, the only one who would be hit with a round would be himself.

"You sucker punched me, cocksucker?"

It was a risky business, but the alternatives weren't so great.

I was about to make my move when a hand shot out, bent Billy ThE's up and back, snatched the revolver out of his hand before either of us could breathe, then cried havoc and let slip the Dog of War.

When primates are properly motivated, we can move with the best of them, and Billy ThE Kiddo was highly motivated. Scrambling backward, he pulled a neighboring table down in front of him, which succeeded in deflecting Dog to the right just long enough for Kiddo to turn and lunge for the alley.

Most everybody in the bar, realizing that a were-monster had been loosed, vacated the immediate area in what I assumed would be an attempt to acquire torches and pitchforks.

Having the advantage of four legs, Dog caught his balance, turned to the left, and shot for the alley where ThE was desperately attempting to flee.

Me? I sipped my beer.

Henry examined the revolver. "Odd gun." He handed it to me. "Consider it a gift."

I took the thing without looking.

There was a great deal of noise from the passageway where the two antagonists had disappeared, and then one agonizing scream. "I guess I'd better go see about that."

Henry sipped his sparkling water and studied the paper on the table. "I suppose you should."

It was about then that I looked down and saw the pink grip of the .38 revolver.

"Where did he get this gun?"

Dougherty looked at the colorful sidearm. "He had a gun?"

Holding the pistol out to him, I glanced around the Hulett Police Department's empty office. "When Kiddo stormed into the bar, he shoved the barrel of this in my ear."

"You searched him. I figured you would've found it if he'd been carrying."

"That's right, I would have. He must've gotten it after you got him up and loaded him into the car. Who else was there?"

"Nobody."

"Who helped you load him?"

"Nutter But— . . . Chief Nutter and a highway patrolman."

"You didn't cuff him?"

"I did, but when I got him back to the jail here, and was walking him in, he was suddenly loose and elbowed me in the face."

"You're lucky you're alive." I gestured toward the holding cell. "Nobody came near him, touched him? Anything?"

"No. Wait." He thought about it. "When I got him over here there were a bunch of bikers out front."

"Men, women?"

"Both. They whooped and hollered and patted him on the back as I was bringing him in." He studied my face. "You're thinking . . ."

"Was Lola one of them?"

"I don't think so, but maybe. I'm not sure. Why?"

I twirled the revolver. "Because this is hers."

We walked to the back where an EMT was tending to Billy ThE Kiddo as he lay on his stomach on a bunk, his left wrist attached to a chain support with a pair of cuffs, and his pants pulled down, exposing his perforated posterior. "I'm gonna own this town when I'm through with you fuckers."

I knelt beside him. "Just a little more piercing done. What's the harm?"

"Fuck you. You aren't supposed to be anywhere near me. I've got a restraining order."

"I don't think that restraining order works when you push gun barrels in my ear."

He grimaced and cried out as the EMT continued to stitch him up. "You hit me!"

I ignored the outburst and held up the pink revolver. "This gun."

He stared at it and then at me. "I never seen that gun before."

"I've got a whole bar full of witnesses who saw you holding it in my ear before my friend Henry took it away from you."

"Yeah, and I've got an entire alley full of people who saw you punch me in the head."

I sounded bored, even to myself. "As you resisted arrest and attempted to visit grievous harm on Officer Dougherty here." I leaned in closer. "ThE, ol' buddy, where did you get the gun? You see, I know who owns it—and I'm betting you do, too. Now, if she gave it to you, that'll make it a lot easier in that I won't have to worry about where she might be if you took it away from her."

"Go fuck yourself."

I stood and gestured to get the EMT's attention. "When you get done, you can sew up this end, too."

Walking back into the bull pen, I turned to Corbin. "Put a general out for Lola and that gold Caddy; she doesn't strike me as the type to go around unarmed."

He sat in a dejected manner and pulled the old stand-up mic toward him. "I screwed up pretty bad, huh?"

"Not really. So far the only one who got hurt in all of this is the human Kong in there." I shrugged as another yelp emanated from the holding cell. "And I'd say he deserved it."

"What are you going to do?"

I spread my hands. "Where in the world is Lola Wojciechowski?"

The Bear and Dog were waiting for me outside, leaning on the MRAP as a group of bikers observed the two of them from a distance. "Are they going to have to put ThE down?"

"I wish."

"What is next?"

I held up the revolver. "Any ideas?"

He glanced down the hill at the throngs of black leather, his eyes narrowing. "Is there a pool table in this town?"

I stepped back toward the office door and yanked it open. "Corbin, is there a pool table around here somewhere?"

"Capt'n Ron's Rodeo Bar, in the back past the dance floor."

"Got it." I shut the door and gestured down the hill. "Conveniently located a hundred feet that way."

The Bear started off with Dog. "I wonder, in the course of recent developments, if they will allow pets?"

We stopped at a large barn door opening into another out-side beer garden. "I keep telling you, he's a service dog."

The bouncer at the door, an amiable-looking cowboy al-most as wide as he was tall, asked, "And what service does he provide?"

"Bomb detection."

He shook his head. "Works for me—there are plenty of them going off in there."

Dodging inside with the beast, we angled to the right and could see Lola taking a shot and stretching across the far-side pocket, revealing more than a little décolletage to the admir-ing members of the sporting life.

"Lola."

Even I was taken aback by the thunder of the Cheyenne Nation's voice in the raucous noise and music of the filled-to-the-gills bar.

She took a second to steady herself and then took the shot with her custom cue, a banking roller that sunk the two ball in the farthest corner. She stood, cocked a leg, and rested her hip against the table as Big Easy, the guard-biker we had last met at the hospital, stepped into our line of sight, speaking in a slight Samoan accent: "Problem?"

I held the revolver up. "A pink one."

"Not your color, my man."

I nodded past him toward Lola. "No, but it's hers. Tell her we'll meet her outside and not to make me come looking for her or I'll see she gets seven months of high-security, low-amenity lodging in Sundance."

As we started to turn and walk out, the big and easy Sa-moan reached over and touched Henry's shoulder, the arm attached having powered the biker's head into the drywall of the Rapid City Regional Hospital. "I know you?"

The Bear smiled the one-crease-at-the-corner-of-his-mouth smile. "Momentarily."

We waited by the door longer than I would've liked, but she finally came sauntering out and stood with her arms crossed. "I'd like my gun back."

I glanced at the revolver tucked in my belt. "You mind telling me how he got it?"

"How who got it?"

"Star of stage, screen, and reality TV, Billy ThE Kiddo."

"And who the hell is Billy ThE Kiddo?"

"A good friend of your son's."

She wrapped her arms around herself and came closer. "Define good."

"Bodaway called him about seventeen times before the accident—if indeed it was an accident."

She straightened up and dropped her arms. "Look, I honestly don't know what you're talking about, let alone *who* you're talking about. You put the gun inside my purse in my car's glove box the last time I saw it."

"Your car, this gun . . . you're kind of lax with your possessions."

She glanced at the Cheyenne Nation. "What can I say? I'm just a material girl in a material world."

The crypt voice returned beside me with enough timber to fill the Black Forest. "Lola, there are lives at stake."

She snorted. "That's funny, 'cause that's what I've been trying to convince you of for days." She hooked her thumbs into the belt loops of her jeans and turned coquettishly to me.

"Imagine my surprise: I came here looking for a red knight in shining armor and all I find is a Watson to your Sherlock Holmes. Feel free to put my gun back where you found it." With this final pronouncement she turned and rejoined the swarm in the bar with her hands raised above her head, snapping her fingers, swaying and singing to Jerry Lee Lewis's "C.C. Rider."

We stood there for a while before he handed me the leash.

"I'm starting to see how this relationship didn't work out."

"Yes."

"I'm sorry."

He glanced at me. "For what?"

"Trying to get you involved in this. It was stupid, and I didn't really know what I was getting you into."

"She is something of a contagion."

I nodded and rubbed Dog's head. "Let's go get you a blood test at the Rapid hospital tomorrow and put this all to rest—then we can head home."

"Deal." We turned and began walking the rest of the way down the hill, stopping at the corner and waiting for another assemblage of motorcycles to go by. "It is funny, but I was just getting used to the idea of being a father, even if it was with Lola." I studied him, and he began talking again. "I watch you with Cady."

"Well, she's yours, too." I sighed. "Sometimes I think she's more yours than mine."

"But she is not."

We crossed the street, and I thought I'd better lighten the subject matter. "Starting to have regrets concerning your ill-spent youth?"

He smiled. "No, no. I just sometimes wonder."

"What your life could've been like?"

"Yes."

"Take my advice—don't do that." Pulling up Dog in front of the Ponderosa Café, I turned and looked at him. "Regret is my turf, buddy."

He smiled a little more broadly. "Sorry."

"You were right about steering clear of her, and I drove us right back in there."

We began walking again. "It's your maiden-in-distress syndrome; you have a difficult time resisting."

I laughed. "Yep, but I'm starting to get the idea that Lola is the kind that ties people to the railroad tracks."

"One of the disadvantages of operating in the contemporary American West is that not all the bad guys have handlebar mustaches."

We crossed the last street toward the motel and walked across the parking lot toward the cabins on the end near the river, where we saw Lola's gold '66 Caddy parked on the grass. The mist from the Belle Fourche almost hid the thing, but the moonlight glistened off the chrome and quarter panels like jewelry.

"Evidently, she also has unique ideas on parking." I pulled the pink-gripped revolver from my belt and handed it to him. "Here, you can put it in her glove box."

"You are giving it back to her?"

I jiggled my jacket where the five rounds rattled in my pocket. "Empty."

He palmed the thing and started off toward the car, only to stop.

I stood there looking after him in the half-mist. "Something?"

He gestured with an open hand, bidding me to follow. "Someone. In the car."

We both walked over to the convertible. ATF field agent Brady Post was sitting in the passenger seat, his head turned to the side with his eyes closed and his mouth gaping open, looking like he was snoring and dead asleep. On closer inspection, however, he was simply dead, a hole in his chest.

10

We couldn't decide what we were going to do with the Caddy, so we leaned against it.

"Need I remind you that what we have here is a dead federal agent?"

"I'm aware of that, but I'm also aware that if this goes public, whoever did it is going to go to ground and we'll never find out what was happening here, let alone who's responsible."

"What do you suggest?"

"They have a vehicle shop at the Hulett Police Department."

"The tin shed?" He studied me. "You want to move both the body and the car as well?"

I glanced over my shoulder toward the bridge, where traffic had appeared to have disappeared, it being the wee hours. "We drive him up there, and then I'll contact McGroder, the AIC in Denver."

Henry looked back at the dead agent and shrugged.

"We'll say we were trying to maintain the integrity of the crime scene."

"By driving it across town."

I held a palm up, feeling for imaginary drops. "It might rain."

He shook his head and reached for Dog's leash. "Do you have gloves?"

I pulled a well-worn pair that I used to shoot with from my jacket. "If you would, put Dog in the room and try and not wake up Vic. I'll meet you at the cop shop."

He inclined his head. "You are not going to give me a ride?"

I skimmed off my jacket as I walked toward Post and carefully placed it over the agent's head. "You were the one getting squeamish."

"I'm over that now; pick me up in the motel lot." And off he went with Dog.

I watched the two of them walk away and then turned back to Brady Post, kneeled down, and looked at him. "What did you get into?" I rested my chin on my arm and studied the dead man, a dull ache starting to form behind my eyes. "And what was it that was important enough to kill you for?" I leaned in close and did something I rarely did. "I'm sorry, but if I'm going to get whoever did this, I'm not going to be able to follow protocol." I patted his arm and gave it a squeeze. "But then, you didn't strike me as a by-the-book kind of guy."

I climbed in the car, started her up, and gently spun the wheels. Easing the accelerator, I backed onto the parking lot and headed for the area between the two buildings. When I pulled on the headlights, the two car thieves were standing in my way.

The shady one who was with the Viking was the first to speak. "Where are you going with Lola's car?"

"I'm parking it in a safe place, as opposed to down by the river."

He continued to talk as Eddy fidgeted. "Does she know that?"

"Everyone in the Western Hemisphere's been driving this car this week, and you guys are going to question me?" I rubbed my hand across my face. "Who are you, anyway?"

"A friend of Lola's."

"Really?" The thick-timbered voice came from behind them, low but loud enough to straighten their backs. The Cheyenne Nation draped an arm over each man. "Because I am a friend of Lola, too, and I do not remember seeing either of your names on the guest list."

They were silent, staring at the asphalt as the weight of his arms curved their spines.

"I will tell you what—when we see Lola next we will tell her you said hello. Eddy the Viking and . . . ?" He hugged the other man, but he didn't appear to want to speak. "And?" I watched as Henry's forearm muscles bunched and the man's face was drawn in close to the Bear's.

"Phil Vesco."

Henry loosened his grip. "Eddy and Phil went up the hill. . . . I will be sure to recommend you to Lola for your sterling service."

I watched as he undraped himself and walked around the car. After slowly getting into the backseat behind the cloaked man in the front, he waved good-bye to the two road agents.

"He's what?"

"He's dead."

Corbin Dougherty's voice rose as he unlocked the steel doors leading to the maintenance shed behind the department's main structure. "Who killed him?"

"We're not clear on that, at least not yet."

He pulled the doors back and flipped the lights on inside. "He's a federal agent?"

"Yep."

"How do you know?"

I turned my head, and Henry and I looked at each other for that briefest of moments as I pulled the Cadillac into the two-bay garage. "He introduced himself to us."

Corbin rapidly closed the doors. "Do they normally do that?"

"Not generally." I climbed out, and Henry flipped the seat and followed. "But the other night at the motel he badged us; he's ATF and working on some kind of gun-running scheme that Bodaway Torres might've been involved with in Arizona."

"Our Bodaway Torres?"

"Yep."

His face was the picture of bewilderment. "Smuggling guns into Wyoming?"

Henry and I looked at each other again. "Kind of sounds like coal to Newcastle, doesn't it? Look, maybe it's not that particularly, but something is going on and the only way we'll find out what it is is by keeping agent Post's death under wraps."

He looked at the enormous car and the dead man. "For how long?"

"I'll ask Mike Novo to get a cashier and some bag boys up from DCI in Cheyenne and have them begin a preliminary while I get ahold of the agency in Denver. Maybe my friends in the FBI can get some information from the ATF and we can get a little more to go on."

"I could see them having that response to me personally, but what in the world could they possibly have against the horse I rode in on?"

"Was that an official response from the ATF?"

Agent-in-Charge Mike McGroder laughed on the phone from Denver. "Pretty much. It would be different if we were all on the same team, but you know, Walt—the federal government is more like a loose coalition of warring tribes."

"Did they even admit that he was theirs?"

"No, and with the number of CIs surrounding them, it's going to be like a minefield as to who knew what he was and who didn't."

"CIs?"

"Confidential Informants. That's the way these guys get in and it's how they get their information."

"What are the chances that he's not ATF at all?"

"Difficult to say, but if he's out of the Phoenix area, I can make some calls to the RAC and the ASAC. I know the guy in charge down there and he might be a little more motivated, especially if I tell him one of his agents is dead."

I continued to advance my education. "RAC?"

"Resident Agent-in-Charge."

"ASAC?"

"Assistant Special Agent-in-Charge."

"Is that what you guys do in your spare time—sit around

and make up acronyms?" I sighed. "I'm trying to keep this from becoming a circus."

"I understand you don't want this to turn into a know-and-go, but the ATF's Special Response Team is going to want its pound of flesh on this, Walt." There was a pause. "With a vengeance."

I looked out the Hulett Police Department's windows, the outside as black as a mine except for the ghostly white fender of the Pequod. "That's fine, but you know as well as I do that if the feds come in here in force, then whoever did it is going to fold up the tents."

There was a pause. "That puts a lot of pressure on you to find out who did it before that happens."

"Yep, it does." I hung up the phone and turned to look at Henry.

"The game is afoot?"

I sighed. "I wish you'd stop doing that."

Dougherty sat in another chair and looked at us. "What now?"

I glanced at the clock on the wall. "The DCI crew should be here in a few hours."

"Before eight?"

"I doubt it. Why?"

Incredulous, he looked at me. "Because then my chief shows up, and I have to explain what a Cadillac and a dead ATF agent are doing in our maintenance shed."

"Blame it on me."

He nodded his head emphatically. "I intend to."

"Well, in answer to your question, I think one of the key elements in the investigation is back in your holding cell." I glanced at Corbin. "He is still back in your holding cell, right?"

"Who?"

"Kiddo."

"Oh, him. Yeah, he's back there." My thought began dawning on him. "Why, are you thinking he's part of this?"

"I don't know, but there's a connection between him and Bodaway and a connection between Bodaway and a dead ATF agent. I'm thinking we take advantage of having the owner-proprietor of The Chop Shop in the holding cell and snoop around and see what he and Bodaway might've had going on over there." I shrugged. "And we can take the Pennington County sheriff's unit back to him; as far as I know, Vic's race car is still in their impound lot."

Henry and I gathered up as Corbin threw me the keys to the Tahoe. "What do I tell the chief, other than it's all your fault?"

"That should do it for now." I paused at the door. "If we don't make it back before the DCI guys get here, just park their vehicle in front of the shed door and try and get them in there as quietly as possible." I reached out and handed him the pink-gripped revolver. "The first thing I want to know is the caliber of the weapon that did the deed."

He stared at the S&W. "You think it was this?"

"If it is, your friend in the back better get used to eating off trays."

The Bear was already in Engelhardt's Tahoe, and I fired the thing up, drifted out of town, and then, gaining speed, turned on the emergency lights.

He buckled his seat belt and settled in. "We are official now?"

"For better or worse."

"Are we going to return the sheriff's car or break and enter first?"

I accelerated toward Moorcroft, figuring the more highway we had, the faster we could go. "In my experience, when you are committing a misdemeanor it's better not to do it in a pur-loined police car." I left the sirens off so that we could talk. "Why kill Post?"

He answered with the obvious response. "They found out he was ATF."

"We could find out where he was staying and see if he left any notes on what he was working on." I took the on-ramp and headed east. "Corbin had a point, though. Why would he reveal himself to us? In my experience, those guys are loath to do anything like that with anybody."

"Perhaps he was worried."

"Turns out he was right to be."

"Whatever he was looking for he discovered it in Hulett."

I thought about it. "Billy ThE Kiddo is involved in this. I'm not sure how, but he's involved."

"How long can you hold him?"

"As long as Nutter Butter is with us. I can press charges myself, if need be, and we can get the court to set bail so high that he has to mortgage his motorcycle shop to walk."

"Well, we know he will not be *sitting* comfortably for some time."

When we got to the Pennington County Jail, it was still

dark, and my eyes were feeling like a sand pit. I pulled the sheriff's car into the entryway of the impound lot as a young deputy, assuming his boss was arriving, snapped to attention in the booth at the gate.

I rolled down the window as he approached. "Hey, troop, we need to make a trade."

He stared at the sheriff's unit. "For what?"

I nodded toward the muscle car nearest his booth. "The Duke of Hazzard in there."

He looked dejected as he went back and retrieved a clipboard from his tiny lodgings. "Bummer. I was kind of hoping that one would go to auction."

There were three streetlights in the parking lot of The Chop Shop, making it impossible to get anywhere near the front of the place without appearing center stage.

"Remind me again why we are doing this?"

"It's the only outstanding lead we've got."

He studied the building in front of us. "Name the un-outstanding ones."

"Lola, which seems to be a dead end other than the fact that we are in possession of her vehicle."

"Along with a dead agent."

I ignored him. "Then we have Bodaway himself, who is in the hospital in a coma."

"There is the rich guy who lives on the golf course."

I nodded. "Yep, but I'm thinking that's just a personal thing between Bodaway and the daughter." I stared at the building

across the lighted expanse of parking lot. "And the establish-
ment in front of us."

"I think we should go around back."

"Agreed." I fired up the Challenger and listened as its exhaust trumpeted, heralding our every move. "I hate this car."

Taking the long way, we put in an extra block with the
lights off and came up on a chain-link fence in the back enclos-
ing what looked to be a salvage yard with a fair amount of
rusting American chrome.

"I do not see a gate."

I looked up at the spiraling razor wire that looped its way
around the perimeter. "I'm not climbing that thing."

He gestured toward a parking spot next to the building.
"Slip in there."

I did as he said and watched as he whirred the window
down and shimmied out, first standing on the sill and then the
top. There was a brief thump as the sheet metal bent, and then
he disappeared.

I turned off the obnoxious engine and sat there thinking
about how we were supposed to be heading back home today,
but that the death of Brady Post had changed all of that. We
were now committed in numerous ways, and if I didn't play
this correctly, I was placing my friend, my brothers in blue,
and myself in a prickly situation with the feds. I hoped that
while we were involved in our covert operations, Mike Mc-
Groder was getting information that might make the nature
of Post's investigation more clear.

I heard more noise as the Bear walked on the roof of the cycle
shop; then the chain-link rattled, and I turned to see Henry stand-

ing on the other side of the fence. I slipped out of the Dodge and joined him, still looking for a gate and still not seeing one.

"There is an electronic security system."

"You're kidding. In this dump?"

"There is a seven-space keypad for an entry code at the back door."

"We're never going to be able to guess the code."

"In my experience you get three tries within a one minute period before the alarms go off and alert the authorities."

"So, our odds are three in, say, a million?"

He shrugged.

"I hate to sound old-school, but what about just breaking a window?"

He turned and walked toward the back door. "If they went to the trouble of installing a keypad, they probably included the windows in said system."

Feeling in my jacket for Bodaway's cell phone, I whispered after him, "You want me to call Corbin and see if we can get Kiddo's birth date or phone number?"

He didn't answer but studied the keypad and then punched in some numbers; evidently, we were now on the clock. He stood there for a moment, and then there was a soft buzz and the sound of a latch being thrown. He pushed open the door and walked in.

Unprepared for this development, I skittered around the exterior of the building, looking all the world like a felon, and soon found him holding open the front door to allow me entry. "What the heck?"

"The Harley-Davidson Motorcycle Company was incorporated on September 17, 1907."

I slid in, and he closed the door behind me. "Hmm . . . 9171907. I'll be damned."

"What one man can invent, another can discover."

"Oh, shut up." I followed as we moved through the office back into the bays of the old service station.

"I wish we had a flashlight."

I pulled a mini Maglite from my hunting jacket.

"What else do you have in there?"

I held up three fingers. "Be prepared."

He took the flashlight and directed it toward the bike that Kiddo had been working on, focusing on what looked like modifications around the gas tank. "What do you think he was doing?"

The Cheyenne Nation stooped, carefully reached under a lip near the back of the tank, and, pulling it up, revealed a hidden compartment about half the size of a small shoe box. "The seams would be covered by a leather strap that goes across the tank."

"Drugs?"

"I do not know. Leaping to conclusions before one has the facts is the mark of a true amateur."

"I warned you about that Sherlock Holmes stuff." We studied the tiny space. "It has to be drugs."

"Need I remind you, Agent Post was investigating guns."

"What gun could be so important that you couldn't just carry it in a saddlebag or on your person?"

He straightened and sighed, as perplexed as I was. "I do not know that, either."

We moved past the vehicle bay where there was a newer addition and a door that read PRIVATE that was padlocked. I studied the thing. "Too bad we don't have a key."

Henry pulled down a pair of bolt cutters with three-foot-long handles from a tool rack on the wall and stepped past me. He placed the clasp of the lock between the jaw-like blades. "This should do the trick."

Before I could say anything, he bit the thing in two, and we both watched as the lock fell on the floor.

I picked it up and stared at him. "How do we explain this?"

He shrugged and pushed open the door. "We do not; we simply take the lock with us and let them think somebody either lost it or did not secure it."

Shaking my head, I stuffed the padlock in my pocket, walked inside, and scanned the walls as we went deeper into a world I'd hoped didn't exist.

The extension that had been added on to the back was poured concrete with reinforced metal beams above—a bunker, in more ways than one. The walls were festooned with Nazi memorabilia and black-and-white photos of Hitler, Goebbels, Goering, Himmler, and Franz Stangl, Paul Blobel, Josef Kramer, and Reinhard Heydrich, to name a few of the other maniacs. There were propaganda posters for the Third Reich with blond-haired, blue-eyed Nazis extolling the virtues of the party, and more cartoon ones expressing the distrust and loathing of Jews and other so-called mongrel races.

There was a large stage at one end draped with assorted Nazi flags and a podium with a swastika.

Along one wall were event tables stacked high with printouts, paper cutters, and pamphlets supporting the KKK, Aryan Brotherhood, and National Alliance. There were books like *The Turner Diaries*, the self-published, apocalyptic, white-supremacist novel that had been found on Timothy McVeigh, and *The Coming War*, a graphic novel of the same ilk, which came with an accompanying DVD. "Looks like we've stumbled into George Lincoln Rockwell's man cave."

The Bear picked up a copy of *The Coming War* and leafed through it, pausing at a point where the white protagonists were hunting Indians with rifles from open Jeeps. "My oh my."

"I guess they've decided to use comics to speak to their intellectual demographic."

"Hmm." He grunted and stuck the graphic novel and DVD under his arm.

"Think we should take a few samples for the FBI?"

He gathered some more. "I do not think they will be missed."

I glanced around the room, unafraid that my flashlight would be seen since there were no windows. "You know what I don't see?"

"Weapons."

"Yep."

He looked at the tables of propaganda. "I do not know if this is not more dangerous."

"The way a lot of these organizations get operating capital is from drugs."

"And gun sales."

"I've said it before and I'll say it again—you can't carry enough guns on a motorcycle to make it profitable."

I looked around some more but couldn't see any trapdoors in the concrete floor or hidden doors in the walls. "But we'd better get out of here."

The Cheyenne Nation followed, giving the room one more

look-over before closing the door behind us. "Why would a Native like Bodaway be trafficking with these people?"

"Maybe he didn't know."

"My experiences lead me to believe that this sort are not very secretive in their political beliefs." He let me out the front and handed me the Nazi propaganda. "I will return the way I came and reset the alarm system."

"See you out back." Skirting around the building, I glanced across the parking lot and didn't see any lights on in the adjacent buildings. Feeling relatively assured, I made the corner at the alley and walked directly into the extended barrel of an S&W .357 Magnum.

"I just wanted you to see how bad planning feels." Engelhardt holstered his revolver. "Got a call about a half hour ago from Mrs. Hirsch, who lives across the way here. She's got an irritable bladder condition and happened to see a large man walking on the roof of this building and another large man entering through the front door."

"Here I thought we were being real stealthy."

"Hard to sneak by an irritable bladder."

"I'm going to have that needlepointed and put on my office wall."

We turned, and I followed him to the alley, where his Tahoe had us boxed in. He watched as Henry set the alarm on the back door, climbed up on the roof, stepped over the razor wire, and lowered himself to the top of the Challenger to join us.

"If you don't mind me asking . . ." Irl's voice stayed low but grew harsh. "What the hell do you guys think you're doing?"

The Bear shrugged. "I needed some parts."

I handed the sheriff a few of the pamphlets. "Looks like Kiddo's got his own little cottage industry."

Irl thumbed through the evidence. "Well, shit."

"Our thoughts exactly."

He gestured with the stack of propaganda. "You mind if I keep these?"

"Seeing as it's inadmissible evidence, sure."

The Bear plucked the DVD from the pile. "I would like to take a look at this."

Engelhardt nodded and then opened the driver's-side door of his unit and tossed the stuff onto the passenger seat as I explained what we'd found. He stroked his chin and listened. "So, we've got a guy who's acting as a mule for some neo-Nazis, but we haven't got any idea what it was he was carrying?"

Henry told him about Brady Post.

"Holy shit." He rubbed his chin some more. "ATF, huh?"

"Yes."

"Well then, it's one of three things." He made a face. "No firearms inside?"

"Nope."

"Then they must have a place somewhere else." He glanced around, taking in the dawn-lit horizon. "Like anywhere in western South Dakota, huh? Well, I've got a file."

"I was hoping you'd say that."

"It sure would be easier if these feds would share their information with us."

"They seem to take that undercover thing pretty seriously."

He shook his head. "But this Brady Post just introduced himself to you guys?"

"To me, but then Henry opened the door and entered the conversation."

Irl shrugged as he slid into his unit. "Let me dig out my files on these shitbirds, and I'll give you a call." He paused. "You know, my uncle was one of the first guys into Buchenwald. He never talked about it except to say one of the buildings they liberated was a stables that was built to hold eighty horses and that they'd had over twelve hundred men in there, five to a bunk. He said the smell was horrific." He sighed. "I'll tell you, if he was still around and knew these turds were in South Dakota, he'd get out his deer rifle and finish the job." My fellow sheriff closed the door behind him and pulled the shiny black Tahoe into the empty streets.

We slid into the Dodge, and I fired up the twin trumpet exhausts, slipping the muscle car into gear and pulling back out onto the main drag. "I'm hungry."

Henry nodded. "I am sleepy."

"We sound like the two dwarfs." Looking for a place to eat, I drove toward Rapid City. "I'll make you a deal: we'll get something and then head back to the motel. I'll wake Vic up and you can have the room."

"When are you going to sleep?"

"When I'm dead."

The food at Ron's, not to be confused with Capt'n Ron's Rodeo Bar, and specifically their world-famous pancakes, was just the thing, but I might've overdone it, ordering a stack as big as dinner plates. "You want some pancakes?"

The Cheyenne Nation was doing his best with an order of

biscuits and gravy that looked like it might feed two men and a hungry boy. "You ordered them, you eat them."

I cleaved off another chunk, dipping it in the syrup and forking it into my mouth. "Do you think we should bring something back for Vic?"

"I do not think her stomach will be ready for solid food."

Sipping my coffee, I thought about a more pressing matter. "What do you want to do about Lola?"

He stared at his plate and continued eating. "Meaning?"

"How hard do you want to lean on her?"

He still didn't look up at me. "She has earned as hard as it takes."

"Have you considered that she might just be concerned for the welfare of her son?" His eyes came up and weighed on me. "Just wondering if you've considered it."

"I have and then immediately dismissed it."

"I know she's manipulative."

"You do not know."

We stared at each other. "Look, I know she hurt your feelings, but do you really think she's involved in the criminal element of this investigation?"

His dark eyes went back to the table. "Why not? What, other than her gender, leads you to believe that she is in any way innocent?"

I thought about it. "Umm, not much."

"Thank you." He went back to his meal.

"Still . . ."

He carefully put his fork on his plate, placed his elbows on the edge of the table, and laced his fingers into a single fist. "When I strike you, I would like you to know why."

"I'm just saying—"

"Yes, and you have said it enough." He leaned back in his chair, the picture of restraint, his eyes closed. "You care."

"Yep, I do."

"It is one of your most annoying traits." He opened his eyes, and the weight of them lay upon me like darkness. "Please do not ever lose it."

There was suddenly a strange noise, and I glanced around, his eyes still on me. "It is Bodaway's cell phone in your shirt pocket."

"Oh." I fumbled with the thing and looked at it, a trick I'd picked up from every other person on the planet. "It's the Hulett Police Department. The guys from DCI must've arrived." He picked up his fork and, instead of stabbing me with it, went back to eating.

I hit the button and held the device to my ear. "Howdy."

"Walt, it's Corbin."

"Hey, Deputy Dawg, what's up?"

"He was wired."

"Excuse me?"

"Brady Post, the ATF agent? He was wearing a wire."

11

"Why didn't they find it?"

"Who?"

DCI combed the interior of the Cadillac, the halogen work lights that they had brought with them augmenting those in the Hulett Police annex building. Mike Novo and I were standing in an area draped with plastic sheets where the agent's body now lay.

"The person who killed him."

Mike pushed some hair from his eyes and stared at the dead man. "They didn't look. Whoever shot him just shot him; there's no evidence that he was searched or tampered with after the murder."

I held the device, about half the size of a pack of matches. "This thing actually records?"

He nodded, handing me the thin wire and the mic bud. "Yeah, much smaller now that they're digital, but you still have to have an exterior mic for sound quality. He wasn't recording at the time of his demise, and it was in the inside pocket of his vest with the mic and cord under his shirt and around his neck."

I held the thing up between us. "I don't have to tell you that this is Christmas, right?"

"No, but you do have to tell the ATF."

I turned to look at the woman with the familiar voice. "Hey, T. J."

T. J. Sherwin, the head of DCI's lab unit, trailed numerous nicknames in her wake. I called her the Little Lady, but there were others who referred to her as the Bitch on Wheels, the Wicked Witch of the West, and the Bag Lady, a sobriquet that referred to the defunct supermarket that served as the Wyoming Division of Criminal Investigation's headquarters in Cheyenne—i.e., cashiers and bag boys and bag girls.

"They're going to want these files before anybody else, and in my experience they don't play well and share, at least not without a federal court order."

"Files?"

"Still a dinosaur, I see." She took the recorder from my hand and held it up to a light. "There's a plug-in that transfers the information to a zip drive and then you download it onto a computer in an audio file. You can actually hear it, just like a real phonograph."

I stared at her. "C'mon, Little Lady, help a cowboy out?"

Sherwin glanced at Novo. "Go away."

He stood there smiling.

"Now."

"Oh. Right." He disappeared, and T.J. indicated that I should follow her toward the back of the shop where they had set up an event table with computers and lab equipment.

"Anything on the weapon?"

She handed me back Lola's .38 in a ziplock bag. "Not this."

"Then what?"

She sat and began attaching cables to the tiny recorder and another thingamajig that attached to a laptop and a small black box, which swallowed a recordable CD. "Forty-gauge semi, probably a Glock, possibly a model 22."

She sat back in the folding chair and studied the freshly bagged gun. "Girlfriend of yours?"

"Henry's."

T. J. glanced past me to where the Bear was leaning against the fender of the DeVille. "Well, that doesn't narrow the field."

"It's Lola's."

Her eyes widened just a bit. "*The* Lola, the one the T-bird is named for?"

"*The* Lola."

"Oh, my."

I took the empty revolver from the bag and stuffed it in my jacket pocket. "It's her son who is in Rapid City Regional Hospital."

"The donor cycle rider?"

I handed her the bag. "Yep."

She tossed it on the table and sighed. "I was wondering what you were doing over here in Crook County."

"Me, too."

She pulled a CD from one of the devices, placed it in a paper cover, and handed it to me. "Just so you know, I have broken numerous state and federal laws by giving you this, so whatever you find, I'd just as soon you listen to it and then destroy it. The ATF will have a copy that's permissible in court as federal evidence, so you've got that to fall back on, but as far as you and I are concerned this CD doesn't exist."

"What CD?" I stuffed it in my jacket. "Anything else I need to know as I attempt to break the big case?"

"He had sex."

"Excuse me?"

"The deceased engaged in copulation with a female no more than an hour before his death."

"That's unfortunate."

"For him or her?"

I glanced at the Cheyenne Nation, who was still leaning on the Caddy but now was looking at us. "Both."

"So, who else could he have fucked?"

I made a gesture for her to lower her voice as the waitress at the Ponderosa Café brought her another medicinal Bloody Mary. "Oh, how about any of the thousands of biker bunnies bouncing around here this week?"

My undersheriff sipped the drink from a straw, the liquid perfectly matching her fingernails. "The fuckee was Lola."

"Boy, both you and Henry have it out for her, huh?"

She raised an eyebrow. "I know women, he knows her, and you don't know shit."

"I'm beginning to think you both might be right."

"So, it was a .40 that killed the agent?"

"Yep."

"Well, that lets her off the hook for this one." She studied me as I stared at the table. "What?"

"Somebody mentioned a model 22 Glock."

"Recently?"

"Yep."

"Well, it would be important to know who that was." She leaned back in her chair and massaged her temples. "So, how come nobody mentioned that I shot myself in the head at the competition last night?"

"You don't think the half-dozen double dirty martinis had something to do with it?"

She yawned. "Your dog takes up the whole bed."

"Yep."

I waited, and she began studying the surface of the table as I had. "Just because it wasn't a .38 doesn't mean she didn't do it."

"No, but—"

"What the hell—did you decide to adopt her while I was knocked out?"

"Gimme a motive. I just don't see what she would've gained by killing Post."

She belched loudly. "Something she couldn't get by fucking him."

I leaned in. "Are there such things?"

"Not with me." She cocked her head coquettishly. "Her son."

"Excuse me?"

She repeated in a remedial fashion, "If the G-man was after her son—"

I had to concede the point but then brought up my own. "Look, as far as we know she's never killed anybody before."

"As far as we know." She studied me now. "More important question: Who else have you got?"

"Billy ThE Kiddo."

"The South Dakota Nazi?"

It took me a long time to respond because suddenly the spokes in my wheel of thought began spinning. "Yep."

"Something?"

"When I was talking to Irl, he mentioned a Glock 22 in Kiddo's past, something about a lawn mower."

"You're kidding."

"Nope; as I recall, he shot his neighbor's lawn mower with a .40 Glock."

She finished off the rest of her Bloody Mary with a strong pull and then set the glass down between us. "Are we really going to go dig up some guy's lawn?"

I gathered my jacket from the back of my chair and looked down at her. "After I take a nap, we go have a chat with Billy ThE himself."

"Where are you taking your nap? Henry has one bed and Dog has the other."

"Probably in Lola."

She shrugged, getting up after me. "Why not? It appears to be where everyone else is sleeping these days."

There wasn't much human traffic, so we made quick time to the Hulett Motel's parking lot. I opened the door to the vintage convertible and looked at the center console in the front and then at the backseat, which didn't look nearly as big as I'd remembered.

"I don't think I'm going to fit."

She glanced in the back, spotting the Cheyenne Nation's blanket, and then, in the passenger seat, she saw the *Annotated Sherlock Holmes*. "Grab the blanket and book and we'll go down by the river and have a picnic."

I retrieved the supplies and shut the door. "We don't have any food."

"No, but I can read and you can put your head in my lap."

"Sold."

"Did you know that Doyle almost named Holmes Sherrinford?"

"In some of the early drafts, but he settled on Sherlock because of a cricket player he remembered." I kept my eyes closed, knowing full well that opening them would only encourage her.

"Did you know the first novel, *A Study in Scarlet*, was a flop?"

"Yep, but the second was a hit after Joseph Stoddart convinced both Doyle and Oscar Wilde to serialize stories for his *Lippincott's Monthly Magazine*. *The Picture of Dorian Gray* was the only novel Wilde ever wrote."

"Does the name Sherlock mean anything?"

"Fair-haired."

I listened as she flipped a page. "Second most-filmed fictional character?"

"Sherlock Holmes."

There was a long pause as she puzzled on something that wasn't annotated in the book suspended above my head. "Who the hell is first?"

"Dracula." I opened my eyes and looked up at her. "Hey, I thought I was supposed to be taking a nap."

"Who's stopping you?"

"You."

"Yeah, I guess I am." She closed the book and set it aside.

"An arrogant, drug-addicted sociopath—why do you suppose the character has been so popular through the years?"

"His perfect humanity."

Her face dropped to look at me. "Explain?"

"He's flawed, but he has an encyclopedic mind and relies on the human element of uncanny intuition, so when scientific method runs amok, he uses his brain. Contrary to popular belief, the method Holmes uses is abduction, not deduction. Abductive reasoning is based on conclusions drawn from observation, whereas deduction is a conclusion drawn from available data and is always true."

"I thought Sherlock Holmes was never wrong?"

"That would be a dreadful disadvantage to a true detective; you have to always be ready to rethink your abductions in the face of the evolving information in any case."

"Elementary, my dear Longmire?"

"He never said that in a single story or novel." I rose up and supported myself with a stiff arm. "How long was I asleep?"

"Less than you want to know."

"I guess I'm done." We stood, and I shook off the blanket, folded it, and placed it under my arm. "Any sign of Henry?"

She closed the book and glanced around. "Nope—must still be asleep in the room."

"I guess we'll leave Dog with him, then, and head over to the police station to have a chat with Billy."

"Sounds like a charmer."

We started toward the T-bird. "Oh, he is."

• • •

"What do you mean, he's gone?"

"Made bail, so he's scot-free."

"How?"

"Somebody moved up the bail schedule, and the judge ruled him a low flight risk in that he's a business owner and a celebrity."

"What about the fact that that business is in another state, as well as the assault with a deadly weapon on a peace officer?"

"The judge let that one slide because of the previous cease and desist that said you weren't supposed to be within a hundred feet of him. Not sure about the rest."

Vic sat on the edge of Corbin's desk. "What was bail?"

The patrolman smiled. "Two hundred and fifty thousand."

"Wowza."

"I guess the judge decided that even though he might be a low flight risk, he was going to make it tough on him by hitting him in the wallet, but Kiddo called the bluff."

"Where did he get a quarter of a million dollars?"

"It was a blanket bond from one of that bunch down in Cheyenne—Liberty Bail Bonds."

"Libby Troon? Hard to believe she'd pop for that without a percentage as collateral."

He picked up a square card and tried to hand it to me. "I've got her number here. You could call her up and ask her who's fronting for Billy?"

"No, she doesn't care for me very much. She's contacted me and Henry about freelancing as bounty hunters for a few of her skip jobs and we've never bit."

"You could tell her it involves a murder case."

"That is the last piece of information I'd want Libby Troon to have." I looked out front and could see Chief Nutter herding some bikers away from the annex building. "Who picked him up?"

"Nobody. He just walked out and disappeared down the street."

"So, you think he's still around?"

"No, he said he was done with the rally and heading home. He also mentioned a lot of stuff about suing you, your dog, me, the city, the county, and all the fish in the Belle Fourche River."

"So, do you really think he went home?"

"It's likely."

"What's the address?" He stared at me. "I'm not hunting him; I just might be able to get a piece of evidence from his next-door neighbor whose lawn mower he may have shot."

He stared at me some more. "You're kidding."

"I wish I were. Address, please?"

He clicked on the computer and wrote it down on a Post-it, and handed it to Vic, who was closer. "It's actually a nice part of town. From what I could tell it was his mother's."

Vic stuffed the piece of paper in her shirt pocket. "I'm sure she'd be proud."

We walked out just as Nutter Butter shooed away the bikers and turned to look at us. "As one professional to another, have you lost your mind?"

"I'm not so sure I had one to begin with, but thanks for adding me to your professional circle."

He lowered his voice. "A dead federal agent in my annex building?"

"We weren't sure where else to put him—or the car."

"You know, this shit seems to follow you wherever you go."

"It's an interesting life." Vic and I leaned against the front grille of the monstrous MRAP. "If you're not nice to me, I won't tell you how to start your truck."

He ignored me and continued. "Plus the entirety of the Division of Criminal Investigation are back there."

"I didn't think you wanted to handle that part."

"I don't want to handle any of it."

I nodded toward the annex. "One of ours is dead." The chief calmed down and took a deep breath as I continued. "Somebody in your town killed him, and I think it has to do with Bodaway Torres. Now, you know as well as I do that if we keep this quiet, whoever did it is going to start worrying, and then they're likely to do something stupid as opposed to doing the smart thing, which is loading up and getting the hell out of here. So, you tell me what you would've done differently."

"It's a hell of a mess."

"And our job."

He sighed. "You think that turd Kiddo had something to do with this, then."

"Yep, but I'm still trying to figure out where he came up with the bail money."

"TV, I guess. You think he's got ties in Cheyenne, too?"

"No, it's just that Liberty Bail Bonds is the only one with pockets deep enough for a surety bond like this, and it just happens to be located in Cheyenne."

He shook his head, and we all sat on the bumper of the military vehicle in a dejected fashion. "Must be a lot of money in fixin' up motorcycles on TV."

"He does have some other rather odd preoccupations."

He turned to look at me. "Like what?"

"The back room of his cycle shop looks like a bunker for the Nazi Rotary League."

He absorbed that one for a while, started to say something, then stopped and started again. "How the hell did you find that out?"

"Broke in last night and had a look-see."

He stood, took two paces, and turned to look at me. "You really have lost your mind, haven't you?" He glanced at Vic. "You wanna talk to your boss here?"

She shrugged. "I'm usually not a calming effect."

"What if they had caught you in there?"

I made a noise between my compressed lips. "They did."

"What?"

"Well, Irl Engelhardt did."

"Is there anybody else that doesn't know what's going on here besides me?"

"No, I think you're about it."

He closed his eyes. "Hey, do me a favor?"

"Sure."

"Let's pretend like this little conversation didn't happen so that I can go back to being as dumb as I have pretended to be."

I laughed, unable to help it. "You're going to pretend that you're oblivious enough to not know that a dead federal agent and an entire field laboratory from DCI have set up shop next door to your office?"

He took a deep breath and hooked his thumbs into his Sam Browne. "I'm about a year and a half from retirement, Sheriff Longmire, and you'd be amazed at the lengths I'm willing to go to to secure the stupidity I have acquired."

I stood up. "Consider yourself untold, then."

"Good." He nodded down the street. "I am now on my way to the Pondo for lunch if you two would like to join me."

"Thanks, but I think we're going to go listen to a new CD I've got."

"Who's on it?"

"You don't want to know."

"Roger that." He started to walk off but then paused. "Just so we're clear: if this turns out to be the case of the century, I'm going to want back in and with full credit for how magnificently I coordinated the whole thing."

"Of course."

He waved and turned his back on us in more ways than one, disappearing into the crowded street.

I turned to Vic. "The brotherhood of blue."

"No shit." She glanced behind her. "What the hell is this thing I'm sitting on?"

"It's an MRAP, or mine-resistant ambush protected vehicle, the centerpiece of the Hulett Police Department's motor pool."

"You're shitting me."

"Nope." I pulled the DCI envelope from my jacket pocket. "And believe it or not, it has a CD player."

Fortunately, Chief Nutter hadn't seen fit to remove the keys from the Pequod, probably because even with the keys most people wouldn't know how to start the damned thing.

The CD player was proving to be almost as difficult. "Where do you suppose the volume is?"

She studied the dash along with me. "Maybe the key needs to be turned to accessory?"

"I thought it was."

She glanced around the cab of the oversized military vehicle. "Why in the world would this thing have a sound system?"

"Nutter ordered it with all the bells and whistles."

She reached overhead to a console and a button that read AUDIO and flipped the switch. "Wonder what this does?" Her voice echoed off the building in front of us as the PA system projected her words over the valley. "Oh shit. . . ." Which also carried through town.

I reached up and flipped the toggle switch. "I don't think that's it." I looked at the dash again. "How about I just stick the thing in and see what lights up?"

"Always been my method of operation."

I ignored the remark and looked for the slot where the disc might be inserted, finally seeing what could've easily been mistaken for a design element. The slot accepted the CD, and it slowly disappeared.

She lodged her feet up on the dash, her Doc Martins in their usual position. "That it?"

"That, or I just lost the only copy we've got."

There was a popping noise and then someone counting. "One, two, three . . . testing one, two, three."

I listened to make sure the PA system was off.

"This is agent Brady Post of the ATF recording a meeting with CI Apelu concerning the activities of the Tre Tre Nomads and specifically Bodaway Torres and Operation Bad God." There was some scrambling and then the mic switched off.

"Who the fuck is Apelu?"

"More important, what's Operation Bad God?"

The mic came back on, and this time there were voices in the background along with some music and ambient noises, probably a bar from the sound of it. Brady's voice was low, as if speaking to someone confidentially. "So, I need a meet."

The next man also spoke quietly, but his voice was powerful, with just a touch of an unidentifiable accent. "No way."

"Hey, I don't work for anybody I never met, man."

"He don't meet people."

"What, he's a fucking hermit?"

"Yeah."

There was a pause. "Look, B-way wants me in on this, but without knowing where the juice is coming from . . ."

"Don't do it, then."

Another pause. "Look, I want in, but I just want to know who I'm in with, you know?"

"I read you, brother, but it ain't gonna happen." There were more noises, and I assumed the other man was adjusting himself in his chair or in the booth, or whatever it was. "This is on a need to know basis—and you don't need to know."

Post mumbled something indiscernible.

"Hey, there's no need to disrespect me, motherfucker."

"Fuck you, asshole!" There was more fumbling around and then the unmistakable sound of the slide mechanism on a semiauto being pulled back. "Hey, man . . ."

The voice became louder, and I was pretty sure the man was leaning in very close. "Let me explain the situation. B-way works for us, and he says you're the real deal, but we don't know that now, do we?"

"B-way and me go back long before Bird City."

"Dude, I don't care." There was another pause, and then the noise of the safety being engaged and the gun being put away. "You don't get to meet the man, and that's it."

There was some more noise, and then the mic cut out.

"Okay, we need to know what Operation Bad God is and who Apelu is, for starters."

"Well, the original name for Devils Tower was Bad God Tower, so it might just be a geographic reference to this area." There were more noises from the sound system, so I hurried the rest. "Torres is supposedly Apache, so this Apelu might've been one of his buddies."

The noise on the CD subsided, and there were mumblings but not much else when suddenly we could hear Post's voice. "Well, I gotta go to the can." We could hear him walking before closing what I assumed was a bathroom door. "Shit, shit, shit." There was more fumbling and then a sudden noise that sounded like a window opening. "Shit, shit, shit."

Vic glanced at me. "What the hell?" More undefinable noise and then nothing. After a moment there was a rhythmical sound. "What is that?"

It took me a moment to place it, but then I laughed. "Frogs."

We sat there listening to the croaking.

"He ripped off the mic?"

"And dropped it out the window, near the river I'd say."

We sat there as the frogs croaked, and I could feel a little ennui overtaking me.

"How long does this shit go on?"

I adjusted my seat back and pulled my hat over my face. "Let me know."

• • •

"More than an hour I listened to croaking frogs."

I yawned. "Nothing else?"

"No, just the sounds of the recently departed coming back to fetch his wire."

"Well, whoever it was, he must've made him plenty nervous." I flipped off the accessory switch, checking the battery levels first to make sure I hadn't killed the Hulett Police Department's apocalyptic auto. "There wasn't a lot on that recording."

"No." She studied me. "Now that you're rested, what's next?"

"We need to go see if we can find anything about where Post was staying—he mentioned the Pioneer Motel to the north of town."

She pulled the handle and began the long climb down. "Did he mention a room number?"

Hopping out myself, I reached up, shut the door, and met her at the front of the Pequod. "No, but I'm betting DCI has already found a key on his person."

Her eyes came back to me as she shook her head. "Pequod—really?"

"It's big, it's white, and it seemed appropriate."

After retrieving the motel's magnetic keycard, we borrowed Chief Nutter's vehicle and drove south a quarter mile to the Pioneer Motel. "Couldn't we have walked?"

I shut the door and headed toward the pleasant-looking strip of rooms only slightly blighted by the bikes and bikers littering the parking lot. "I didn't think you liked walking."

"I don't, but jeez, this seems a little like overkill." She stopped by the office and turned to look at me. "How are we playing this? I mean if we just go over and walk in, isn't anybody involved going to be suspicious?"

"We'll just flip the place and look around and maybe there'll be something else we might find along the way."

"There's this thing called a warrant? And inadmissable evidence?" She sighed and followed me into the office, the doorbell tinkling from the facing.

"Howdy."

A middle-aged woman looked up from reading the *Rapid City Journal*. "Sorry, we're full up through the rally."

"We're not looking for a room to stay in; we were just wondering if you might know which room this key goes to?"

She took it from me and examined it. "No way to tell; we just punch in the room number and then slide it through and encode it magnetically."

"Hmm." I took the key back. "You wouldn't happen to have a room registered to a gentleman by the name of Brady Post?"

She opened an honest to goodness file box and pulled a card out. "Room number twelve, on the end out there."

"Do you mind if we take a look?"

She stared at her paper again and then at me. "Well, I don't know who he is, but it can't be good if Sheriff Walt Longmire is looking for him." She turned the Rapid City paper around and held it up for me so that I could read the feature article about the progress of the Save Jen campaign and the High Plains Dinosaur Museum—along with an enormous photo of me.

12

"That case was a good two and a half months ago; what the heck are they doing running an article on it now?"

Vic continued to read the borrowed paper. "It's more about the addition to the museum than the case. More to the point, where did they get this really hideous photo of you?"

I ignored her and slipped the card into the electronic mechanism, watched as it blinked from red to green, and pushed the door open. I have, in my time as the father of a teenage daughter, seen scenes of chaos and anarchy that no man should ever witness, and this was another of those. The furniture was turned over with the bed pushed against the wall, clothes and personal effects everywhere. Pictures had been thrown on the floor, and the closet doors had been pulled from the sliders.

Vic peered in after me. "So, you think they were looking for something?"

I tipped the mattress from the wall for a look behind it, just making sure there weren't any bodies lying about, and then leaned it back. "Where do you want to start?"

She stepped over a pile of clothes and put the newspaper on a windowsill. "Can we rent a backhoe?"

Carrying the larger pieces of furniture outside onto the

sidewalk under the curious eyes of the bikers coming and going from the parking lot, we finally got to where we could move around in the place without tripping.

Vic started by going through the clothes that were scattered all over the room, making a pile in the corner with the ones that she had examined, as I went through the drawers and the closet. "This was a real toss. If they found what they were looking for, it wasn't till the end of the search."

I felt along the top shelf of the closet under a blanket. "Whatever it was, they were looking hard."

There was a noise at the door, and we turned to find a drunk biker in a leather jacket and do-rag standing in the doorway with a bottle of beer in one hand and a cigarette in the other. "Hey, what are you guys doing in Brady's room?"

"Straightening up a little." I glanced around and then studied him. "Somebody trashed the place."

He nodded. "Yeah. Why did they do that?"

"Probably looking to see if the tags were still on the mattress."

"Do they still check those?"

I ignored the question. "Were you here when the place got torn up?"

He threw a thumb. "Two doors down."

"What time?"

"Late—after midnight."

"What'd they look like?"

"I don't know, a couple of guys in black polo shirts. One of 'em was really big."

"Bigger than me?"

"Yeah. Hey, are you guys cops?"

I ignored this question, too. "What about the other one?"

He leaned against the doorjamb. "He was smaller, but still a big fucker."

"What did they look like, other than their size?"

"I don't know."

"I thought you said you saw them?"

"Well, for a minute. I mean, I wasn't wearing any clothes, and there was all this noise, so I stuck my head out the door and yelled, but they told me to shut the hell up and disappear or they were gonna stuff me in a trash can." He thought about it. "And it was dark."

"How do you know Brady?"

He shrugged. "We had a beer out here at the picnic table a couple of nights back."

I nodded, figuring I'd gotten as much out of him as I was going to get. "What's your name?"

He deposited the cigarette into his beer bottle and stuck out his free hand. "Gogo."

"Gogo?"

"George, George Lance, but everybody just calls me Gogo."

I shook the hand and gave him one of my cards. "Nice to meet you, Gogo. Walt Longmire, sheriff of Absaroka County."

He studied the card. "Cool."

"If you think of anything else, you might let us know?"

"Sure." He pushed off the door facing and disappeared.

"You want to know what's amazing about that exchange?"

I turned to look at her. "What's that?"

"That you actually had cards." She went back to sorting through Brady's personal effects. "What phone number have you got on there, anyway?"

"The office number." She mumbled something—I wasn't sure what it was, but I figured that it wasn't complimentary—and went back to searching. "I'm checking the bathroom."

"I'll alert the press. You want some reading material? There's a lovely article in the paper on the sill you can wipe with."

"Thanks. I don't plan on being that long." Thinking it was a heck of a lot easier to search for something when you knew what it was you were searching for, I went into the bathroom. Knowing that the space for contraband on motorcycles was relatively small helped but not much.

I opened and closed the medicine cabinet and tried not to look into my tired eyes in the mirror. The shower curtain had been torn off the rings, and the towels were on the floor. After checking the back of the toilet, I piled the stuff on the seat and looked in the shower stall, the trash can, and on the window-sill.

Nothing.

I was about to turn and walk out when one of those old-fashioned ceiling fixtures with a rectangular glass shade caught my eye. I had had one just like it when I was a kid, with cowboys roping from horses painted on the inside of the surface, but there was a small shaded square in one corner on this one that didn't match.

I carefully stepped up on the toilet in the hopes that I wouldn't rip it from the floor and unthreaded the nut on the bottom of the shade, palming it so that I could pluck out the strange item.

I put the shade back on, and looked at the small object. It was a plastic cube of some sort, khaki in color, and about two inches square. If it was a box, I had no idea how you would open it since there were no ridges, creases, or cracks. "Hey, Vic?" I came out and offered the thing to her. "Any idea what this is?"

"A ring box?"

I handed it to her. "Open it."

She turned it in her fingers just as I had and then weighed it in her palm. "It's plastic but heavy." She examined it closer. "Where did you find it?"

"In the light fixture."

"No way it's part of the thing?"

"No, and it's a strange color if it's for any kind of construction."

She handed it back to me. "A Rubik's Cube for morons?"

"I have no idea."

"Well, this pisses me off. We go through the place with a fine-tooth comb and all we find is something that we have no idea what it is?"

"It's a plastic cube." Mike Novo turned the thing in his hand. "Solid, by all accounts."

Vic was annoyed. "So, what's it for?"

"Hell if I know. I mean it's not styrene or anything—it's hard." He handed it back to me. "Maybe it's a spacer of some kind."

I handed it back to him. "I need to know."

"You want me to send it to Cheyenne?"

"Yep."

"And then what?"

"X-ray it, test it. A federal agent possibly lost his life because of it, Mike. Do whatever it is you people do and find out what the heck it is."

"Okay." He stood and pulled out a FedEx box.

"T.J. get anything more from the body?"

He nodded toward the back. "You can ask her—she's finishing up the autopsy in the pop-up lab." He snapped his fingers and pointed at me. "Henry was by here looking for you. He had your dog with him."

"He say where he was going?"

"The Ponderosa Café. He said Dog was hungry, and they were going for a late lunch/early dinner."

I turned to look at Vic. "Hungry?"

"Starved."

"Let's go talk to T. J., and then we'll grab something to eat."

She followed me as I led the way. "Dead people and dinner, my favorite night out."

The Little Lady was pulling off her latex gloves when we shoved the plastic aside and stepped in. "No other traces. The killer placed the muzzle of the .40 against his chest and pulled the trigger." She threw the gloves in a nearby trash can. "From the angle of the shot, I'd say your friend here was asleep."

"Nothing else?"

She picked up a clipboard and began writing. "As noted, the decedent had sex before being shot; he'd eaten a little before that, and he also ingested a schedule IV controlled substance, probably Lorazepam, a high-potency, intermediate-duration, 3-hydroxy benzodiazepine drug, often used to treat anxiety disorders."

"Like being worried that somebody might shoot you in the chest?"

T.J. glanced at Vic, noting the fact that she had on her sunglasses in the gloom of the annex. "Exactly like that." Sherwin extended a hand. "How do you feel, Vic?"

My undersheriff looked dubiously at the hand for a moment and then shook. "Still hung over; how 'bout you?"

"Just tired. At least hung over means you *had* fun."

She glanced at me.

"You ordered without us?"

The Bear chewed a bite of his cheeseburger. "Dog was hungry." He fed him another fry. "He is always hungry."

Vic and I pulled out chairs and sat. "We found a plastic cube in Brady's motel room."

Henry wiped his hands on his napkin. "A what?"

"Plastic cube, about two inches by two inches by two inches—perfectly square and khaki in color. Any ideas?"

He puzzled. "Hard plastic?"

"Very."

He shrugged. "Let me see it."

"DCI's job. I gave it to Mike Novo to ship off just now."

Dragging another fry through the ketchup, he fed it to Dog. "Nothing else?"

"Nope, no more wire equipment, computer, nothing." The waitress arrived, and we ordered up. "Somebody destroyed the place, and I'm assuming they got everything."

"Except the cube. Whatever that is."

I glanced out the window at the comings and goings of a couple thousand motorcycles in the early evening. "He hid it in the light fixture, so he knew it was a possibility that someone was going to be looking for it."

The Bear nodded and split the last fry with Dog. "It would be nice if we had access to the ATF agent's control officer. It is possible that he might know what Post was working on."

I leaned back in my seat. "I'm still waiting on McGroder to get back to me."

Vic rested an elbow on the table, pushing a wave of blue-black hair from her face and supporting her chin with a palm. "How?"

"Excuse me?"

"How is he supposed to get in touch with you?"

Satisfied with myself, I smiled and patted my jacket pocket. "I've got Bodaway Torres's cell phone."

"Have you checked it?" I suddenly felt a little less sure of myself as she reached over and pulled the phone from my pocket, thumbed a few buttons, and studied the screen as the waitress came back with our drinks and I sipped my iced tea.

The Cheyenne Nation studied Vic, still wearing her sunglasses. "How is your head?"

"Shitty. How's yours?"

"Fine, but I did not drink a vat of dirty martinis last night."

She turned the screen toward me. "Eight phone messages and three texts from the regional office in Denver, Colorado, of the FB of I."

"Oh."

"You hit the button that silenced it."

"Oh."

The phone suddenly spoke. "Hello?"

Vic gestured with the device. "Take it; it's McGroder."

I took the thing and held it to my ear. "Hey, Mike."

"Where the hell have you been? I've been trying to get you for what seems like days."

"This cell phone thing is kind of new to me. Have you got something?"

"This is a shit storm of incomparable magnitude, and none of us have an umbrella. This Post guy was a real deal, and an undercover operative for the last thirteen years with all the biker gangs. He was involved in a major bust on weapons in the Southwest, but evidently he had gotten into something even bigger."

"Like what?"

"The control officer wouldn't say."

"So big the ATF won't tell the FBI?"

"Apparently."

I thought about it. "What's he want done with Post?"

"Amazingly enough, he went along with your assessment of the know-and-go, but get ready because he's on his way there."

"Coming to Hulett?"

"Left today from Phoenix."

"Okay."

"His name is John Stainbrook." There was a long pause, and I listened as the FBI man shuffled papers on his desk. "Walt, don't jerk this guy around; he's the real juice, and unless you and your pals up there in the Wild West want to end up in an undisclosed facility in the Arizona desert, just tell him everything you know."

"Well, that won't take long, considering we don't know a lot." I reached down to pet Dog. "Hey, Mike, we found something in Post's motel room—"

"You searched his room?"

"Don't worry about it; we weren't the first. Anyway, we found a plastic cube, khaki in color, about two inches square—any idea what that might be?"

He sighed. "Walt, are you on drugs?"

"That's the only thing of interest we found."

He sighed. "I have no idea."

"Oh, well. Maybe the Stainbrook guy can help us out."

"There's one more thing."

"I'm listening."

"Post wasn't alone."

"What's that supposed to mean?"

"The ATF has two undercover agents there in Hulett."

I watched as Henry continued to tinker with the metal detector we'd purchased at High Plains Pawn, in an attempt to get the thing to light up or do something that might indicate it was operable.

Vic looked out the window of the Dodge at the gathering gloom of one of suburban Rapid City's nicer neighborhoods, her eyes rising to the gigantic cottonwoods that wreathed the street. "I figure if I lived in a place like this I'd shoot myself."

"Why?"

"The incredible normalcy of it." She turned to look at me. "So, two ATF birds in one bush? Any guesses?"

"Not a one."

"So, this is not an informant or someone but an actual secret agent?"

"I don't think they call them secret agents."

"I know, but I like the sound of it—makes it sound espionage-y and shit."

I let that one settle. "According to McGroder and this John Stainbrook character, there are two undercover operatives."

"Undercover operatives—I like that, too." She went back to watching a particular house down the street. "Well, be careful what you wish for; an hour ago you were wishing you could talk to these ATF guys about what Post was working on, and now you've got his boss hotfooting it up here."

"It must be important." I turned and looked at the Cheyenne Nation. "How's it going?"

"I do not know." He put the top back on the plastic case and pushed a button, which resulted in a high-pitched squeal from the thing. "I think it is working." He extended the wand with a disc on it toward the dash, and the thing started screaming again.

"Can you turn the volume down?"

Vic peered at the instrumentation on the Dodge. "Wow, who would've figured there was real metal in the dash."

The Bear adjusted the knob and fiddled some more. "It is set on the highest level of sensitivity, but I will adjust it when we get on the lawn."

Vic glanced at the sky. "Dark enough?"

I pulled the door handle and climbed out. "Unless we're going to hang around here all night." I met the two of them at the back of the pumpkin chiffon muscle car, the perfect vehicle for undercover work. "It must be the Tudor-looking one three houses up—the one next to the house with the cars parked on the lawn."

Vic shook her head as Henry continued to calibrate the metal detector. "So, tell me again what the hell we're doing out here?"

I opened the trunk and pulled out the new shovel I'd purchased at Shipton's Ranch Supply. "When I was talking to Engelhardt, he said that one of the run-ins he had had with Billy ThE Kiddo was when he shot his neighbor's lawn mower with a .40 Glock. Post was shot with a .40, so I thought we'd get the slug and hand it over to DCI and see if they could get a match—case solved."

She looked at the oversized lawns. "You're kidding."

I closed the trunk and balanced the shovel on my shoulder. "Got a better idea?"

She studied the house next to the Tudor. "Yeah, we get a warrant, go into the jackass's house, find the gun, and hand it over to DCI for testing."

"You think he's stupid enough to still have it?"

"I think he's stupid enough to open a wholesale stupid store and sell franchises."

Following the Bear, I started off down the street. "Well, if this doesn't work—"

She sighed and brought up the rear.

Staying to the far side of Kiddo's house, Henry dropped the wand and started detecting, moving it across the newly mown grass, whereupon it squealed softly and the yellow light on the instrument panel lit up. "A little too sensitive." He recalibrated it again, but this time the thing did nothing at all. "Hmm, a little too desensitized perhaps."

While he fiddled with the adjustments, Vic and I looked around. There were no lights on in either of the two houses, and it looked as though there was no one home in either one.

She leaned against a large cottonwood and studied the Kiddo abode. "So, in a nice neighborhood, this asshole parks his cars and motorcycles in the yard."

There was a noise behind us, and I turned to see Henry waving the metal detector over a small patch of God's little acre. I walked over. "Something?"

"Possibly."

Looking around one last time, I placed the edge of the blade into the turf and dug in. I lifted a chunk of sod, tipped it to the side, and then stomped another shovel full from the ground, carefully placing it beside the hole for reinterment. "How far down does that thing read?"

He shrugged. "I have no idea."

I shoveled again and this time felt something scrape. I handed the spade to Henry, took out my Maglite, shined it in the hole, and poked around, finally recovering an old railroad spike. "Hmm."

"Not what we are looking for?"

"No." I returned the dirt to the hole and then replaced the sod, stomping on it, as the Bear continued working the massive lawn. "This is going to take all night." I glanced around for Vic, but she'd obviously gotten bored and wandered off.

The machine made another noise, and I followed Henry to a spot about twenty feet away and repeated the procedure, which resulted in another spike. "What'd we find, the transcontinental railroad here?"

He shrugged again and moved on, but after another five

railroad spikes, I was losing my enthusiasm. "I don't suppose you could dial that thing down again?"

"I could, but the difference between a railroad spike and a slug might be beyond this particular model's abilities." He adjusted the thing again. "It would be helpful if we had an approximate area where the shooting took place."

"Yep, I know."

I looked up and could see Vic standing just a little ways away.

"How's it going?" She stepped closer and raised a glass to her lips, sipped some wine, and glanced around in the darkness. "Don't quit your day job."

It took me a moment to ask. "I'm almost afraid to know, but where'd you get the wine?"

"Earl Heiple, who owns the yard we're digging in."

"Did you go introduce yourself to Mr. Heiple?"

"I did. He was reading in his den, so I knocked on his back door."

"And he gave you a glass of wine?"

"He's ready to give you one, too. He says he hates that riotous prick next door." She paused. "He's like a hundred years old, but called Kiddo a riotous prick—used those exact words." She took another sip. "I like him."

"He didn't happen to tell you where Billy ThE shot the lawn mower, did he?"

She gestured with the wineglass. "Yeah, out there in the middle someplace; he said he'd show us."

• • •

"They used railroad ties near the sidewalk. They backfilled the front lawn in '27, but I guess the spikes are still there."

"Has your family always lived here?"

He nodded his gray head and pushed his glasses farther up on his nose. "Fourth generation South Dakota."

He noticed Henry's glass was a little low and reached an unsteady hand out to pour the Bear a little more cabernet. "This is the 2012—it's very good."

"Thank you."

He gestured toward my glass, but I waved him off and he smiled. "I would've thought all that digging would've given you a thirst."

I returned the smile. "So, you didn't know we were out there?"

"Not until this beautiful young lady appeared at my door."

I picked up my glass and took a sip. "I'm thinking I should be apologizing."

He set the bottle back on the counter. "No need."

The house was massive and well furnished, the kitchen a wooden structure that had been added on to the backside of the stone house, a precaution that had been made in the days when such rooms periodically burnt down. His den looked to be an old porch that had been converted, and I couldn't help but wonder why he appeared to live the majority of his life in the more modest portions of the huge house.

I glanced around the kitchen—homey, but a little run down. "You live here alone?"

He nodded and sat on a stool opposite the three of us. "Ever since Evelyn died seventeen years ago."

"Children?"

"A son in Florida and a daughter in Alabama; I think the Midwest winters took a toll on them." He sighed and looked around. "It's a museum, I know. They keep trying to get me to move, but so far I've resisted. I've lived here my whole life, and I'm not sure I'd know myself anywhere else."

The Cheyenne Nation warmed to the old man. "What did you do? For a living."

He gestured toward the book lying on the counter to our left, Herodotus's *The Histories*. "I taught world history at Black Hills State."

"'Men trust their ears less than their eyes.'"

He nodded and looked sad. "He is rather one-sided, but he's still the most reliable historian of the ancient world." The old scholar considered me. "I find it hard to believe that a Wyoming sheriff quotes Herodotus."

"It's a magnificent book."

He placed a wrinkled hand lovingly on the tome. "I read it periodically to convince myself that we live in more civilized times."

"Where people shoot each other's lawn mowers?"

"'From great wrongdoing there are great punishments from the gods.'" He glanced at me through the tops of his bifocals. "Are you here to punish wrongdoers?"

"Yep."

He stood and moved toward the door, and we followed. "The Kiddos were marvelous people, but their son's actions have always been questionable, to say the least."

We gathered our primitive equipment from the back stoop, and I watched as Vic surreptitiously slipped an arm through one of his, carefully steering him along the sidewalk toward the front lawn.

The old fellow was spry enough and led us to a spot near the property line but thankfully with an obstructed view of Billy's house next door. "I was mowing the grass myself when he came out of his house shooting like a madman. I think the first shot landed somewhere out near the middle of the lawn, but the second I'm sure of since it missed my foot by only a yard or so." He tapped a house shoe on a spot in the grass. "I would say here."

The three of us stepped back, and Henry ran the wand over the patch; the device immediately squealed and lit up.

I stepped forward with the shovel and repeated the procedure. I was starting to feel like a grave digger.

He watched me. "How far will a bullet go into the ground?"

I looked up at him. "Usually about a foot, depending on the weapon and the composition of the soil." I shoveled out another scoop. "Rocks can deflect a bullet quite a ways, so you can never be completely sure where they might go. How far away was he when he fired?"

He thought about it. "Twenty yards. He was truly crazed."

I scooped out another. "He still is."

Henry moved in and passed the wand over the hole, but the detector didn't respond. We looked at each other, and then he waved the thing over the pile of dirt I'd shoveled to the side; suddenly, it lit up and squealed.

"Bingo." I kneeled down and began sifting through the dirt with my fingers, feeling for the slug. "I'd say your powers of recollection are pretty amazing, Mr. Heiple."

He stood there, arm in arm with my undersheriff. "Perhaps, but if you've ever been shot at, and I'm sure you have, you tend to remember it." He paused for a moment and then continued, almost apologetically. "I was with Company One, Thirty-third Armored Regiment, Third Armored Division, First U.S. Army in the Battle of the Bulge. We were raw recruits brought in to replace the men who had been killed in the initial German offensive. On my first night, there we were deployed in the third Sherman tank that my crew had been given, the first two having been destroyed. We were guarding the fuel dump at Francorchamps above Stavelot late one night. I was smoking a cigarette and listening to the bats flying around my head outside my assistant-driver hole. After a moment the older and much more experienced driver poked his head out of his hatch, looked at me, and said, "You do know you're being shot at with that damned cigarette, don't you?" So I threw it over the side and scrambled in; then he told me that I'd just flicked a lit cigarette into a field of cans containing 124,000 gallons of gasoline."

I breathed a laugh and thought about the neo-Nazi reality star living next door as I carefully plucked the bullet from the dirt. I brushed it off and held it up into the moonlight—a perfectly mushroomed .40 slug. "You never forget your first time."

13

"What good is it having a daughter who works for the attorney general if I can't get a confidential piece of information every once in a while?" I could feel her fuming three hundred miles to the south as I sat there watching the sun come up, thankful that I'd finally gotten some sleep. "That information is with the courts, and I don't have any pull over there." She paused and then growled, "I just started last week—I don't have any pull over here, either. If it's a blanket bail, then they don't have to disclose who supplied the money, Dad."

"Could you make a few phone calls for me?"

"I can't believe you're asking me to compromise my position."

"Heck, if you weren't there, I'd be calling the attorney general himself and hitting him up." I waited a moment before changing the subject. "How's the painting going?"

Her tone brightened a little but not much. "It looks really great, and Lola seems to like it. Speaking of, how's her namesake?"

I yawned. "Probably going to the women's prison in Lusk before this is all over with."

"Really?"

"I don't know. I'm concerned about her son being hurt, but with the death of a federal agent, that's kind of taken a back-seat. Every time I think I've got something nailed down in this case, something worse happens that just complicates it."

"You'll figure it out; you always do."

"Right."

"There was a big article in the Cheyenne paper that they got from the AP wire about the Save Jen campaign and the High Plains Dinosaur Museum. Wasn't a very good photo of you, though."

"Yep, I saw it in the Rapid City paper."

She laughed. "You're a big deal."

"Right."

"Stop saying 'right.'"

I held my tongue.

"I found a nice lady who's been doing day care for *our* Lola. Her name is Alexia Mendez; they've got an extended family here in Cheyenne."

"She's nice?"

"Yes, and she's over six feet tall and probably three hundred pounds."

"Does Lola like her?"

"Crazy about her."

"Well then, she's okay by me."

"When are you and Henry coming down here for a visit?"

I sighed and leaned back in the folding chair on the old flagstone patio near our room at the motel and watched Dog as he watered the vicinity. "What about Dog?"

"Dog is always welcome, even when you're not."

The phone went dead in my hand. I deposited it in my jacket

pocket as the aforementioned beast came over and set his hundred and fifty pounds on my foot. "How you doin', buddy?"

He wagged and lolled his head back to look at me.

"I gave up breakfast so we could have quality time, so have some time of quality, will you?"

I scratched the fur under his chin just as a man in full motorcycle regalia—boots, torn jeans, black T-shirt, well-worn leather jacket, hair tied back under an American flag do-rag, Ray-Ban sunglasses over his eyes—made the corner at the other end of the motel. I watched him approach the door to our room.

I cleared my throat loudly. "Can I help you?"

He looked at me and walked over the rest of the way but slowed a little when Dog stood. "Is he friendly?"

I got up and extended a hand. "Unless you're a honey-baked ham."

He patted Dog's head, and we shook. "Sheriff Longmire, I presume?" His voice was soft with a bit of California in it.

"Yep. You John Stainbrook?"

He pulled out a badge wallet hanging on a chain under his T-shirt and showed me his credentials, then dropped the badge back in its hiding place and gestured with a hand that had a lot of rings and tattoos on it. "If you could gimme some ID."

I pulled my badge wallet from my pocket and handed it to him.

"Sorry. Saw that photo of you in the paper yesterday, but you can't be too careful in my line of business." He took his time looking at it and then handed it back. "What have you got for me?"

"Other than the slug we dropped off last night with DCI?"

His face stiffened under what looked like a beard on a Persian statue, ringlets and all. "I'd just like to hear your version before we go any further."

I gestured toward the other chair, and he sat. "Not much I can tell you other than what you already know, but I was hoping that if we shared our collective info we could make some headway on this."

He nodded. "I'm hoping as well, but to do that I need to know what you know. This is a federal investigation, and even though I appreciate your intimacy with the situation, I'm going to need to see your cards first."

"Okay." I leaned back in my chair and told him about the first meeting with Post and, more important, about the second, when he had told Henry and me who he was.

"He told you who and what he was?"

"Yep."

Stainbrook, looking all the world like some ancient philosopher, shook his head and pulled at the beard. "Then he must've been under a lot of pressure. Brady never did that anywhere with anybody."

"I've got a trustworthy face."

He stood and walked a little away, finally standing at the edge of the patio and looking at the river. "Tell me about the hit."

"Textbook. Somebody, and we think we know who, placed the barrel of a .40 at his chest while he was either sleeping or resting in the Cadillac. No prints, nothing."

"Lola Wojciechowski's Caddy?"

"Yep." I stood up. "Hey, do you want to tell me what her connection to all of this might be?"

He turned and looked at me, even going to the trouble of

taking off his sunglasses. "Her son, Bodaway, was moving guns for the Tre Tre Nomads, but then he got into business with some folks up this way and things got a lot heavier."

"In what way?"

"Know anything about ASPs?"

I shook my head and thought about it, finally throwing out a feeble bone. "Alleged Sensory Perception?"

"Advanced synthetic polymers."

"Well, look what the cat dragged in!"

We both turned to see Lola standing on the ramp of the parking lot that led to the cabins, hands on her hips.

Stainbrook was faster than I was. "Lola, baby! I was just askin' this cowboy where I could find you." He walked over to her, and they shared an embrace before turning back to me, arm in arm.

She gave me a hard look, flipping the black and silver hair from her face. "Where the hell is my car?"

"Excuse me?" I had to think fast and come up with a story so that she didn't just stroll into the Hulett Police Department looking for it.

"My Caddy, where the hell is it?"

I struck on a scenario. "Impound in Rapid City—evidently there was a speeding violation and a number of parking tickets."

She stared at me. "You've got to be joking."

"Wish I were."

She turned back to Stainbrook. "Have you two met formally?"

He immediately stuck the same hand out I'd shook before, but this time he had a newfound name. "Ray Swift. Good to meet you. Any friend of Lola's is a friend of mine."

I shook the hand now turned covert. "Well, I don't know if I'd call us friends—maybe just acquaintances."

"Oh, Sheriff, now you've hurt my feelings."

He made a show of double-taking me. "Sheriff?"

"Yep."

He glanced at her again. "You hangin' with law-dawgs now?"

"Friend of a friend." She hugged him closer. "Buy me breakfast and gimme a ride over to Rapid City so I can get my car?"

"Well, there's a problem with that." He turned her, and they started to head back toward the center of town. "Let's go have breakfast, Lola, and I'll explain." He looked over his shoulder at me and winked. "I'll catch you later, Sheriff . . . ?"

"Longmire. Walt Longmire."

"Right." He made a gun with a forefinger and cocked it at me, firing wide.

"I'm sure we'll be seeing each other." I patted my leg and Dog came over, sitting on my foot again as we watched them jangle up the hill and across the parking lot, leaving me to thank the heavens that my facet of law enforcement was a little more straightforward. I'd briefly dipped into undercover work, but I always had trouble remembering who I was—and that stuff wore me out.

I scratched behind Dog's ears again and thought about the two-inch cube of plastic I'd found in Post's motel room. "Advanced synthetic polymers—that ring any bells with you?"

He wagged, and I took it as a yes.

"Well, it sure doesn't with me."

• • •

"Advanced synthetic polymers."

"That's what he said, but then Lola showed up, as she is wont to do, and we had to change gears. Evidently she knows him as Ray Swift."

Vic shook her head. "I need a player card."

"I know." We leaned on the trunk of the Orange Blossom Special as the Bear finished up an interview with *Iron Horse*, a biker/girlie magazine. "So, the cube we found in Post's room takes on a new importance. I'm not sure what it is exactly, but at least we know it's part of the equation." I looked at Vic. "I'll just have to get Stainbrook/Swift alone so that we can acquire more information."

She studied Henry as he talked to the reporter. "Well, we know the one thing that'll distract her more than anything else."

"True."

She reached in the window and petted Dog, who was commanding the driver's seat. "You think they're going to make him take his clothes off?"

"I think it's only naked women in that magazine, but times change."

"You're just jealous, because he's getting as much print as you are." She studied me for a moment and then took my arm and led me around to the other side of the vehicle, where we were relatively shaded from public view. Once there, she reached underneath her leather jacket, pulled her signature Glock 19, and handed it to me.

"What's this?" I glanced at the Bear and the interviewer, who were paying us no mind. "You want me to speed up the interview?"

"You know, I'm glad that you came to me with this, because if you had gone to Stainbrook or DCI, they would've said, 'You know, we gotta get rid of this dumb-ass Longmire, because he's so amazingly stupid.'" She pointed at the wicked-looking semi-automatic in my hands. "Advanced synthetic polymer."

"Plastic guns?"

"Partially." She shook her head at me. "Realizing your technical advancement pretty much stops at muzzle loaders, I thought I'd save you some embarrassment." She pointed at the plastic portions of her sidearm. "ASPs."

"Oh." I handled the Glock, feeling again how lightweight it was compared to my Colt 1911. "So, how long have they been doing these things again?"

"There were earlier versions, but the ones that are popular now stemmed from the Austrian military and police service in the early '80s."

"Gaston Glock, right?"

"The Safe Action pistol, polymer-framed, short-recoil-operated, locked-breech semiautomatic." She leaned against the car's shiny flanks. "There was a bunch of shit about the reliability of a *plastic* gun, but that little baby right there holds the lion's share of sales to American law enforcement agencies, at, like, sixty-five percent."

"So what's the big deal about advanced synthetic polymers if they've been around for thirty-five years?"

"I don't know." She took her sidearm and stuffed it back in her pancake holster. "Even the tan color of the cube is no big deal—they've been making that color for years. Hell, three-quarters of the guys in Afghanistan and Iraq are carrying them." She stretched, raising her arms, which drew her shirt from her jeans, revealing her midriff. "And we still don't know who the second ATF agent happens to be?"

"Nope."

"I don't think it's Lola."

I couldn't help but chuckle. "I don't think so, either."

The Cheyenne Nation finished up with the fourth estate and came over, resting his back on the Tangerine Dream along with us.

"You make the centerfold?"

"I refused to be airbrushed." He raised an eyebrow and shook his head at her. "I feel like such a piece of meat."

"We have a job for you. Your ex has attached herself to the ATF CO, and I need to talk to him about this ASP thing."

We loaded into the General Lee and drove toward the center of all things Hulett. Vic shut the growling engine off and glanced around at the milling motorcyclists, just now dragging themselves out of bed after their previous night's revelries. "When are all these people going to go home and return to being a problem for their local law enforcement agencies?"

I pulled the handle, stepped into the alley, and caught a chorus of a garage-band version of Lynyrd Skynyrd's "Simple Man." "It'll start winding down the day after tomorrow."

"So, the clock is ticking?"

"In more ways than one." I turned to Henry. "How do you want to play this?"

He clasped the bridge of his nose with a thumb and forefinger. "It will not be hard; as soon as she figures out that he does not have a car, she will attempt to employ her namesake."

"You think you can get word to Stainbrook that we're out back?"

"I think so. What do you want me to tell Lola when we get to Rapid and her car is not there?"

"Knowing her, she's not going to go into the sheriff's office voluntarily, so you can just come back out and tell her that it was returned to Hulett, compliments of the South Dakota tax-payers."

"You are sure that DCI will be through with it later today?"

"One can hope, but if not, we'll deal with that burning bridge when we get to it." Without another word, we watched as he disappeared through the beer garden into the restaurant proper.

I turned to Vic. "I guess when Stainbrook comes out we'll pretend that we're taking him into custody and walk him up to the HPD and talk."

"I don't think it's Eddy the Viking, either."

"What?"

"The second ATF agent."

"You keep narrowing the field." I shook my head. "Let me know when you get it down to one."

Agent Stainbrook was impressed with the interior of the USS Pequod, even if Vic, sitting in the back with Dog, wasn't. "I think we should hang a shingle on this thing and let every-body know that we're establishing squatter rights in it and opening up an office."

Stainbrook glanced around the interior of the behemoth. "What are they intending to do with this thing, anyway?"

"I don't honestly know—go fishing, I guess." I turned in

the seat and looked at his profile. "So, what's the big deal about ASPs?"

"All right, first off, I want you to know that it is against agency policy to give you this information in any form, and I'm placing myself and my people in a precarious position by telling you any of this."

I nodded, and then he looked back at Vic, who made the motion of locking her mouth and throwing away the key. I assumed Dog was exempt.

He took a deep breath and started in. "In 1986 the Congressional Office of Technology Assessment reported that a ninety-nine percent metal-less gun could feasibly be made of advanced synthetic polymers, with metal used just for springs, but that it was only a possibility." He pulled out his own sidearm, which looked remarkably like Vic's only slightly larger. "This is a Gen4 Glock G22, and it's got ASP parts like the grip and trigger guard. Now, it's difficult to recognize one of these on an X-ray scanner when it's disassembled, but it can be done." He handed it to me. "This weapon is eighty-three percent metal by weight."

I held the lightweight .40. "So?"

"In '88 there was a company based in Scottsdale, Arizona, called Dust Devil Development that claimed it was going to have a prototype of a completely ASP weapon in less than a year. Well, a lot of agencies figured it was just hot air to get investors interested in the company, but Congress lost their minds over the fact that these weapons could be impossible to detect. They ordered an investigation, and suddenly Dust Devil Development ceased to exist. Shortly after that, Congress passed laws that banned the production of any kind of fully ASP weapons."

"Scottsdale, huh?"

He nodded. "You see, the difficulty had been in the parts of the mechanism that would wear out. Those had to be made with metal; there just wasn't any ASP that was able to stand up to that kind of punishment."

"Till now?"

"You got it. Enter Bill Tichenor, a polymer technician out of Silicon Valley's Special Materials Division. Tichenor develops a ceramic material that's supposed to replace the metal exhaust valves in automobile engines, and this stuff is supposed to be as strong as steel. Well, this does not go unnoticed by the FBI, and they clamp down on the Special Materials Division and classify the formula for the stuff."

Vic leaned forward. "If they were so spooked by this, then why didn't they shut down production completely?"

"They did that for the car exhaust valves, but when they went through Tichenor's files they found designs for all kinds of applications, especially worrisome being the concept drawings for a small automatic pistol."

"Uh-oh."

"Wait, it gets worse. The CIA, seeing an opportunity, tried to argue with Congress about the viability of continued development."

Vic pulled herself up between us. "The CIA?"

"The agency's position was that the weapon would be used for antiterrorism purposes, and in situations where foreign powers had magnetometer security, they could still get weapons into hostage situations."

Vic laughed. "And vice versa."

"It all got shut down eventually, but here's an interesting tidbit: six weeks after the Department of Justice shuts Special Materials Division down for good in 1996, Bill Tichenor is found without a head or hands in a dumpster behind 4014 North Goldwater Avenue in Scottsdale, Arizona."

"That's where Dust Devil Development was working on the plastic gun?"

"Precisely. There was communication between Tichenor and Dust Devil, a go-between." He paused. "That turned out to be Delshay Torres."

I thought about the conversation I'd had with Lola the first time we'd met: "Chief cook and bottle washer of the Crossbones Custom bike shop somewhere in the Phoenix area."

Stainbrook nodded again. "Maryvale, yeah."

"So, I'm assuming that Delshay got involved, and therefore Bodaway, because he was familiar with the fabrication of different materials and not likely to notify the Congress of his advancements?"

The ATF man leaned back in his seat. "Not likely then or now—suspicious hit and run in Nogales, just this side of the Mexican border, last year."

"So, what are the chances they've actually developed a fully ASP weapon?"

He laughed, but it wasn't funny. "Since my man Post got his hands on that sample you found in his motel room? I'd say pretty good."

"So that's what the cube was, a sample of metal-tensile-strength advanced synthetic polymer?"

He nodded. "We've already got people in Cheyenne with your DCI, and they've confirmed that that's what it is."

Vic looked at the two of us. "So, how does a shitbird like Billy ThE Kiddo get involved in something like this?"

Stainbrook sighed. "Material fabrication at his shop."

"We've been there."

"Where?"

"The Chop Shop—Kiddo's place in Rapid City." I was aware that he was staring at me. "It was after hours. Not that I'd know the difference, but it didn't look like they were up to anything that complicated, just the usual bodywork and paint." I took a breath. "And there's something more I should let you in on. Kiddo's got an entire shrine in his back room that looks like the beginning of the Fourth Reich."

He waved a hand at me. "I'm not surprised, and I don't give a shit. I don't want to appear callous, but when you've been doing this job as long as I have, you get used to seeing all kinds of bizarre stuff. I really don't care what their screwed-up belief system is; I just want to keep dangerous weapons out of their hands."

"And make sure that they pay their taxes."

"Yeah, that, too." He thought about it. "Billy ThE doesn't strike me as being all that smart."

"Well, he doesn't know the meaning of the word 'fear,' but then he doesn't know the meaning of a lot of words."

The ATF agent cocked his head and looked at both of us. "But he does know material fabrication."

"Yep."

Vic smiled. "Kind of a chopper savant?" She shrugged. "And muscle?"

He turned to look at her. "For who?"

She looked out the side window at the throngs of bikers down the street. "Good question."

We parted company with Agent Stainbrook at the Hulett Police Department annex and were assured by DCI that Lola's Cadillac would be released and sitting outside by the time she and the Cheyenne Nation returned from their round-trip.

DCI's mobile lab unit was preparing to return to Cheyenne, and T. J. was helping pack up the equipment. "We don't have the ability up here to match the slugs, but I already shipped the one you gave us ahead, so as soon as I hear anything I'll let you know."

"Sounds good." I glanced around. "Speaking of, has anybody seen or heard of the whereabouts of the presumed shooter, Billy ThE Kiddo?"

"You'd have to ask the locals about that."

I nodded, and we shook. "Thanks, T. J."

She held my hand. "You look like hell. I don't suppose it would do any good to tell you to head home and go to bed?"

"You know, women are always trying to get me to go to bed."

The chief of the Wyoming Division of Criminal Investigation's Lab Unit shook her head and glanced at Vic. "Take care of him, will you?"

She went out the door, and Vic stepped into my line of sight. "You know, if I wasn't in the picture, I've got a feeling you could have a pretty active social life."

I turned her by the shoulder, and we started toward the

police department's office. "I don't think I'd have the energy for it."

Pushing open the door of the HPD, we found Chief Nutter in a heated conversation with a couple of bikers. "Look, it's not our responsibility to make sure your bike is safe if it's parked in a questionable area."

The leather-clad dudester howled, "It was parked on Main Street!"

Nutter shrugged. "What can I tell you? It's a tough town this week." He showed the disgruntled bikers the door and turned to us as they made their way out. "What do you want?"

"In the interest of interdepartmental cooperation, I was wondering if there had been any sightings of Billy ThE?"

"Probably back beneath the rhinestone-encrusted rock he crawled out from under."

"So, that would be a no."

Nutter glanced around. "Hell, find Deputy Dog; he's making arrests at a banner rate around here. As of last night, I don't have any more room in my holding cells. What'd you do to him, anyway?"

"Oh, just gave him a little confidence."

The phone rang, and the chief answered. "Hulett Police Department." There was a pause, and then he continued, "Well, when was the last time you saw your boyfriend? Really, that hardly ever happens during rally week. . . ."

I waved good-bye, and we made a hasty retreat outside, Vic looking past me and then down Main. "I don't think Nutter is ATF, either."

"Agreed."

The streets were a little subdued, but it was still early as we made our way downtown, a half block away. Vic checked across the street for the possibility of a Kiddo sighting, and I kept an eye to the right, peering behind the tents that sold T-shirts, hats, jewelry, and biker paraphernalia. "How come you didn't ask Stainbrook who his number two was?"

"It didn't seem appropriate."

"Not Billy ThE."

"Probably not." I shook my head. "Maybe rather than trying to figure out who's undercover, we should be focusing on the case?"

She smiled. "My, aren't we testy this morning."

"I'm beginning to think that I can't operate without sleep as well as I used to." There was some noise coming from the area behind one of the tents on Vic's side, and I could just make out the back of Dougherty's head.

Vic was already on the move, and I did my best to keep up.

I figured we were going to have to do another intervention, but we were mildly surprised to find Corbin with a forefinger bouncing off the chest of a tall, skinny biker. "And if you don't get your act together, you're going to have to call your accountant boss on Monday and explain to him why you're spending the workweek in the Crook County jail in Sundance, Wyoming." The biker looked a little shell-shocked and started to say something, but Dougherty cut him off. "Not another word." He pointed down the dirt alleyway. "Go."

He gestured in the other direction at another man, and I had to cover a smile while the entire crowd drifted away, having been denied the drama. He was turning to go himself when he saw Vic and me standing there. "Hey."

"Hey, yourself." I nodded toward the dissipating crowd. "Looks like you've got things under control."

He rested a hand on his sidearm and nodded. "I think I'm starting to get the hang of this."

Vic put her hands on her hips and couldn't help but smile along with me as we followed him back onto Main Street. He held a hand up and paused traffic as we crossed.

"Hey, troop, you haven't seen Kiddo around, have you?"

"No." He slowed and glanced at me. "I'd imagine as much trouble as he's in, he's probably going to lie low until his court date. Why?"

"Just curious as to where he's hanging out and with whom."

"Probably back in Rapid, don't you think?"

"Maybe."

He stepped up his pace, yelling at a guy down the block who had just shoved another. "Hey, knock it off over there!" He turned to look at us as he sprinted away. "If you find out anything, let me know."

Vic stepped up beside me, and we watched him separate the two individuals. I glanced at her from the corner of one eye. "What do you think?"

"I think you've created a monster."

"Hmm . . ." There was a buzzing in my jacket that I'd slowly come to realize meant either Bodaway Torres or I was receiving a phone call. "I've been meaning to hand it over, but I keep forgetting that I have it." With Vic looking at me questioningly, I pulled the cell phone out, studied the screen, and hit the button. "Hello, Punk."

"You owe me."

"I always owe you."

"Yeah, but you owe me big-time now."

"Did you find out who sprung Kiddo?"

She readjusted her phone. "You don't really owe me, Dad. I just went over to courts and mentioned your name and they made me a copy of the blanket bail receipt. If I'd known how much of an effect your name had, I'd have been throwing it around a lot sooner."

"It's only effective in certain circles."

"The other thing I've discovered is that helping you with cases is a great way of getting and holding your attention."

"So, who fronted the bail for Billy ThE?"

"I bought a new couch at Sofa Mart in Fort Collins—it's called the Homerun Sofa. It's a recliner in red leather with white stitching, and they don't deliver."

"Cady."

"I need you and the Bear to go down and get it and bring it up the fire escape in the back. It's kind of tight around the corners, but I think you can make it."

"Cady, please?"

I could hear her rustling a piece of paper. "Does the name Robert J. Nance mean anything to you?"

14

"Why would Bob Nance put up Kiddo's bail if he wasn't involved?"

"I don't know."

"He's smart and at the same time dumb enough, with plenty of cash, to front an operation like the one that Stainbrook described." She sipped her lemonade and watched the traffic two-wheeling by as we sat on the running board of the Pequod again. "So, why don't we go in there and get the chief to look up his buddy Nance and see what he's been up to?"

"Because he's Nance's buddy; so, I'd just as soon Dougherty assisted us with this."

"You think Nutter is somehow in on it?"

"No, I just think it's an uncomfortable situation with the two of them being so cozy." I patted the fender of the military vehicle. "Nance bought him this battleship, among other things. I think if we're going to make a run at Nance, then we'd better make sure we've got our ducks in a row."

"Really."

"He's just the type to be able to buy or arrange a way to get out of this, and I'm not here just to get the outlaw bikers. If Nance is the money behind this operation, he's not going to just let it go. If he's using these fabricators to get a prototype together, then he's likely to take it to the next level and become an arms dealer."

"Internationally?"

"Just because the mainstream government doesn't want the things made doesn't mean there isn't somebody else who wouldn't."

"Like the CIA?"

"Exactly."

"So, we need a rundown on Bob Nance to see if there's anything in his background that might connect him to all this before we do anything?"

"Yep."

"You don't think he's crossed his t's and dotted his i's?"

"I'm beginning to wonder if anybody's ever given him a good, hard look."

"But this crap's been going on since when, '88 or '89?"

"Yep, with Tichenor killed in '96 and Torres Senior just last year."

"That's some pretty slow development."

"Hard to get it done when no reputable manufacturer will touch it with a ten-foot advanced synthetic polymer stick."

"And your technicians keep ending up dead." She sighed. "When does the blue knight get off?"

I pulled out my pocket watch. "About five minutes ago." Almost on cue, the young patrolman crossed the street toward us with a familiar man, his hands cuffed behind his back. "Speak of the devil and associate."

Dougherty slowed as we stood, bringing Eddy the Viking to a stop with him. "Hey, any news?"

"Some, but we'd rather speak confidentially, if possible." I glanced at the biker, who was, as usual, pretty well inebriated. "What'd Eddy do now?"

"Tried to get a random woman to show him some body parts, and when she wouldn't, he showed her some of his in hopes of some sort of trade-off."

I looked down at the man, who continued staring at the sidewalk, giving us the impression that he might charge us with his plastic horns. "Really, Eddy?"

He muttered. "I was set up."

"How?"

"You should've seen those tits."

I shook my head and turned to Corbin. "Hey, can we use one of your computers to hook into the National Crime Information Center and do a little research?"

"Sure."

He disappeared inside, and we waited a few moments before Chief Nutter appeared and started toward Main Street without looking at us.

"Let's go."

The office reception area was overrun with the hired guns from other counties, towns, and the Highway Patrol. The only quiet place with a computer was Chief Nutter's office to the left. "You mind if we use Nutter Butter's office?"

He glanced up from fingerprinting the Viking. "Go right ahead."

Once inside, I pulled the chair out and indicated to Vic that she should sit in it. "You're a lot faster on these things than I am."

"You got that right." She eased herself into the rolling chair and began working her magic. "This is going to take a while with just his name. I wonder how many Robert Nances there are in the U.S.?"

I pulled out the borrowed phone. "Cady took a photo of the copy of the bail application, and I think that might have a lot of Nance's pertinent info on it." I handed her the phone. "I just don't know how to get at it."

She shook her head and brought the photo onto the screen. "You are so helpless." She stared at it and began reading the information. "Oh, we can find him with all of this."

As she worked, I glanced around Nutter's office, taking in the photos and plaques that you accumulate over decades in law enforcement, and thought about how the stuff on his walls looked a lot like the stuff on mine, although a lot of mine was left over from Lucian Connally.

"Okay, nothing till '97 when he was charged by a federal grand jury in California for conspiring to defraud the IRS and tax evasion that had to do with money owed for the two previous years. His wife was also charged."

"He said they were divorced, and she'd gotten three houses out of him."

Vic continued reading from the computer screen. "I can see how there was trouble in paradise. He sold a business in California, then didn't report it, and then tried to conceal the two years of monetary installments by filing false tax returns." She looked up at me. "It looks like he might have gotten his daughter to do it, too."

"Uh-oh."

"And then the whole happy family concealed the assets by opening a foreign bank account in a Caribbean island, using purported trusts. Over the next year or so he deposited more than six million into the account, but then they got divorced and I'm betting she dropped a dime on his ass."

I rested my face in my hands. "Then what?"

"He sold his business, probably in an attempt to pay off some of the taxes and accrued penalties." She looked up. "I mean, this guy was going to the big stony lonesome—Club Fed."

Leaving my face in my hands, I spoke through my fingers. "What was the name of his business?"

She scanned the screen. "Doesn't say."

"Which California grand jury address?"

"Oakland."

"Near Silicon Valley."

She nodded and took in a deep breath. "Home of Special Materials, who first came up with the formula for this particular ASP."

"Then what?"

Her tarnished gold eyes went back to the screen. "The next mention is when he wired the remainder of the proceeds to a law firm in Dearborn Heights, Michigan, but then he instructed them to wire 3.7 million to an account in, of all places . . ." She looked at me. "Scottsdale, Arizona."

"Home of Dust Devil Development and the dumpster where Tichenor was found the year before."

"Holy shit."

"It's all circumstantial."

"Are you fucking kidding?"

"Do me a favor? I'm curious about the Detroit connection, so type his name in along with Detroit and see what comes up."

"Nothing—no . . . wait. There's a picture of him, much

younger, winning some kind of prize or award as an alumnus of the University of Michigan back in the seventies." She turned the screen so that I could see. "Isn't that him?"

"Yep. Put in automobile industry."

She tapped a few more keys. "Here he is again. He worked for GM for most of his early career."

"And was involved in engine and acoustical tile development?"

She nodded. "Yeah. And exhaust systems."

"Stainbrook mentioned that the first time they stumbled across this stuff was when they were developing polymer exhaust valves that were supposed to be as strong as steel."

"Shit. I'm betting he was in on developing it first."

"Yep, or at least got it started."

She slumped back in Nutter's chair. "Why wouldn't you just patent this stuff and sell it to the government for bags of money. I mean, the CIA wanted it."

"Just from the small amount we've gleaned from this, I don't think Nance has a very good opinion of the federal government, especially as a business partner."

"So, he gets Tichenor to advance the polymer further and then gets rid of him when he hands it over to research and development."

"Torres."

"And then when he's got a workable material, he gets rid of him."

"Or somebody does."

"C'mon, Walt, the guy is Professor Moriarty—he's leaving bodies around like the Black Plague."

"Well, by getting in bed with the Tre Tre Nomads via Delshay and Bodaway, he's certainly been introduced to the criminal element."

"Introduced?" She touched up the lipstick at the corner of her perfect mouth with the tip of a pinkie and stared at the computer screen. "Hell, they're fucking engaged."

"So, what have we got?"

My undersheriff leaned against the front counter of the office, the three of us enjoying the brief lull. "Well, it's complex."

Corbin nodded and chewed his sandwich. "I figured."

I leaned on the other side of the patrolman and came clean. "It's looking more and more like Nutter's friend Bob Nance may be involved in all of this."

"Nance involved with Kiddo?"

"I think it's all connected to the investigation the ATF has been working on and why Agent Post was murdered."

"What's the deal?"

"Plastic guns." Vic went on to explain, adding Nance's industrial background as the last piece of the puzzle.

"But now we have to come up with some kind of concrete evidence that connects Kiddo to Nance. Henry and I did a little snooping in Billy ThE's shop, but there was nothing advanced enough to indicate that he was doing anything out of the ordinary, other than modifying bikes to carry either samples of the plastic or prototypes of the guns themselves." I stepped away from the counter and turned to look at Corbin. "Does Nance have any other properties around here where they might have a facility large enough to produce the ASPs?"

Having lost his appetite, he set his sandwich down. "I have no idea."

"I assume we'd have to go down to Sundance to go through the records and find out where all his real estate holdings are."

"Yeah, I guess." He thought about it. "Wait, you're looking for some sort of connection between Kiddo and Nance, right?"

"Yep."

"Well, Eddy worked for Kiddo for about two years before Billy ThE fired him this last winter."

Vic was incredulous. "Our Eddy—the drunk Viking?"

"Yeah."

"Go get him."

We could hear Dougherty's keys jangling as he disappeared into the back holding cells where the lawless awaited transport to the Crook County jail in Sundance.

Vic walked over with her head down, speaking softly as she chewed a nail. "I am having trouble thinking of a less reliable informant."

"Me, too."

Dougherty returned with Eddy and sat him on a chair, his Viking helmet a little askew. It looked like Corbin had woken him up. A little goggle-eyed, he glanced at my undersheriff. "Is she going to show me her tits?"

"Probably not." I placed my hands on my knees and bent down to look him in the eyes. "Hey, Eddy?"

"Yeah?"

"You worked for Billy ThE Kiddo for a few years, right?"

"Yeah." He belched. "He's a prick."

I glanced at the others. "Yep, we kind of got that."

Still quite drunk, his eyes wobbled around the room. "Fired me. Said I didn't know shit. I told him—"

"Eddy." I reached out and took his chin to try to hold his attention. "Do you remember if Kiddo had another shop that he worked in?"

"Prick."

"The Chop Shop, Billy's place; was there another one?"

"No."

"You're sure?"

"Yeah."

"What about a guy by the name of Bob Nance—did Billy ThE ever have any dealings with Nance?"

"The rich prick?"

I tried to keep from laughing. "Could be."

"Asshole lives on a golf course. Has a jet that we went for a ride in. Went all the way to Daytona. . . . Fast, man."

"So, what did Kiddo do with Nance?"

"Stuff, man. He did stuff."

I grabbed his chin again. "Did Billy ThE work for Nance, and if he did, where? Did you ever go to his house?"

He pulled loose and flapped his hands in an attempt to keep mine away. "Yeah, man. I did a couple of times, and then we went to that bunker thing of his."

I stood, glancing at the others and then back down at him. "What bunker thing?"

"The hut, man. That half-round thing that sticks up out of the ground."

"A Quonset hut?"

"Yeah—I mean, that's what it started as."

"Where?"

He threw a thumb over his shoulder, gesturing toward who knows where. "On that road."

"What road?"

He gestured in another direction this time. "To the airport—the airport road."

"In Rapid City?"

"No, man. Here."

I turned to look at Dougherty. "Hulett, with a population of under four hundred people, has an airport?"

"It's the only airport in Crook County—took ten years to get it built."

Driving past the clubhouse, we headed south along the ridge where Vic had won the skeet event. "The only way to get to the airport is this road through the golf course?"

"Yeah."

"Convenient for Nance."

Vic slowed the Challenger and stopped at the precipice where we could see the 5,500-foot runway angling southwest to our right about a mile.

Corbin pointed toward a branch road that led north around a ridge. "That's the only other road, so it must be up there."

"Vic, park at that pull-off and we'll hike. I don't see any reason to advertise." She did as I said, and as we all piled out, I glanced at Dougherty. "Do you have any binoculars with you?"

He reached into a shooting bag and produced a pair in a plastic case. "Believe it or not, I use them for bird-watching."

Vic struck out in front. "I believe you."

We weaved our way through the pines that gave the Black

Hills their name and up a wash where the hillside must've collapsed after the road had been put in. There was some brush at the top and a lot more trees, so we could move without being seen toward the southern point of the high ground.

When we got there, I kneeled down and studied the small box canyon below. It was a relatively impossible site to sneak up on, with rock walls on three sides, and if I were a betting man, I would've guessed that the canyon had started out shallow but had at one point been excavated and used as a quarry, the walls now creeping up quickly around the structure.

If Nance was looking to build an impregnable fortress, he could've done worse. The bunker that Eddy the Viking had made reference to was about halfway up, and if it had started as a Quonset hut, it had evolved from there. The building was a concrete fortress with no windows and a razor-wire perimeter, and there were concrete vehicle blockades leading toward the entrance down by the main road.

"Hell."

Dougherty handed me the binoculars, and I lay down on the edge to take a closer look. There were security guards in black polo shirts near the entrance and down by the gate, including Frick and Frack, the same men I'd seen at Nance's house and the shooting event.

There were a couple of black Jeeps parked close to the building, black being the new black, but nothing else out in the open. "So, what could Nance be doing down there that's so important that he has to have armed guards around the place?"

Corbin was the first to respond. "Something worth a lot of money."

Vic was more succinct. "Something illegal."

Tired of resting my weight on my elbows, I rolled over onto my back and handed the binoculars to my undersheriff. "It's the Alamo."

She held the glasses up to her eyes and kept them there for a long look. "Then let's go get a couple hundred thousand Mexicans and take 'em."

"No, this is where we hand the stick off to Stainbrook and the ATF—they're set up for this kind of foolishness. We'll head back into town and tell them to get a task force out here to shut down Nance and Kiddo's operation."

Vic continued to focus the binoculars on the compound below. "I'd say just Nance's operation, 'cause it sure looks to me like they're taking Billy ThE Kiddo for a proverbial ride."

I rolled back over. "What?"

She handed the binoculars back to me. "Isn't that shit-for-brains getting loaded into one of the Jeeps?"

I focused in and sure enough, Frick was stuffing the Holly-wood biker into the passenger seat of one of the Wranglers as Frack climbed in the back. "Could you see if Kiddo was hand-cuffed?"

"Yeah, he was."

I watched as they pulled out, were let through the gate, and then headed toward the main road. I turned to Dougherty. "Where do you think they're going?"

"This way, I'd imagine; the only thing in the other direction is the airport." We stood and hustled back toward the Dodge. "You think they're going to fly him out of here?"

"If he's lucky."

When we got back to Vic's rental, you could clearly see down the hill and there was no Jeep Wrangler coming our way.

"They must be going to the airport." Corbin opened the door and tossed his bag in the back. "Nance has a jet, one of those twin-engine Cessnas, so we'd better hustle if we're going to catch them."

Vic was already in the driver's seat, and I threw myself in in the nick of time, the Dodge roaring sideways as we shot by the precipice and down the long slope. "Slow down when you go past the cutoff; we don't want to draw their attention when we go by."

Dougherty hung between the bucket seats. "The cutoff to the bunker is past the airport road, so just slow down when you get there. You can't see the hangars from the bunker, either—it's too far up the canyon."

We slowly turned at the airport and drove down into the parking lot. I drew my .45 as we did a quick circle around the half-dozen buildings, still seeing no Jeep.

"You think they're inside one of the hangars?"

"Not with the kind of aircraft you described. They would have to have that thing out here and warming up with a crew." I glanced at the gravel road that ran alongside the runway. "Where does that road go?"

He looked through the windshield past us. "There are a few hay fields down that way and some dirt roads that peter out into the forest before you get over to 24 or 183."

Vic turned to look at him. "So, there's nothing down there?"

"Not really."

She gunned the Challenger and laid a twenty-foot black strip on the tarmac. "They're going to kill him."

We swung around another corner as Vic leveled out the

Dodge and lit up all the cylinders, bringing the Hemi on line like an orange javelin. Dougherty flew across the backseat and crashed into the other side.

"I'd put my seat belt on if I were you, troop."

The big straightaway along the airport gave us the advantage by allowing the muscle car to flex and catch up with the cloud of dust roiling from behind what we assumed was the Jeep. "I sure am going to be disappointed if we're following some rancher on his tractor."

She put her foot even farther into the Dodge's accelerator. "I'll tell you here in a second." There was another turn, and I had to admire the way she flat-tracked the Challenger, throwing it into the gravel curve and keeping her foot in it the whole way as she focused on her prey. "Oh, you are mine, chickenshit."

The vehicle ahead had followed the road to the left and quickly passed over an elevated bridge, where I could see that it was, indeed, the Wrangler. "It's them."

Vic sawed the wheel, and we shot off the road into the hay pasture, taking a more direct route to the bridge. "Got it."

Even though we were pounding the undercarriage of the low-slung muscle car, we made time, but I wasn't sure what was going to happen when we attempted to get back on the elevated gravel road or, worse yet, the bridge.

We screamed along, the bridge appearing to be approaching at an alarming rate; if we missed it, we would most certainly end up crashing into the guardrail buttresses or flying into the creek.

I braced a hand against the dash. ". . . Vic."

"Got it."

The Dodge flew up the embankment, skipped the edge, and, slamming onto the road's uneven surface, slid completely sideways, the buttress of the bridge looking more and more like a gigantic, swinging cudgel. ". . . Vic."

"Got it."

From the back, Corbin's voice sounded surprisingly conversational. "We are all going to die."

Whipping the wheel to the right, she nosed the hood of the car forward into the narrow aperture. We all held our breath as the tires pulled free, but the car met the road and blistered the wood planks, soared over the downgrade, and blew into the hundred feet of remaining gravel road before thundering over a cattle guard into an expansive hay field still scattered with the thousand-pound square bales.

The Wrangler, traveling at a slightly more sedate pace, was running along to our right. Frick turned and looked at us as if we were crazy.

"I think we've caught up to them."

The Jeep swerved, and one of the hay bales, very green with alfalfa, shot between us. On the other side, we regained sight of each other, and I could see Frick had his window down and was giving us a questioning look.

Hoping to avoid anything dramatic, I pulled my badge wallet from my pocket and flashed it at him about the time that Vic swerved to miss another bale.

My hopes of keeping things civil were dashed as the back window on the Jeep began rolling down, and I could see Frack brandishing some sort of automatic machine pistol.

I gave it one last try, yelling over the noise of the two engines. "Absaroka Sheriff's Department—pull over!"

Frick ignored me, and Frack pointed the pistol at us.

"Vic."

"Got it." She locked up the brakes on the car and then swung hard, careening behind the Wrangler and then gunning it and coming up on the other side.

Corbin's voice rose from the back. "Won't the doors stop bullets?"

"No, they won't; even a .22 will go through most modern car doors, and maybe through the other side as well. Roll your window down—it'll give you another layer of insulation, if it makes you feel better."

"The window will stop a bullet?"

"Can't hurt."

Thank goodness the hay field was relatively smooth from years of plowing, and thank more goodness it had just been swathed, so that Vic could at least see where the really rough patches were. She swerved around another bale and angled toward the Jeep as he attempted to steer clear of her.

I could see that Billy ThE was handcuffed to the dash and didn't look too comfortable with the situation. It was about then that the rear window on the other side of the Jeep began rolling down and the automatic pistol made another appearance.

"I don't think they want to talk." She sliced around another bale and came in hard this time, clipping the back quarter of the Jeep, but Frick corrected and continued on.

Dougherty swung up between the seats again. "Do you want me to shoot?"

Vic and I both answered as one: "Just put your seat belt on!"

Pulling to one side, I slid my Colt from the holster just as Vic handed me her Glock. "Shoot 'em."

"I'm going to give them one more opportunity to stop."

"You're going to get us killed." She slid in behind the Jeep as Frick began a slow turn to the left in an attempt to stay in the field. "Hopefully Frack won't shoot out of the back." Watching Frick slalom through the bales, Vic stayed close but then swung out again, positioning us on the left as I hung my badge out for them to see.

"Absaroka County Sheriff. Stop the vehicle. Now!"

We hit some bumps, and there was some noise, but it was only when I saw the barrel of the automatic smoking that I realized that Frack had fired.

I glanced into the rear and could see that Corbin's eyes were wide as he looked at the holes punched in the interior panels of the car. "Are you hit?"

"No, and I'd just as soon not be."

Vic swerved around another bale, and I turned to see that Frack was aiming at us again. I extended both of my arms, a weapon in each hand, aiming low at the Jeep's tires, and began pulling the triggers until there was nothing left.

In a second I had blown out both tires, but the Wrangler was veering toward us now, and I could see Frick lowering his window, both men attempting to take careful aim at me.

Grabbing the extra magazines from my belt, I dropped the empty and jammed the fresh rounds into my Colt as Vic locked up the brakes, using another bale for cover and swinging behind the still speeding Jeep. "Okay, I'm ready to shoot them now."

"About time!" She turned the leather-clad wheel, and we feinted to the right—getting the backseat gunner to move to the other side—but then swung the Dodge's seven hundred horses back up on the driver's side. We overshot a bit, but by the time we drew even, I had the .45 fully extended and aimed directly at the driver's head, just hoping I didn't miss and hit Billy ThE.

As is usually the case, that split-second hesitation cost me.

There was a swale in the field, and both vehicles were thrown to the right, causing me to lose my position in the seat and hit my face on the door. I could feel the blood spilling from my nose as I clambered back up and swiped at my face in an attempt to clear my eyes; once I did, I could see both Frick and Frack extending their pistols and smiling.

It was about then that they ran head-on into one of the thousand-pound bales.

15

"That's something you don't see every day."

We'd pulled up beside the Jeep; the driver had buried its front into the bale, and its rear end was now sticking up off the ground at about a thirty-degree angle.

Keeping my sidearm on the door, I tossed Vic hers, and she went around to the other side with Corbin following her with his own drawn. "You two get Frick and Frack, and I'll get Kiddo."

The body of the Wrangler was crumpled and had impinged the door, but I pulled the handle and bent the door back on its hinges as the airbags deflated. Kiddo was slumped in his seat, handcuffed to it with the chain running through the chicken bar. I felt for a pulse and it was strong, so he wasn't dead. "He's out cold."

Vic had opened the other side and unceremoniously pulled the driver out, allowing him to sag onto the ground. "This one's alive—barely, but alive."

Reaching up, I pried open the rear door and stepped aside as Frack tumbled out. I went through the motions—flipped him over and took the machine gun—but could plainly see that he'd shot himself a number of times on impact. "This one's dead, a bunch of times over."

I went back to the front, adjusted Billy ThE's seat, slipped off the safety belt, and pushed him back. "Check the driver for cuff keys, would you?"

Corbin was already on it and patted the now-moaning Frick as Vic collected weapons. Dougherty brought the keys around, and I uncuffed Kiddo, pulled him from the vehicle, and placed him on my shoulder. I carried him around and laid him on the trunk lid of the Dodge, where I noticed he'd pissed himself.

Corbin looked around my shoulder. "Are you sure he's alive?"

"He's breathing." I glanced over at Vic, who was kneeling by Frick. "Can he talk?"

She reached down and none too gently smacked his face. "Hey, asshole, can you talk?" His face rolled a little to the side, and then he sputtered and raised a hand, which Vic immediately grabbed and placed under her knee. "I said talk, not move." He cried out, and she shook her head. "Stop being a pussy."

He gargled something about his knee killing him, and it was possible that he had a point, in that it was bleeding and had already swollen to the size of a cantaloupe even with the constriction of his BDU pants.

My undersheriff kneeled a little more pointedly on his arm. "Talk, asshole. My experience with types like you is that your mouths always work."

I moved in, getting the wayward attention of the driver. His eyes steadied on mine. "How are you doing, Mr. Frick?"

He gasped. "How the hell do you think I'm doing?"

I studied his knee, broken nose, sloped collarbone, and

what looked to be a couple of broken fingers on his other hand. "Well, you look like shit."

"We need medical attention."

I glanced through the open doors of the Jeep at the body on the other side. "We? Nope, I don't think so. Your buddy's dead as Kelsey's nuts—must've shot himself about nine times—and I think your prisoner just has a case of the vapors." I studied him. "Where were you headed?"

"Lawyer."

I glanced around. "I don't think you're going to find one out here."

He yelled it this time. "I want a lawyer!"

"And I want answers—maybe we can work out a trade."

Spitting the words, he repeated himself. "Lawyer."

Vic picked up the bloody machine pistol from the ground— where I had put it down in order to get Kiddo out of the vehicle—and sprayed the fender of the Wrangler with a frightening series of shots, then carefully placed the muzzle close to the guy's eye. "You feel the heat from that, shithead? Try and imagine how hot it'll be at over fifteen hundred feet per second when I pull the trigger again."

Frick still said nothing, choosing instead to exhale, blowing the coagulated blood from his nose.

Vic obliged him by closing up one of the nostrils with the automatic, the heat of the muzzle sizzling the blood before he could turn his head away. "I'm betting there's another twenty rounds in this thing that I can use to fill up that empty head of yours if you don't start talking."

"I'm not incriminating myself." He closed his eyes and

swallowed. "But . . . um, whatta you want to know? I mean, off the record."

I glanced back toward the municipal airport. "Somebody taking an early flight?"

"Yeah."

"Were you guys supposed to join the bunker bunch on board?"

He said nothing until Vic tapped his temple with the Sig Sauer. "Maybe, all right?"

"How long before they start figuring out something went wrong?"

He thought about it. "The head guy, he's making financial arrangements, so they can't get out of here till he gets that stuff done, but it won't be long." He winced. "Look, my fucking knee is killing me. . . ."

Vic moved and again reminded him about the 9mm.

"How fortified is the bunker?"

He snorted. "Forget it, Andy Griffith, you'll never get in there."

I nodded. "These guys, do they have a stake or are they just hired?"

"Hired, but they're good."

I looked down at him and smiled. "As good as you?"

I made Frick ride in the trunk with the dead Frack, mostly because there wasn't a lot of room but also because I thought he needed a lesson in humility.

We followed another series of hay fields, reconnected with

the gravel road that led around the airport, and swung back north to where we joined route 209 and finally 24, thereby getting back into Hulett without having to go near the bunker and raising suspicions. Vic parked the Dodge at the police station, and we tried not to draw too much attention to ourselves as we carried the bodies into the office, putting Frick in the holding cell.

"What in the hell?"

Chief Nutter held the door as we returned with Billy ThE draped between Corbin and me, finally placing him in the office chair. "Call in the EMTs down the street for the one in the cell and they can take the dead one, too." I turned to Vic. "Grab one of those handheld radios, get back on that ridge, and keep an eye on them. Give us a call if anybody moves, okay?"

She grabbed a radio and, with an extended burnout from the parking lot, was gone.

Nutter placed his hands on his knees and studied Kiddo's still unconscious face. "This one alive?"

"Enough to piss himself." I tapped the face of the star of *Chopper Off* with the back of my hand. "I would've figured he'd have been awake by now, but I guess not."

Nutter disappeared into the back and came out with a couple of paper tabs in one hand.

"Ammonium carbonate?"

He nodded. "Smelling salts. Leftovers from my boxing days—they smell too bad to expire."

He snapped one of the tiny envelopes under Billy ThE's nose and his head jerked back, his instinct to avoid the burning sensation in his mucous membranes foremost.

Catching his shoulder, I held Billy upright as he glanced around, stretched his jaw, and then began retching. I grabbed the trash can from under the desk and set it in his lap as he accommodated me by vehemently throwing up into it.

I held the can as I pointed for Corbin to get some towels from the bathroom. After a few moments Kiddo's stomach settled, or he ran out of things to throw up, and I handed him one of the towels Dougherty had brought back, trading the patrolman the trash can. "You might want to take that outside."

I watched as he exited with the wastebasket and gave Kiddo a moment. "You know they were going to kill you, right?"

He took a breath, dry retching this time, and then fell back into the chair.

"They didn't need you anymore after you did all the polymer fabrication for Nance, and you'd become a liability, which is actually something you're probably used to being."

He stared at me.

"So, Nance and his friends are going to try and fly the coop?"

He finally nodded. "He's got connections in Mexico. . . . Oh man, this whole situation has turned to shit."

"I'd say that's the understatement of the year."

The front door opened, and Henry entered with Agent Stainbrook, both of them wearing quizzical looks.

Corbin closed the door behind them. "It's Nance, and he's got his private army bunkered up over near the airport where they've got a jet warming up for a clean getaway."

Stainbrook approached and shook his head at the biker. "You know, I had my doubts about you, but I didn't think you were this stupid."

Kiddo shook his head. "You're one of them?"

The ATF agent slipped his badge from under his shirt and held it out to Billy ThE so that he could get a better than good look. "Yeah, and so was my buddy, Brady Post."

Kiddo raised his hands. "I had nothing to do with that."

Stainbrook's face stiffened. "To do with what?"

"I overheard some of them talking while I was hiding out about somebody shooting the main enforcer on the Tre Tre Nomads, but it wasn't me that did it."

"Then who did?"

"I don't know—I don't kill people."

"Your gun did."

He made a face and appeared a little paler through the stylish facial hair and tattoos. "What are you talking about?"

"That .40 of yours was the weapon that did the deed, and we got an absolute ballistic match with the slug the sheriff here was able to dig out of your neighbor's yard from the time you attempted to shoot his lawn mower."

He glanced at me. "You have got to be fucking kidding."

I stuffed my hands in my pockets. "Nope."

"I haven't had that gun in forever—I think Nance had it when we were working on the design for . . ." He wiped the tears from his face. "It was just for show."

Stainbrook pulled out another chair and slid in close to the former TV star. "Then you put on quite a show, my friend."

Kiddo hung his head. "Look, this guy comes to me and says he's got this new space-age shit that's stronger than steel, says he's got it patented and everything, but that he's got to keep it under wraps to maintain his competitive edge. He had a shit-load of money, and I had debts—with the production companies and ex-wives and shit. . . . Then my show gets cancelled. When I started helping him, it was all about bikes, but then he started talking about the government and how that's where the real money was—you know, in guns."

I sat on the edge of the desk. "Did he also mention it was highly illegal?"

"Oh, man, it was a business deal." He sobbed. "I even came up with the idea of moving the samples in the hidden containers of the gas tanks. I was trying so hard to get him back on track and out of the gun thing."

"I don't suppose you're aware of what happened to his previous business associate who ended up in a dumpster in Scottsdale with no hands and no head."

He stared at me.

"I'm just trying to get a read on where your allegiances lie in all of this. Now, you can partner up with the ATF and me, or you can continue to play ball with the guys who were on their way to shooting you in the back of the head and burying you in a ditch beside a hay field—choice is yours."

His eyes flicked among all of us like a raccoon fresh out of trees. "What do you want to know?"

"How many men does he have in there?"

"I really don't know; they kept me in the front with a blanket over my head."

"What would you guess?"

"A half dozen, maybe."

"Are they armed?"

"I don't think so. I mean, they're just going to Mexico."

I let the absurdity of that statement pass. "Do they have supplies?"

"Like what?"

I fought the urge to pick him up by his Adam's apple. "Food, water?"

"I don't think so."

Stainbrook's eyes met with mine. "You thinking what I'm thinking?"

I stood, not liking the option, but knowing it was the most prudent. "Bottle 'em up and just hold 'em there till the cavalry gets here?"

He nodded. "They'll destroy the evidence, or as much of it as they can, but I don't want this asshole getting away."

"I think we're all in agreement on that."

There was a disruption at the door as somebody made to come in, but with the Cheyenne Nation blocking it, the chances of that were just about nil. But then the Bear stepped to the side and swept the door wide, reached out and grabbed whoever it was, and pulled him into the room one-handed.

After landing, Eddy the Viking stood there trying to look as if entering this way had been his idea. "Hey."

Corbin, the one who knew him best, seemed to be the person he was talking to. "Can I help you, Eddy? We're, um, kind of busy here."

"There's a gang of guys out front and they saw you carrying Billy in here and they say they're going to stir some shit up if you don't turn him loose or something." The Viking shrugged. "I guess they're big fans of the show."

Nutter shook his head and followed him toward the door. "Good grief."

I pointed to the patrolman. "Corbin, go with them."

"Right."

He followed, and Henry let them pass but then held the door open after them just to give the troublemakers a look at the reinforcements. You could hear voices outside, but after a moment they died down, the Bear keeping his eye on them as he closed the door.

"There's probably something else you should know." We all turned at Kiddo's voice as his head dropped to his chest. "I mean, something kinda important?"

"What?"

His head came up slowly. "They've got a hostage."

"Who?"

Kiddo looked toward Stainbrook. "I want immunity. I want total immunity, or I stop talking right now."

Stainbrook stood, spun the chair, and then sat again, laying his thick arms on the back and scooting in close. "Let me explain something to you. One of my best men is dead. A guy who has two kids and a loving wife in San Diego is never going to get to see his family again, because you or one of your scumbag friends shot him in the chest. Now, if you don't tell us everything you know right now, I'm going to find one of those really hideous federal prisons and drop you in gen-pop and let them see how they like that tough-guy, movie-star ass of yours."

We all sat there staring at him as the front door opened again, and we watched as Corbin and Nutter strong-armed a handcuffed biker through the bull pen toward the holding cells. "We got your back, Billy ThE!"

Kiddo's head sagged. "Jesus." The Hollywood biker took a few breaths, stoking his courage, and finally spoke. "Lola."

I glanced at Henry, who was back to leaning against the

front door like a sphinx, and it was as if Billy had commented on the weather.

He shifted in his seat. "And I guess that's partially my fault."

Henry's voice echoed against the concrete walls like a jackhammer. "Do tell."

Kiddo turned and looked at him but then evidently felt safer looking at me. "She wanted to meet Nance, and I didn't see any reason why not."

The Bear pushed off the wall. "You are sure she is in there?"

The reality star nodded. "Yeah, I heard her voice."

The Cheyenne Nation studied him for a moment, then turned to walk back and look out the window.

I ventured an opinion. "If we get them trapped, there's no way they'll hurt her."

The Bear glanced at me over his shoulder. "You are sure of that?"

I shrugged. "Of course not."

It was then that the radio console on the desk chattered.

Static. "Walt, are you there?"

Pushing Kiddo aside, I grabbed the desk mic and answered, "Yep, what's up?"

Static. "They're loading a cargo container onto a flatbed."

Stainbrook's hand came into view. "We need that stuff."

I spoke into the mic again. "Anything else? I mean are they loading people, or just the samples and equipment?"

Static. "Just stuff for now, but it's not going to be too much longer and they're gonna be headed for the friendly skies."

I leaned in again. "All right, keep me posted. And Vic?"

Static. "Yeah?"

"Keep a lookout for Lola."

There was a pause.

Static. "You're shitting me."

"Nope. Over." I stood and looked around the room for an answer, and, not finding one, asked in general, "Anybody got any ideas?"

Nutter volunteered from the doorway. "Call Ellsworth Air Force Base and have them shoot the sons-a-bitches out of the air."

"Anybody have anything a little less drastic?"

"Yes, but just barely."

I turned and could see that Henry was still looking out the window but was now pointing outside. "'I think that there are certain crimes which the law cannot touch, and which therefore, to some extent, justify private revenge.'"

Ignoring the Sherlock quote, I walked over to where my best friend was standing, peering through the dusty slats of the venetian blinds in the late-afternoon sun at what filled the parking lot: the fifteen tons of white, mine-resistant ambush protected military juggernaut—the mighty Pequod.

16

"You have to admit that there's a certain dramatic irony in driving this thing up Nance's rear end, seeing as how he bought it and all." Rumbling through the cutoff to the golf course, I revved the monstrous thing into second gear as it effortlessly climbed the hill.

Henry was silent as I made small talk with Stainbrook. "So, tell me Eddy the Viking isn't your second agent on scene."

"Eddy the Viking is not my second agent on scene."

"Do you mean that?"

"Yes."

"I'm relieved. I thought we were in real trouble there for a minute." I rounded the turns that flattened into the parking lot beside the clubhouse where the skeet shoot competition had been what seemed a long time ago. "So, Apelu, aka Big Easy, was Post's confidential informant within the Tre Tre Nomads?"

The ATF agent hung on to two of the straps, trying to keep himself centered in the backseat so that he could see through the windshield. "Big Easy was the primary, but there are others. We thought of approaching Kiddo, but he seemed like

such a loose cannon we figured a week later he'd be attempting to negotiate another cable reality show." His voice assumed a fake TV announcer tone: "Billy ThE Kiddo, ATF!"

"It could still happen." I spun the wheel starboard and sent
the Pequod down the road past the utility buildings toward
the airport. "So, Nance tags the original scientist who came up
with the polymer, then works with Torres, Bodaway's father,
then gets rid of him, and partners up with Kiddo?"

"That's the way it looks."

"How did he ever think he could get rid of a celebrity like
Billy ThE and get away with it?"

"I'd say he's desperate."

"Why try and kill Bodaway?"

"I have no idea. Maybe it just had to do with the daughter,
but you can see from the score card that when these guys go
to kill you they generally don't miss, especially on a lonesome
road at night." There was a pause. "You really give a shit about
this kid?"

I glanced at Henry and sighed. "I do. That's the case that
I'm working on."

"Is that why you're driving an armored military vehicle
through a golf course right now?"

"Ancillary; Nance and his plastic guns are your problem,
but if I can work my case by helping you with yours, so be it."

"The daughter."

"Chloe."

"She says she found him on the side of the road?"

I shrugged. "Maybe she did."

"Do we have any idea where she is?"

I glanced back at him. "I was hoping you did."

He shook his head. "Not on our radar, but I'm sure we can find out."

"There were a lot of cell phone calls going back and forth between her and Bodaway."

"Maybe she was in on it."

"A beautiful girl, a handsome boy. Maybe they're just a thing."

The ATF agent paused. "I never thought of that."

I pulled the MRAP around the corner and parked beside the Oriental poppy colored Challenger. "Agent, you've got to get out more."

Vic was standing on the hillside at the top of the berm, pretty much eye level with us as I opened the door of the Pequod and gestured like the lovely Carol Merrill.

She put her hands on both sides of her face in mock enthusiasm and spoke in a voice loud enough to be heard over the diesel engine. "Oh my, the fleet's in."

I smiled at our conveyance. "I think we've got enough fuel to get the job done and make it back to a gas station—maybe."

She dropped her hands and looked at me. "Where's Nutter and Dougherty?"

"Babysitting Dog and waiting for the squad of highway patrolmen that are on their way."

"So, our job is to . . . ?"

"Bottle them up till reinforcements arrive." I climbed out and watched as she negotiated her way down the embankment. "Have they finished loading the stuff?"

She swung the binoculars on her neck. "They're finishing

up now, but I'm thinking that they'll likely go back to the bunker before finally heading out."

"I don't think the air crew are armed, but we've got to keep that thing on the ground."

"Split up?"

"Yep. You can take Stainbrook, and Henry and I will park the Pequod and blockade the bunker gate. We'll see what their plastic guns can do against it."

"What are you going to do about Lola?"

"What would they gain by hurting her?"

"A threat—she's the only ticket they've got to get out of here."

"They kill her, and they go nowhere."

She punched my arm and moved toward the Dodge as the ATF agent joined her on the other side. "That's your negotiation stance?"

I threw a thumb back at Henry, still seated in the passenger seat of the Pequod. "Got it from the Cheyenne."

She rolled her eyes and slipped inside, starting the Challenger with a subdued rumble.

Stainbrook looked back at me with the door handle in his hand, more than a little concerned. "Does she know how to drive this thing?"

The flatbed was making the return trip to the bunker, and fortunately the occupants weren't paying any attention to the road on the hill leading back into town. I'd let Vic advance a hundred yards ahead of me. I figured when she made her move I'd make mine, only slower, much slower.

I glanced at Henry, who sat there studying the road ahead and bouncing in his palm the foregrip of the Sig Sauer machine pistol we'd confiscated from Nance's dead gunman. "How are you doing?"

"I am not sure."

Nodding my head, my eyes followed his to where Vic had inched forward a few feet, probably for a better vantage point. "I can tell. Mixed feelings?"

"You could call it that."

"It's not important what I call it." I leaned back in my seat. "You're sure you still don't have any feeling for Lola?"

He turned and looked at me.

"Bodaway?"

His eyes went back to the windshield, and I watched as his breathing slowed. "He has not had many advantages in this life."

"No, he hasn't, and unfortunately I don't think he's going to be getting any anytime soon." I waited before saying the rest. "I know this is a case of the pot calling the kettle black, but you can't do everything for everybody, Henry."

"No, but the least I can do is keep his mother from dying."

I glanced around at the plethora of military overkill. "Hey, it was your idea to bring this behemoth to the party; you got something else in mind now?"

He leaned forward, trying to get a better look at the bunker. "If you roll up to the front with this, that should provide enough of a distraction to allow me to come in from the back."

"If there is a back. There aren't any windows, so I'm not so sure there's a door other than the one in front."

"What have we got to lose? You are going to need someone outside the vehicle, short of driving through the structure, which you cannot do without imperiling Lola."

"Shock and awe, huh?"

He finally smiled. "You be the awe, and I will provide the shock." He pulled the handle and climbed out, slinging the machine pistol over his shoulder and looking all the world like some high plains merc. "I will need ten minutes."

I pointed toward the muscle car. "Tell Bo and Luke Duke up ahead of us there." As he started to close the door, I asked, "How long were you going to sit there before telling me what you were thinking?"

The smile lingered, and he quoted me some more Arthur Conan Doyle: "'When I glanced again his face had resumed that red-Indian composure which had made so many regard him as a machine rather than a man.'"

I took out my Colt and lodged it in the seat he'd been occupying up to now. "Get out of here before I shoot you myself."

The door closed, and he was gone into the twilight of early evening like an afterthought.

Ten minutes can be a long time, and this was one of those instances.

I stuffed my pocket watch back into my jeans and cracked the door open, the windows being inoperable, as Vic walked up alongside, stepping onto the running board of the Pequod. "It's been nine and a half minutes."

She glanced down the road. "They're loading up smaller items for the final run, so I think it's now or never."

"Okay. You guys head over to the airport and shut it down; I don't even want that thing capable of flight."

"Take the keys?"

"I don't know if jets have keys."

"We'll steal the distributor cap."

"I don't know if they have those, either."

"Fuckin' whatever, we'll stop it, okay?"

"If it seems secure, you can come over and help me."

"Deal."

"Don't shoot anybody unless you have to."

She made a face, looking at my ride. "And don't you run over anybody unless you have to." She then bit my arm and was gone, more like a forethought.

As I'd anticipated, she blasted the Dodge down the hill like an internally combusted luge sled, sliding through the s-curve and skidding onto the municipal airport tarmac next to the Citation jet.

My approach was a bit slower but carried a great deal more majesty, kind of like a house on wheels. Approaching an astonishing twenty miles an hour, I wheeled the MRAP into the cutoff leading up the box canyon to the bunker.

There were five men standing by the flatbed and a Suburban near the entrance, and they all turned to watch as I approached. I was wishing that Nutter had sprung for the sirens but figured the PA system would have to suffice.

Lodging the oversize vehicle in the fourteen-foot opening of the closed gate, I parked in close enough so that the only thing that could possibly pass on either side would be a man on foot.

I plucked the mic from the dash, flipped the toggle switch

overhead, and heard my voice echo off the surrounding rock walls. "Howdy."

They didn't move.

So far, the awe thing was working pretty well.

"This is Sheriff Walt Longmire, and I hate to ruin your day, but you're all under arrest."

They still didn't move, and I started thinking it was maybe too much shock. This particular thought was belayed by their next action, which was to draw their collective weapons and begin pointing them at me. My next thought was to wonder whether Chief Nutter had opted for the bulletproof glass option.

I decided to bluff my way in and keyed the mic. "I wouldn't make a bad situation worse by doing that. We've shut down your escape plane over at the airport, and there are about a hundred Wyoming peace officers converging on this area as we speak." I watched as they glanced around, but they didn't seem awed or shocked anymore. "Honest."

I'm not sure who fired first, or if it was even one of them, but at the report of the gunshot they jumped and one of them fired a round into the windshield of the MRAP, spidering the bulletproof glass.

As a reflex, I shied against the door as another volley cracked the rest of the screen, but it held. "Oh, Nutter . . . you magnificent bastard."

Figuring there wasn't much else for it, I slipped my foot from the brake and stomped on the gas. Until the thing came to a stop, I would just duck between the seats, along for the ride.

There was a burst of noise as the giant wheels of the Pequod rammed into the closest truck and began climbing up its rear. There was more noise and a lot of yelling, which I hoped meant that the shooters were running for their lives, which is what I would've been doing. The Pequod kind of settled out as it ran over the pickup, but then I felt another lurch as it slammed into the flatbed that had ferried the supplies to the airport.

I felt its tires give way and could hear the entire body being crushed under the weight of the fifteen ton military vehicle; at least Nutter hadn't put the Pequod on a diet.

The big truck lurched and grunted and, using the two civilian vehicles as traction, began grinding into the reinforced Quonset hut, taking the buttressed concrete front with it. The thing kept going, and I started getting the feeling that I should let up or I would be likely to run right over the building and flatten whoever might happen to be inside, including Henry, most likely Lola, and Nance.

Letting up on the accelerator, I felt the Pequod reluctantly lose speed, and it felt like it might have grounded its front suspension into the collapsed wall. It settled like a whale in a deep surf. Carefully lifting my head, I glanced around but couldn't see much on account of the amazing amount of dust in the air. As it abated in the slight breeze, I could see that my surmise had been pretty much on target.

The gunmen were on the surrounding hillsides running for the tree line, and I didn't blame them.

The radio rattled on the dash of the big truck. Static. "Stainbrook and I heard shots; are you all right?"

I gripped and keyed the mic. "Couldn't be better."

Static. "What happened?"

"They threw a few shots at me, so I ran over two of their trucks and into their building."

Static. "Where are the shooters?"

"Scattered hither and yon."

Static. "Did you get Nance?"

"Not yet, but I'm working on it. So is Henry."

No one seemed to be interested in turning and throwing a potshot at me, so I pulled the handle and opened the MRAP's unencumbered driver's door. Stepping out onto the concrete rubble that had been the front wall of the bunker, I still held the mic. "What's the status on the plane?"

Static. "Grounded. There was one tough guy, but I popped him in the nose with the butt of my Glock and things calmed down."

I keyed the mic again. "Well, keep them there, and I'll ring in when we get the rest." I let go of the mic and watched as it launched back into the cab and ricocheted off the steering wheel.

I glanced back at the two flattened vehicles behind me. "Wow, that worked."

Slipping my Colt from my holster, I carefully picked my way down the rubble and, peering under the lip of the Quonset hut into the darkness of the very long building, tried to figure out how I was going to get in. Whatever door had been at the front of the structure was now buried, so, crabbing along the side and using the running boards as a railing, I went around the back of the Pequod and spotted a portion of the concrete wall that had collapsed to the inside.

Giving one more glance to the surrounding area, I could see that Nance's rental army had gotten to the rock walls, but I was pretty sure they wouldn't get much farther with the noose tightening.

Scrambling down the rubble, I raised a hand to steady myself on the Quonset's arced metal ridge and swung into what must've been a waiting room or reception area. Fortunately, there were no bodies, and I was feeling relatively sure that my impromptu frontal assault hadn't cost any lives.

I listened, but there didn't appear to be any noise coming from within. Stepping down onto the concrete floor, I could see a doorway to my left that must've led further inside, but with the interior wall having shifted, the jamb looked a little crooked, and when I tried the knob, it wouldn't budge.

Stepping back, I put a size 13 warrant into use, and the cheap, hollow-core door split in two. Leading with the Colt, I stepped inside.

There were a few sparks from the fractured overhead lighting, but other than that, not much illumination. It was definitely a manufacturing setup, and a lot of the equipment was still here, obviously too heavy to be loaded on the jet.

Working my way down the single aisle into the darkness, I thought about what a great target I must be presenting, backlit from behind. I figured that Henry must've found them and either had the situation in hand or was involved in some sort of standoff. Either way, I figured it was okay to yell. "Henry!"

There was some movement in the shadows about thirty yards away, and I raised the barrel of the .45, taking aim. "Henry?"

"Stop yelling; it is undignified."

I made out his familiar shape as he approached with the machine pistol at his shoulder. "Where were you?"

He glanced past me at the wreckage. "Running in the other direction because a madman drove a truck into the building."

"See anybody?"

He turned and started back. "Only a lowly gunsel whom I have tied to a chair."

"You only got one?"

"Where are yours?"

"Running for the Black Hills." I caught up with him. "Does he know where Nance and Lola are?"

"I was about to ask him when you attempted your drive-through."

True to the Bear's word, there was a middle-aged individual sitting in an office chair, tied with what looked to be an extension cord. I gestured toward him. "Hey, Phil."

He was sweating profusely. "Would you please tell him to let me go?"

"And that would be because you are the number two agent on scene from the ATF?"

He glanced at Henry and then back at me. "I have no idea what you're talking about."

"Look, Post is dead and your AIC, John Stainbrook or Ray Swift, whichever one he's going by today, is also on scene, so if you want to spend the rest of the afternoon tied to a chair . . ."

"How did you know it was me?"

"You were always around, and I don't think anybody in

their right mind would voluntarily spend time with Eddy the Viking." I looked toward the back door. "Where's Nance?"

"Not here."

"Yep, we got that much. Does he have Lola with him?"

"The biker chick, yeah." He shifted in the seat but then remembered that he was tied. "He said something about taking her to his house for something special."

I glanced at the Cheyenne Nation, but his face remained neutral. "Special, huh?"

"That's what he said." His eyes darted between us. "Look, I don't think he has any idea you people are here. He was going to take her to his place and be back in an hour."

"Was he armed?"

"He's always armed."

"Right." I stood and started back toward the MRAP. "Well, let's go to the golf course."

"Aren't you going to untie me?"

I paused, holstered my Colt, and threw a thumb at the Bear. "Ask him, Agent Vesco; he's the one who tied you up."

Getting the Pequod disentangled from the bunker wreckage and backed over the two vehicles I'd crushed was surprisingly easy, and I smiled at Henry as the giant, run-flat tires thumped back onto solid ground. "You know, I'm starting to think I do need one of these."

Henry rose up and peered through the cracks in the bulletproof glass. "It would take up your entire parking lot."

I wheeled the Pequod around to the lee side and started back for the gate. "It'd be great for rodeo parades."

I drove through, turned right, and headed up the hill. "So, why take Lola to his house? To kill her?"

Henry shrugged, placing the MPX in his lap. "Probably."

"You don't seem too upset."

"What good would it do?"

"So, you really don't care about her anymore."

"I care about her enough to keep her alive for the sake of her son, but beyond that, no."

The radio rattled on the dash, and Henry fished the mic from the floor.

Static. "Hey, did you assholes just turn and drive up the road?"

Wisely, he handed the mic to me.

I took it and answered. "We found the other ATF agent on scene."

Static. "Who was it?"

"The little guy, Phil Vesco, Eddy the Viking's running buddy."

Static. "Him? I never would've figured it."

"I think that's what they count on. Anyway, tell Stainbrook he's walking down from the bunker, so don't shoot him. Nance took Lola up to his house, so we're on the way up there."

Static. "I wanna go."

"No, he's up there alone. Stay with the plane, just in case he gets by us or isn't there. The only way out is that jet, so keep it bottled up."

Static. "You suck."

"Roger that."

It only took a few minutes to get to Nance's house, and I

was tempted to run into it—a thought the Bear must've read. "It is a nice house, and he is going to lose it by going to prison, so why not do the future owners a favor and spare it?"

Pulling in behind the Range Rover in the driveway, I bumped it and parked. "Just a love tap." We climbed out and looked around but didn't see anybody peeking from the windows, or any rifle barrels, for that matter. "How could they not hear us?"

The Cheyenne Nation ignored me and went for the door, which was unlocked. I watched as he used the barrel of the Sig Sauer to swing it open silently; then he looked one way and the other. "Clear."

Following him in, I slid the 1911 from my holster and trained it on the balcony above, then dropped it back toward the entryway that led toward the kitchen. Indicating that Henry should go one way and I would go the other, I moved through the kitchen and trained the .45 on the great room where Nance and I had had our discussion just a few days before.

The Bear moved silently across that room toward the other end, which must've led to the garage, as I went the opposite way toward a split staircase in the living room.

When I looked back, I could see Henry shaking his head no. I nodded and gestured for him to take the upstairs and began my descent.

It was a wide stairway with custom-made treads that looked like ironwood. There was a security door at the bottom of a landing, heavy with small windows that I could tell were two-way mirrors.

I stepped to the side and turned the gold handle, quietly

pushing the door open and waiting a moment before stepping into the empty, carpeted hallway.

There were photographs on the walls, lots of them, with Nance and celebrities on boats, in planes, and in race cars. I started down the hall, only to have Lola open the door on the end and move toward me with her head down, wearing nothing but a large white towel.

I waited till she was easily in reach and then stepped forward, placing my hand over her mouth and gently pushing her to the wall and holding her there.

"Mphhhlph." Her eyes were wide as I held the barrel of the .45 to my lips to shush her.

She tried to speak, but I held my hand firmly over her mouth. "From this point on, you don't make a sound; you simply nod your head yes or shake your head no. Got it?"

She did.

"He in there?"

She nodded.

"Is he alone?"

She nodded again.

"Is he armed?"

She nodded once more.

"Does he know we're here?"

This time she shook her head.

"Good." I loosened my grip. "Whisper. Where were you going?"

I could barely hear her when she finally spoke. "Bathroom."

"Go there and lock the door behind you. Henry's here, too." I glanced at the towel. "And he might just shoot you himself."

I watched as she slid back to the wall and disappeared behind me, quietly closing and locking the door. I waited a moment and then turned back toward the end of the hallway.

Another set of mirrors looked blankly at me, and I could only hope that Nance wasn't standing on the other side with one of his nifty little plastic guns pointed at me.

Considering the thought, I stepped forward and pushed open one of the mirrored doors. I moved to the side, slipped in, and stood there in the half-light. There was a series of weapon lockers to my left and a gun safe beyond that, leading to a firing range about twenty-five yards in length with a standard man-shaped silhouette target hanging from a motorized track at the far end. The walls and ceiling were covered in cone-shaped, noise-absorbing foam, and there was a shooter's station with a number of what I assumed were Nance's polymer pistols in different states of disassembly lying on the counter.

There was a small observation area to the right behind a bulletproof glass wall and door, where a naked Bob Nance had his back to me and was evidently pouring himself a drink. "You okay, baby?"

I waited a moment before answering. "Yeah, I'm good."

His head turned slightly, but his hands stayed where I couldn't see them, his voice slightly muffled by the heavy glass. "Sheriff?"

"Yep." I trained the barrel of my Colt on his midsection. "You want to put those hands where I can see them?"

He didn't move. "Would you like a drink?"

"I want to see your hands."

He lifted a tumbler holding a few cubes of ice and probably a healthy dollop of scotch up past his shoulder. "Highland Park, twenty-five-year-old. As I recall, you enjoyed it."

"The other hand."

"C'mon, let's have a drink and discuss this like gentlemen." He turned a little but still kept the other hand hidden. "You've kind of caught me at an awkward time. I'm assuming you saw Lola?"

"The hand."

He sighed. "Um, actually, I've got one of my guns—would you like to see it?"

"Yep, I would."

He turned slowly, holding the tumbler in one hand and in the other, one of the completely assembled polymer weapons, but this was a strange one, a blocky, desert-tan revolver, which he had pointed toward the ceiling. "Are you sure you won't have a drink?"

"Put the weapon on the counter."

He didn't move the gun hand but did bring the glass up and sip his scotch. "Do you have any idea how much this thing cost?"

"In lives?"

He smiled. "In dollars."

"I don't care."

"It's a prototype. I wanted to see just how much power the new stuff could handle, so we made this all-polymer revolver in a .454 Casull model, the line of thought being that if the new plastic could hold up to this round, it could hold up to anything."

"Put it on the counter."

"You know one of the great things about the .454? It can

deliver a 250-grain bullet with a muzzle velocity of over 1,900 feet per second and about 2,000 foot-pounds of energy, meaning it'll shoot through bulletproof glass like this one between us like a hot knife through butter." He sipped his scotch some more and lowered the barrel of the revolver on me. "And you know what the worst caliber to shoot through bulletproof glass is?" He continued to point the revolver at me. "That .45 ACP you're carrying. It'll make a dent, but it won't go through—muzzle velocity is just too slow." He gestured with the plastic gun. "Not like this."

I glanced at the closed glass door to my right.

"Don't do it; I'll shoot you before you make it."

I sighed. "Then what?"

"What do you mean?"

"I've got backup."

He smiled some more, and I really wanted to shoot at him, bulletproof glass be damned. "So do I."

"No, you don't. They're all running for the hills." He looked a little unsure now. "We've grounded your plane, and I ran over two of your trucks and crashed into your bunker with that MRAP you bought the police department." His eyes widened a little. "I guess you're not enjoying the irony in that, huh?" I pulled out my pocket watch and looked at it. "And in less than an hour every cop in Wyoming is going to be all over this place, not to mention the federal government and a really pissed-off Indian who is roaming your house with some kind of 9mm machine pistol which probably won't go through this glass either, but you're going to have to come out of that fishbowl sometime, Nance."

I glanced around at the acoustical foam walls of the million-dollar basement. Even when you talked, you could hear your voice sticking there, which made the delivery of the next words that much more enjoyable. "And when you do, nobody's going to hear you die."

EPILOGUE

I sipped my beer at the Ponderosa Café and watched Henry and Vic talking with another long-haired individual I didn't know. This guy looked a little different from the rest in that he was carrying a guitar case.

Things had settled back down into a regular August high plains summer day: the streets were pretty much cleared of tourist biker traffic, the vendors were striking their tents, and the whole town of Hulett had that after-the-carnival feel to it, as if the world had packed up and left the place behind.

Melancholy.

Or maybe it was just me.

I'd wanted to head home, but Stainbrook and the feds had asked us to stick around for the depositions that would assure Nance spent the rest of his life in rooms without light switches. Heck, I would've stayed in hell for that. Truth to be told, Hulett was a beautiful little town when not in biker season, and I was attempting to enjoy the down time, aside from being on the phone in negotiation with the Greatest Legal Mind of Our Time about moving sofas and helping to paint ceilings.

"You're tall, and you don't have to use a ladder."

"I could bring Henry; he doesn't have to use a ladder and he actually knows how to paint."

"One of you can sleep on the new sofa after you go pick it up."

"Right." I held Bodaway's phone against my ear and reached over and petted Dog. "I've got a weapons recertification in Douglas and a parole hearing to sit through down there in Cheyenne, so we'll be heading that way soon."

"That Western Star thing?"

"Yep."

"Oh, Daddy, isn't it time to let that go?" It was silent on the line for a few moments. "So, have you seen Lola?"

"Other than when we passed her on our way in to make our statements to the feds, no."

"Do you suppose she's in Rapid City at the hospital?"

"It's where I'd be."

"It's where you've been." There was another pause. "So, everybody goes to jail?"

"Prison." I sighed, wishing I were in another line of work so that my daughter and I would have nicer things to chat about on the phone. "Nance is lawyered up, but he's never going to see the light of day. And they picked up his daughter in Rapid City for tax evasion, but it's looking more and more like she didn't have anything to do with all this; she and Bodaway were just in love. . . . Go figure."

"What about Billy ThE Kiddo?"

"Conspiracy and a number of other charges, but he's singing like Janice Joplin and he'll probably get away with suspended sentences and have another outlaw pelt for his resume. By the time he's done spinning it, he'll probably have saved all

of the ATF and us single-handedly. There were some produc-
ers here already, looking to develop a new reality show with
the inked idiot."

"You're kidding."

"I wish I were."

"What about the Nazi thing?"

"Not for public consumption and probably not good for
ratings—part of the deal he made with the ATF; besides, it
would all be inadmissible. I'm not worried about it, though,
his type always ends up getting what they deserve eventually."

"Who killed the ATF agent Post?"

I sighed and continued on, figuring lawyering wasn't that
much more pleasant than sheriffing after all. "Nance. They
found Kiddo's pistol in Bob's collection in his private little
shooting gallery downstairs, along with a bunch of others,
like trophies—blowback on the barrels and still carrying his
fingerprints. I wouldn't be surprised if they didn't connect him
to a whole slew of other homicides before it was all over."

"But it is all over."

"Yep."

"So, when are you heading home?"

"Henry and Vic just got back from returning her rental car
in Rapid City. They seem to be talking to a couple of guys
from the garage band that's been playing here all week. We
still have to hook up the motorcycle trailer, but then we'll be
heading home."

"Be careful and don't get any more guns pointed at you,
'kay?"

"Sure thing, Punk."

"I love you."

"Love you, too." I pressed the button and disconnected—whatever happened to hanging up the phone?—and placed the mobile on the table as the two came ambling over; I noticed Vic holding a CD, still in the cellophane. "I can't believe that guy talked you into buying his music." I glanced past them and could see roadies still packing up the band's equipment. "I hope you told them to broaden their musical horizons; you can't get far in life just doing covers of Lynyrd Skynyrd."

Henry nodded. "Unless you are Lynyrd Skynyrd."

"What?"

Vic held out the *Best of* CD. "They *are* Lynyrd Skynyrd." She glanced behind, but the band members were gone. "At least they were."

I finished my beer, smiled, and quickly backtracked. "I thought they sounded awfully good for a garage band."

The Cheyenne Nation decided that in celebration of winning the Jackpine Gypsies Hill Climb, he would ride Lucie home with his trophy tied to the headlight a la Marlon Brando in *The Wild One*. We were to follow in the T-bird with Rosalie and Bodaway's Harley in tow on the trailer.

We watched as he checked the tie-down straps on them and then put on a pair of goggles and a Bell Boss helmet and straddled the four-cylinder Indian. "Are you sure you want to ride that thing all the way back to Absaroka County?"

"That is what it is for."

I glanced at Vic and gestured toward the sidecar. "Would you like to join him?"

She walked back and cracked the door of the Baltic blue

convertible and ushered Dog into the back before flipping the seat and climbing in. "Thanks, but no thanks."

The Bear shrugged, kicked the vintage Indian to life, and throttled away as I walked back and climbed in the Thunderbird, pulling out from the Hulett Motel and circling the parking lot in a wide arc after him.

It was late in the afternoon, and the sun had already reached its zenith, slanting its rays in a golden horizontal that highlighted the landscape to its fullest effect. We rolled out of town, following the Indian on the Indian, and I couldn't help but feel a certain anticipation for the geologic wonder just ahead.

"What the hell is that?"

Bad God Tower must've had a peek at her as we topped one of the tiny hillocks and drifted south. I didn't say anything but just eased the big Thunderbird through the curves until we topped the last hill and swept down an easy slope on route 24 that opened into the wide straightaway where Henry and I had stopped on the way into town.

"Holy shit."

It was the effect that Devils Tower had on folks the first time they actually saw it. Photographs don't really prepare you for just how impressive the first United States monument is. I slowed the convertible, allowing Vic the full impact of the Matho Tipila as the Cheyenne referred to it. "It's something, huh?"

As we drifted slowly along, I saw that the Cheyenne Nation had pulled onto the turnoff to Devils Tower, possibly to idle a little in the majesty of the natural wonder; I then saw that it was an unnatural wonder that had caught his attention.

Slowing down still more, I stopped the convertible along-side the road at a little distance, allowing them some privacy.

Vic was paying no attention, her focus still on the tower as she unbuckled and kneeled in the passenger seat, her hands on the doorsill, to study the geologic wonder. "Wow."

Even Dog moved over to the right side of the backseat for a gander, but my attention was drawn ahead, where a red 1948 Indian sat in a wide pullover parked opposite a gold '66 Cadillac.

"Can we go see it?"

My attention was drawn back to Vic. "Um, probably not now."

"C'mon. . . ." She turned in the seat toward me but stopped when she saw the tableau up ahead. "Hmm."

The Bear was still seated on the motorcycle now with his helmet off, but Lola Wojciechowski had pushed off the grille of the Caddy and was standing in a provocative manner with hands on swiveling hips.

"Boy, I wish I was a fly in a sidecar right now."

"Not me."

Vic turned and slid back in her seat, and Dog, recognizing the emotionally charged situation even from afar, registered a low whine. My undersheriff reached back and ran her hand across his muzzle. "Easy, boy."

"Are you talking to him or me?"

"Both." We sat there in the silence with a light breeze drift-ing from Devils Tower, the smell of the juniper and jack pines better than incense. "I wonder what they're talking about?"

"I think it's more of a 'who.'"

Lola moved closer, even going so far as to drape a wrist

over the handlebars of the big Indian motorcycle. Henry didn't move, and she upped the ante by arching her back, her black leather jacket and cropped white T-shirt riding up, displaying the ring in her belly button. "Boy, she's playing it for all it's worth, huh?"

"Maybe, but I don't think he's in the game."

There was a little more conversation, but you could tell that Lola wasn't getting what she wanted.

After a few more exchanges, the Bear placed his helmet back on his head, pulled the goggles down, and slipped on his gloves. He cocked his head at something she said and then stood, kicking the Indian to life. He gave her a jaunty salute as she hugged herself with one arm, and then he throttled up and pulled out.

I fired up the Thunderbird and slipped it in gear, easing the convertible and trailer onto the state route. As we approached Lola, she stepped onto the road and held up a hand like a traffic cop.

"Just keep going."

As much as I wanted to heed Vic's advice, the gentleman in me slowed and stopped as the dark-haired woman with the silver shot through it rounded the front of the T-bird, laid an arm across the top of the windshield, and smiled down exclusively at me. "Hi."

"Hello, Lola."

She finally glanced at Vic, extending the other hand across me and bringing the scent of perfume, leather, and utter abandonment into my nostrils as they politely shook. "Lola Wojciechowski."

Vic batted her eyelashes, and her tone was buttery strychnine. "I've heard so much about you." She glanced back and then cracked open the passenger side door, stepping out and allowing Dog to follow. "We're taking a short walk." She glanced at me. "A short walk, and then we'll be right back." My undersheriff and my Dog strolled into the high grass, both of them gazing at the monolith in the distance.

"Kind of got you on a short leash, doesn't she?"

Tipping my hat to provide a little personal shade, I glanced up at her. "What do you want, Lola? I've got to catch up with Henry."

She grinned the killer smile and studied me. "I just wanted to say thanks."

"For what?"

"For everything—you were very nice to me, and I don't get that a lot."

I didn't say anything.

"See, still nice." Her eyes played over to Devils Tower, and I was beginning to lose my patience. "You probably think I need to be in jail, huh?"

"Not my problem."

She studied the landscape some more and then nodded. "I play the percentages, Sheriff—it's how I survive."

"And what were the percentages on having sex with Brady Post just before he died?" Her turn to say nothing, but she did swivel her head back to study me. "I'm fighting the thought that Nance put you up to it so that he could kill Post, postcoitus. What's it like to have sex with a man knowing he's going to die?"

She smiled and shook her head in a dismissive fashion, the silver streak falling over her forehead like a lightning bolt as her scary green eyes focused on me through the tangle of lush hair. "You're all dying, whether I decide to screw you or not."

I hit the starter on the Thunderbird and, ready to go, leaned back in my seat.

She grinned the wicked grin again and cocked her head, giving the impression that she was willing to hop in and give me one of her free samples, samples being all that Lola ever gave for free. "I'm not sure why it is that I'm thanking you, though." Her expression became a little graver. "You never did find out who ran my son off the road."

Hearing the motor on the big bird idling, Vic returned with Dog and let him climb in the back before taking her seat and closing the door after her.

I shrugged. "I would've thought it was an obvious fact, Lola—you did."

Delivering a pitch-perfect performance, she laughed and shook her head. "You're crazy."

I pulled the young man's phone from my pocket and handed it to her. "Either because he had Chloe Nance on the back of the bike or because you wanted him out of Bob Nance's gun business, you and that Cadillac of yours were what sent Bodaway off the road that night. I'll give you the benefit of the doubt and think you didn't know about the culvert that did the majority of the damage, but those are the facts, for what it's worth."

Her expression remained the same as she palmed her son's phone, staring at it.

"Now, if you don't mind, and even if you do, we'd like to go home."

She smirked a little and still held on to her vehicular namesake as if it were a life preserver. "If you believed that, Sheriff, you'd have me in jail."

I took a deep breath in an attempt not to be cruel, but some situations are deserving of it and some people, too. "Not really, because when I think about your son lying down there in the Rapid City Regional ICU, I figure there's nothing that the ATF, I, or the law could do to you that could possibly compare to the punishment you've constructed for yourself."

I slipped the lever into gear, but she still didn't move, maybe because she couldn't.

"Good-bye, Lola."

She had no resort but to let the shiny chrome molding of the windshield slip from her grasp as we pulled away, and I wasn't tempted to look into the rearview mirror, not even once.